DATE DUE

OCT 0 6 1997			
NOV 2 2 2004			
2 2004			
JUL			
5/12/06			

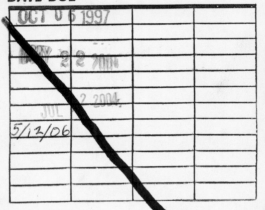
on
the
above rule.

3. All injuries to books beyond reasonable
wear and all losses shall be made good to the
satisfaction of the librarian.

4. Each borrower is held responsible for all
books drawn on his card and for all fines accruing
on the same.

DEMCO

The
Caravaggio
Obsession

By the same author
in Thorndike Large Print

The Rembrandt Panel

The Caravaggio Obsession

Oliver Banks

THORNDIKE PRESS • THORNDIKE, MAINE

Library of Congress Cataloging in Publication Data:

Banks, Oliver T.
  The Caravaggio obsession.

  "Thorndike large print"—P.
  1. Large type books. I. Title.
  [PS3552.A488C3 1984b]   813'.54   84–5977
  ISBN 0–89621–538–5 (lg. print)

Large Print edition available through arrangement with
Little, Brown and Company

Cover design by Gustav Szabo

For my father

PART I

Rome

1

At quarter of eight the cramped streets of the Campo Marzio became quieter, and the bright bustle of the day modulated into the calm and penumbrous Roman evening. It was the time when stray cats began to glide between the shadows, and old men with pushcarts claimed the streets which, an hour earlier, had been glutted with the angry snarl of traffic.

In a narrow cul-de-sac only two blocks away from the great thoroughfare of the Corso Vittorio Emanuele, a man sat waiting in a car. The car, a dirty gray Fiat, seemed too small for the figure huddled in the driver's seat.

The man, whose name was Mario, could feel his legs stiffening. He looked at his watch and cursed. He hated the waiting.

He had a newspaper propped against the steering wheel. It was opened to the sports section, and he nervously read for the third time the account of the fluke goal that had allowed Roma to beat Lazio the day before, hoping that it was an omen. Mario was a great believer in omens.

He was a big man with bony, jutting features dominated by deep-set but curiously expressionless eyes under bushy brows which grew together, forming a thick black line across the broad plane of his forehead. His overemphatic jaw gave him a slightly belligerent look. His face didn't bother him any more than his nickname: *il gigantesco*, which in Italian means both giant and monster.

Over the top of his newspaper, Mario glanced once more at the target. Flanked by much larger buildings, the Palazzo Caprese seemed to puff itself up with baroque embellishments. The heavy marble cartouche decorated with the Caprese coat-of-arms, which tilted precariously over the entrance portico, the massive Doric columns of the windows, the niches, scrolls, and pediments, had seemed pompous and silly to Mario when he had seen the building in the slides for the first time. Now the palazzo seemed vaguely threatening.

Mario checked his watch, decided that the time was close enough, opened the door, and slid out. He felt better as soon as he got free of the car. He walked quickly to the corner diagonally across the street from the Palazzo Caprese, staying in the shadows as much as possible until he reached his post.

The cool air of the evening had helped to clear his head, but Mario was still nervous. He had been in the car too long: only an hour by his watch, perhaps, but still too long. The man Mario knew only as *il Capo*, the Boss, wanted to be certain there were no other visitors to the palazzo, so Mario had been chosen to stake it out. Mario got the jobs that were particularly nasty or particularly boring; that was the order of things. No sense whining about it.

He hoped that the porter would be punctual.

Mario checked the doorway across the street, then the street itself. Except for a few noisy students, it was clear. In a minute or so the students would be gone.

Mario took a cigarette out of the pocket

of his scarred and greasy leather jacket, lit it, and took a series of short puffs to make sure the coal at the end would be large and visible. He looked to his right and spotted the green Citroën *deux-chevaux* in place, parked thirty meters or so from the front of the palazzo. He flicked the ash off his cigarette, took another hard puff on it, and felt under the flap of his jacket for the length of pipe in his pants pocket. Then he heard the sound he was waiting for.

It was a harsh rasping sound, wood and metal against stone. Mario threw the cigarette in front of him into the street. It described a high arc, spinning like a Catherine wheel, and by the time it hit the cobblestones he could hear the car starting its engine.

The rasping sound was caused by one of the massive oak doors of the palazzo, moving grudgingly on its antique wrought-iron hinges. It took the porter almost a full minute to close it, and another half-minute to position the heavy rod attached to it so that it fell plumb in the hole sunk in the marble plinth of the entrance. Occupied in coaxing the rod into position, on his hands and knees, the porter was unaware of both the large man crossing the street diagonally toward him on one side, and the green car edging toward him on the other.

The porter was a heavy, bull-necked, round-shouldered man in a dirty gray uniform. Finishing with the first door, he struggled to his feet, wiped his rust-stained hands on a large rag, sighed, and began to trudge back toward the second door. He managed only three steps.

The porter never heard the man behind him. Mario swung his left arm over the porter's shoulder, grabbing the lapel of his jacket a fraction of a second before he brought the pipe down on his head. The pipe was six inches of lead, triple-wrapped in burlap to muffle both the sound and the blow. The idea was to knock the porter out rather than kill him. Mario had been amused at this, and had told the *Capo* that he could promise the porter unconscious or the porter alive, but not necessarily both. A skull is a skull and a lead pipe is a lead pipe. Unconscious, Mario had been told. But try. . . .

The crack was loud enough even through the burlap, and for a moment the porter seemed to hang suspended and weightless before his knees buckled and he started to pitch forward. Mario caught him from behind and pulled him into the shadowed corner behind the closed oak portal. By now the green car was parked directly in front of the door of the palazzo, blocking the view from the street.

Mario checked the unconscious man quickly. His breath was coming in short irregular gasps. His eyes, half-closed, showed only the whites, and his limbs twitched in palsied spasms. Mario knew these symptoms and decided that the blow had been too hard. He made a silent apology, realized there was no time, and promised to be sorry later. A mass, perhaps. Anonymous flowers to the widow. . . .

Two men from the green Citroën were already inside. They didn't look at Mario or speak to him, but quickly completed the porter's unfinished duties, closing the door and slamming the bolt into place.

The two men who joined Mario were a study in contrasts. The first, Alberto, was tall and gangling, with an expressive face dominated by sad, soulful eyes. The second man was small, thin, and fine-boned, with youthful and delicate features which betrayed nothing. Mario respected

14

both of them, but he feared only the small man, the *Capo*.

Alberto carried a long nylon duffel bag and the *Capo* an ordinary-looking, cheap suitcase, the kind hawkers sell by the cartload to tourists near the Termini Station. With a nod, the smaller man directed the others to the drab little cubbyhole of the porter's office, where the team went quickly to work.

Alberto placed the duffel on the middle of the porter's desk and unzipped it. Inside were two bundles wrapped in towels. Alberto removed the towels, revealing a small arsenal. The first bundle contained two nasty-looking Israeli Uzis with long magazines and short barrels, and a heavy German .45-caliber pistol. The second held a sledgehammer which Mario picked up, hefted, and rested against his shoulder.

Underneath these bundles, protected by several layers of cloth, was a long metal tool-tray. Alberto extracted it and laid it on the table next to the rifles. He took a pair of rubber-handled wire cutters from the tray, stuck them in his belt, and left the office. Still no one had spoken.

When he returned a couple of minutes

later, he nodded to the others and replaced the wire cutters in the tray. Then the *Capo* took a final item from the duffel: three woolen ski masks, black, but with red borders around the skull-like apertures for the mouth and eyes.

After they put on the masks they left the office, with Mario carrying one automatic rifle and the sledgehammer, Alberto the second rifle, and the small man the pistol and the suitcase. They ran in a low crouch, Indian file, to the end of the long barrel-vaulted entrance hall, which terminated in an open courtyard. They turned right, stopping at the foot of an elaborately carved marble staircase.

The *Capo* gestured to the others to stay close to the wall, while he crept forward until he was in the shadow of one of the columns that ringed the courtyard. From this vantage point, he could see three sides of the inner court. He scanned the windows above, but they were dark. The only light in the courtyard was a flickering greenish glow from lights installed at the bottom of a fountain in the back wall of the yard, and the only sound was the faint gurgle of water.

The small man turned back toward the

others, and a moment later they carefully ascended the staircase. At the top they flattened themselves against the pilasters flanking the doorway leading to the central room of the palazzo, the *gran salone*. The *Capo*, crouching, looked at his watch and gestured to Mario, who propped his gun against the wall and stood up in front of the door, the sledgehammer loosely held in front of his body.

Still with his eyes on the watch, the crouching figure raised his right hand and listened for the signal. A moment later the stillness was broken by the sound of a motorcycle in the street outside. As the engine retched and settled into a loud drone Mario jerked the hammer back and, when the motorcycle was revved again, swung it forward as hard as he could at the brass doorknob.

The sledgehammer was the kind workmen use to pound the heavy basalt cobbles into the Roman streets. By Mario's third swing, the knob had been driven through the door and the plate with the locking mechanism was separated from its shattered wooden matrix. This left a chain lock, which needed only a sharp kick. Mario tossed the hammer aside, picked up

17

his gun, and burst through what was left of the door, followed by the others.

They were running hard. There was a short hallway that ended in a pair of French doors. They pushed these back and entered the *gran salone*, where they found what they were looking for.

The *gran salone* was a huge, almost cubic room, which still clung to shreds of its former grandeur. The coved ceiling was decorated with a peeling fresco of Apollo driving his chariot across the sky. A crystal chandelier, some sconces, and some period furniture remained from the time when the room had been a stage for masked balls and elaborate formal dinners. Now it looked a little shabby, and much too large for its single occupant.

Guglielmo Caprese stood behind his desk, a useless telephone clutched in his hand. He was a tall fat man with a small fleshy mouth, quivering jowls, and eyes filled with fear, but there was a kind of spluttering bravado in his voice when he started to yell at them.

"Nothing, you bastards, not one lira . ."

The two men with the rifles fanned out to the sides while the *Capo* walked across the room, his pistol pointed at Caprese.

"Nothing. Understand that. My company will pay you nothing; my wife, nothing; my lawyers . . ."

The small man's voice, when he finally spoke, was calm and cold.

"Enough, *Signore Porco*. Put the telephone back, put your hands on your head, and sit down. Don't move and don't speak."

He stepped around the desk and walked up to Caprese, the pistol aimed at the middle of Caprese's ample stomach. Caprese sat down.

"So. You can kill me —"

"— and will, if you don't shut up."

"Signore Porco" did as he was told. In fact he looked less like a pig than a large and bewildered fish, with its mouth opening and closing spasmodically and its round button eyes darting among the three armed men. There was one final splutter.

"If you think you can —"

This was as far as he got. The small man took a step forward. Caprese, terrified, thrust his hands in front of the gun. The other man raised the pistol slightly and swung it with both arms. The barrel caught Caprese high on the left temple and sent him sprawling backward into his chair. The chair spun out from under him and Caprese crumpled to the floor, his head caught and held by the leather seat.

The *Capo* put his pistol down, grabbed Caprese by the lapel, kicked the chair out of the way, and lowered him to the floor. Then he leaned over and patted the unconscious man on the cheek.

"*Buona notte, Signore Porco.* Sweet dreams. Try not to bleed too much on the nice parquet floor."

As the *Capo* straightened up, Alberto returned from a quick search of the palazzo to report that they were alone. There were three doors leading off the *gran salone.* After checking the first two, Alberto and the *Capo* turned to the third door. While Alberto examined it, Mario went over to guard Caprese, on the off chance that he would need to be taken care of again. Having seen the small man swing his pistol, Mario doubted that this would be necessary. With any luck, Mario's job was almost finished.

The doorway that occupied his companions was small but impressive, and evidently part of the original palace. Like the one Mario had demolished earlier, the door was oak, elaborately carved with floral patterns, and in the center, the Caprese coat of arms. Alberto dropped to one knee to examine the lock and the old wrought-iron key imbedded in it, but he didn't touch either the key or the brass knob just above it.

This was Alberto's game. Before becoming involved with the radicals at the university, he had been a student in electrical engineering as well as political philosophy. He liked to joke with the *Capo* that the reason he had joined the cell was that it was the only way he could find to combine his interests.

The *Capo* brought the suitcase to Alberto, who opened it, took off his ski mask, and mopped his brow.

"Perhaps we're that lucky, perhaps not. I want to test it."

Alberto took two objects from the case: a flashlight which was larger and more lethal-looking than the *Capo*'s pistol, and a black box roughly the size and shape of an automobile battery, to which several sets of wires were attached. One set led to a pair of earphones, the other to an object that looked like a doctor's stethoscope.

The tall man put on the earphones,

flipped a toggle switch on the black box, and watched the needles in the gauges on the box fluctuate, then quiver and hold steady. Then he took the stethoscope and placed it next to the lock; he nodded and tried it again next to the set of hinges, and finally along the joint. Then he took off the earphones.

He shook his head to the smaller man.

"Maybe we are that lucky."

He turned the handle slowly, then pushed the door with his left hand. He took a deep breath, exhaled slowly, wiped his hands on his shirt, and reached for the key. The key grated in the lock but turned, and the door swung open a fraction of an inch.

Still squatting, the tall man crossed himself and pushed the door all the way open.

The room was a small octagon without windows; the only illumination was a wedge of light from the doorway. The smaller man tried to enter, but he was restrained by his companion.

"No. Wait."

The tall man pushed the switch on his flashlight and knelt in front of the doorway, training the beam back and forth across the walls, and more slowly along the joins at the floor and ceiling. As the light flickered over the gilt, crystal, and silver decorations it seemed to leave a glistening stream behind it, like the phosphorescent wake of a ship in the night.

"I don't see anything. No wires, no infrared beams. If he has motion sensors we're screwed."

"All I see is a light switch."

"Good. Let's just turn it on and pray."

The sudden blaze of light from tubes hidden in the molding of the coved ceiling disclosed a stunning array of riches: furniture, sculpture, paintings, ornamental decorations of all sorts. One wall held books: ancient vellum-covered manuscripts and huge tooled-leather Bibles, histories, and account books. Another held shelf upon shelf of small sculptural objects: Renaissance bronzes and medals, silver and gilt and bronze statuettes. In one corner stood a mahogany case inlaid with exquisite intarsia designs, and within it were gold and silver cups and ewers encrusted with embossed figures.

This was the *Capo*'s game. He put on a pair of thin cotton gloves and began to move through the room, picking things up, looking at them, and replacing them carefully. At the same time, he talked excitedly in a half-whisper. Alberto understood only about half of what he said, and hardly knew if he was being addressed at all.

"So, the pig was even fatter than I thought. We call a room like this a *studiolo* — a little study — but the Germans are right; it is a *Wunderkammer*, a room of wonders. All of this from Caprese's rotten wine and his workers' sweat. Alberto, get the bags and the case."

When he returned, Alberto found the other man holding a bronze statuette of Venus which he was examining carefully from different angles. The nude figure was elegantly lithe, and its polished surfaces glinted as he rotated it in his hand. He gave it to Alberto.

"This goes. Wrap it up carefully. A single nick or scratch could ruin it."

He picked up another sculpture, inspected it, and handed it to his friend. It was an inkwell in the form of a small, shaggy satyr.

"This, too. A playmate for Venus. Look at the horny little bastard — I hope he doesn't knock her up."

From a shelf of Renaissance bronze medals, the small man selected one.

"And this Pisanello. Maybe it's a late cast, but if it's original, it's priceless. Now for the paintings."

The paintings occupied one wall of the cubicle. They were all fairly small, even miniature, and were evidently chosen with the same taste for jewel-like color and delicacy that governed the room as a whole. They ran from waist-height right to the ceiling, and were fitted tightly together, like the pieces of a jigsaw puzzle.

Here the choices evidently became more difficult. The small man stalked back and forth, pausing periodically to scrutinize a signature or detail through a pocket magnifier, muttering to himself, struggling. Alberto glanced at his watch. They had already been in the palazzo eighteen minutes. He was about to mention this when the other man gestured to him to come over.

"I want those."

He tapped four of the frames lightly with his lens.

All of the pictures were small. None of the dimensions of any of them could have been more than eight or ten inches. They were all attached to the wall in the same way: an eye-screw hung on a nail at the top, and a metal tab attached to the wall by another screw at the bottom. Stealing them simply involved removing some screws.

Each of the four frames had a gilt plate at the bottom with the name and dates of the artist on it, and Alberto read these as he detached the pictures from the wall: Saraceni, Elsheimer, Brueghel, Bosschaert. None of the names meant much to him. "Brueghel" sounded familiar; he vaguely remembered something he had once seen in a reproduction, a painting of hunters in the snow. But that hadn't looked anything like this.

Albert shrugged.

"Just those?"

"Just those four. Make two packages and cut cardboard between them. I don't want the frames broken. They'll fit in the suitcase."

While Alberto arranged the paintings in the case, the *Capo* made one more slow circuit of the room, and when he returned the job was done. Alberto looked at the other man in anticipation.

"*Va bene.* Let's go."

"What? You mean that's all? Look at that stuff over there. That's gold and silver, man . . ."

"So? What can I do with it — take it down to the Porta Portese and sell it to tourists?"

"It can be melted . . ."

"No."

"Why not?"

"Not by me. My job is stealing things, not destroying them."

"Are you crazy? There's a man out there with a concussion, another half dead, maybe more than half . . ."

"I said it's over. I have what I came to get." The slight man lowered his voice to a whisper. "Don't be greedy, Alberto."

The tall man nodded, hearing the threat behind the admonition.

Before they left, the *Capo* wrote a message across one wall of the *salone* in huge letters with a spray can of red paint. It was a graffito written in the same childish scrawl as the political graffiti that desecrated most of the great Roman public buildings, and had the same childish flavor: *Ti ho in culo, polizia assassina.*

Roughly translated, it meant, "Shove it

up your ass, police assassins."

The other two men looked at each other, hesitated, but said nothing. It seemed like a pointless and idiotic act. The small man did not explain it, but then he never explained anything more than necessary.

It's not even good Italian, Alberto thought, as he descended the stairs a moment later.

2

Tonio had gone to bed mad and woken up mad. The croissants smeared with jam, the boiled egg and espresso he'd had for breakfast had filled his stomach and cleared his head, but they hadn't improved his mood.

Tonio was a large, slow-moving, essentially humorless man. He was also a creature of habit, and became annoyed whenever the daily rituals of his life were disrupted. Today, it seemed to him, the carefully cultivated balance of his existence had been reduced to chaos.

True, he still had his job, the same job he'd held for over fifteen years. He drove a van. He never thought of himself as a driver anymore, though. He had been accorded the title of "Security Officer" several years ago, and his ego inflated to accommodate this new rank. When asked what he did, however, Tonio invariably answered simply that he "worked at the museum." This left open the possibility (however small) that Tonio was perhaps the director of the museum, or at least a curator.

From the museum's point of view, Tonio had several shining virtues. He was a good driver, for one thing. The van he drove was invariably in impeccable condition, since Tonio was a scrupulous mechanic. He was always punctual, reliable in an emergency, and, if not brave, at least stubborn. He was also blessed (from the museum's point of view) with an enviable lack of imagination on any subject other than himself.

When the workmen loaded the van, Tonio demanded an exact reckoning of the weight of the objects, the materials involved, the presence or absence of glass — all questions that would influence his speed, the way he approached a curve, even, on occasion, his route. Other than that, he seemed to have no interest at all in what they put in his truck. A painting by Titian, a sculpture by Michelangelo, or drawing by Leonardo was, for Tonio, simply a part of a load.

The one time a hijacking attempt had been made on the truck, Tonio had emerged something of a hero. There had been a roadblock, a huge semi driven diagonally across a road near Siena, a black car, figures waving guns. Tonio simply stopped the van, flipped the safety lock, and waited. He couldn't think of anything to do, so he did nothing. The cab of the van was bullet-proof and jimmy-proof, as was the door in back, and the thieves apparently decided that explosives would not be such a good idea since the cargo they were trying to expropriate consisted of a number of Renaissance ceramics and terra cottas. Tonio listened to a certain amount of banging around and then disappeared for a moment, reaching over onto the floor of the cab. When he reappeared he was holding a sandwich, which he proceeded to munch with a slow, bovine imperturbability. This was the last straw; the thugs jumped back in their vehicles and roared off, leaving Tonio to finish his lunch.

The trouble at the museum had started several months back, with the advent of the new Director of Security. He was young, ambitious, and energetic, three qualities Tonio found highly suspicious. Worse, he had lots of new ideas. It was several of these "new ideas" which led Tonio to his present misery.

In the past few weeks, signs reading *Sicurezza!* had been sprouting all over the museum. Memos, graphs, essays on museum security, and lectures and films (both obligatory) had been hurled at everyone from curators to janitors. Tonio's personal doom was sealed by a short memo with a title that sounded like a philosophical treatise: "Concerning the Security of Works of Art in Process of Transport."

The new rules laid down in the memo seemed idiotic to Tonio, who said so to anyone who cared to listen. In the first place, the memo decreed that in the future all transportation of art works would be carried out with two trucks rather than one. The first van to leave the museum would be empty, merely a decoy. This would always be the museum's usual van, and it would proceed to its destination following the most obvious and direct route. The art would actually be transported in a second van, which would be disguised. This van would leave the museum an hour or so after the first, and travel a complicated, indirect route carefully designed so as to hide both its destination and its origin.

This new system annoyed Tonio on several scores. In the first place it meant that Tonio would no longer be able to drive what he thought of as *his* van. Worse, it meant that his partner Maurizio would be driving the empty van. With effort, Tonio could accept the implied elevation of Maurizio to equal status with himself, but he did not like the idea of making long drives alone. As Tonio pointed out, for the price of a new van the museum could afford at least two armed guards, which would have made a great deal more sense from the point of view of security.

The business about the routes also annoyed him. Until now this had been left largely up to Tonio. Tonio prided himself on knowing the best and most secure roads from the Accademia in Venice to the Capodimonte Museum in Naples, and he viewed any interference in this matter as a professional slight as well as a practical nuisance.

Finally, there was the idiotic business of the "disguised van." The van itself was all right; Tonio had, at least, been consulted on this matter. The disguise was another thing altogether. At first the van was covered with the insignia of a well-known radio and television company, but it had occurred to the new Director of Security that thieves would perhaps be as likely to hijack a van they thought contained electronic equipment as one they thought contained works of art.

Which led to the final indignity. On this particular hot summer morning Tonio found himself driving through the outskirts of Rome in a powder-blue van decorated with stylized sprays of flowers and emblazoned with the legend *Campanula — Carta Igienica.*

"Bluebell Toilet Paper." An hour before Tonio had sat huddled over a thermos of coffee at the loading dock of the museum while the workmen arranged the crates in the back of the van and had tried to maintain a semblance of dignity in the face of a continual stream of smutty remarks. It was a moment Tonio had been dreading for days.

Only now, as the industrial clutter of

the city's outskirts began to thin out and fall away, did Tonio begin to feel relaxed. In fact, it was a beautiful day. The Roman *campagna* spread out on either side of him like a lush green carpet, and the slight haze softened and gilded the hills in the distance. To his left was a field where sheep grazed, and in the distance the rippling arcade of the claudian aqueduct, and, beyond that, a row of umbrella pines which seemed to pick up the rhythms of the aqueduct and extend them into the landscape.

The route Tonio had been handed was absurdly circuitous, but at least it got him away from the *autostrada* traffic. There were only a handful of other cars on the road, and the countryside around him began to open up with sweeping vistas punctuated only by small farms and vineyards. With a growing sense of liberation, Tonio began to settle into the pleasant monotony of the drive.

The harsh sound of a horn surprised him. He looked in the mirror and saw the gray car swing out to pass him, and quickly slid over on the road to give it room. It was a small Fiat, and it was going much too fast.

Tonio watched it swing back into his lane, and wondered about it. Then curiosity became alarm. As the car diminished it seemed to pick up speed, and at the same time, its path became erratic, slewing back and forth across the road. A drunk on the road at noon, on a weekday? Perhaps, Tonio decided, but not here, and not driving a cheap Fiat.

In the distance Tonio could see that the car had stopped. It had swung off the road onto the shoulder, and was parked awkwardly, the back end projecting out onto the pavement, the driver's door open. Instinctively Tonio slowed the van to see if there was any trouble.

As he approached the car its driver emerged and the situation became obvious, even at a distance. It was a young woman, and as she stumbled from the car she had to grab at the door for support.. As her right hand clung to the door frame, her left was clutching her hugely distended abdomen, and Tonio, a father, knew all too well what the trouble was.

As she saw the van coming up behind her the woman managed a weak wave, and then suddenly doubled over. Tonio, muttering, *"Madonna, Cristo,"* swung the van onto the shoulder and braked hard. He jumped from the cab and ran toward the woman. She had slid to the ground and was rocking back and forth, her arms across her stomach, her back propped against the car, moaning. Tonio looked around and saw nothing, not a car, not a house, and swore again. Just before he got to her he yelled, "Don't worry!"

She looked up at Tonio and smiled, and the smile told Tonio what a fool he had been. In a way, the smile was worse, and more of a shock, than the small pistol she held in her right hand.

"Calm yourself, Signore. No *bambini* today; just a matter of some pictures."

Tonio stopped dead, panting and sputtering, and looked at her in dumb amazement. For some reason he wished she were't so young, or so beautiful. She quickly got to her feet, brushed off the back of her maternity dress, and leaned casually against the car door, and it was not until the door of the passenger seat opened that Tonio was aware of her companion.

He was a small, thin man with quick movements, whose smooth face, large eyes, and small teeth reminded Tonio of an Indian he knew. This man also held a gun, and he took charge of the scene with a series of crisp orders.

"Over to the other side of the truck. Lean against it and put your hands behind your back. Don't be stupid, and don't forget there are two of us."

It seemed to Tonio that he'd been nothing but stupid for the past ten minutes, but he didn't say anything as he was trussed up. If there had been anything he could have thought of to do he might have done it, out of sheer perversity; but there was nothing. The small man tied Tonio's hands together and pushed him up into the passenger seat of the van, where he tied Tonio's feet together. He also took a long end of the cord that bound Tonio's hands and tied it to the window frame of the van. Tonio didn't immediately understand this, and then he realized that it was to keep him from wriggling over onto the driver's seat and leaning on the horn with his forehead. Finally, with a nasty grin, the small man took Tonio's keys.

Tonio was gagged but not blindfolded. With nothing else to do, he watched the woman unstrap the pillows from under her dress and toss them into the back seat of the car. She had a large mane of dark red hair that glinted cooper in the sun, and she threw it off her forehead with a proud toss of her head. Vain, he thought, watching her tug at the maternity dress and pat it down over her torso.

There was a wild moment of hope when Tonio heard another vehicle approach, slow down, and stop behind them. But the petulant, slightly bored expression on the woman's face didn't change, and Tonio quickly understood that the help was for them, not him. By craning his neck, he could catch a glimpse in the driver's mirror of another van pulling off the road.

A little later he could hear two men talking. After that he heard them opening the van and dull metallic banging as the cargo was shifted from one truck to the other.

Tonio thought about the Director of Security at the museum, and began to swear silently to himself. It was the imbecile director who had got him out in the middle of nowhere, a place where minutes passed between automobiles. If anyone sensed there was trouble, the woman was stationed by the side of the road to wave him smilingly on.

And if anyone suspected a hijacking, they would see the inscription on the side of the van: Bluebell Toilet Paper. Who would steal toilet paper?

Yet, as angry as he was, Tonio knew, with absolute, bitter certainty, who was going to bear the blame.

3

As usual, the redhead was one of the first people in the museum. She showed her student card and was given a green ticket marked *gratuito*, and as she passed through the turnstile she opened the huge black purse for the guard's inspection. It was more of a carryall than a purse, actually, and at first the guards had tried to make her check it. She had explained that she needed it to carry notes and books to the museum library, where she was doing her research.

The guard had confirmed this the first week she came to the museum. He didn't like her. She was beautiful, of course, but he sensed something supercilious about her manner that bothered him. Something about the way she looked at him, or something about the way she tossed her head. Something, anyway.

So he made her show her card every day, and every day he poked around in her bag in a perfunctory way. He also made her open it when she left. If she'd smiled at him, or flirted with him, or even greeted him on occasion, things might have been different.

Snotty bitch, he thought, as he watched her march off to work.

The museum was described in the guidebooks as "small but exquisite," which was accurate. It was based on a Palladian villa and had an open court in the middle, flanked on both sides by long wings. In the wings were a series of painting galleries opening off the wide corridors, and at the end of the corridors flights of steps led down to a basement area containing a library, the new restoration laboratores, and a large storage area. The central court was reserved for sculpture, and the balconies above it exhibited cases of antique ceramics, coins, and jewelry. Though small, it was about the only museum in the city where one could view the history of art in its entirety.

Following her custom, the young woman

passed the counters that held the cards and guidebooks and immediately turned left down one of the long corridors. She did not head for the stairs leading down to the library, however, but immediately ducked into the first gallery on the left off the corridor, which contained large, brooding Italian baroque paintings. She passed through it quickly into the adjacent gallery, nodded pleasantly to the guard, and stopped to feign interest in some lively oil sketches of Venice by Guardi, a highlight of the museum's eighteenth-century collection.

This part was easy, and the next part just slightly trickier. She emerged from the gallery by the door at the far end, quickly crossed the central corridor, and entered the room marked *Signore*.

Again she was in luck. The guards had remembered to unlock it this time, and she found herself alone. She went to the stall farthest from the entrance, closed the door, and went to work.

At the bottom of the black bag was a white smock rolled up in a tight cylinder. She unrolled it and slipped it on. Inside one pocket was a white linen scarf, which in turn held a small pile of hairpins. She pinned up her hair and covered it with the scarf. From the other pocket she took out a pair of dark framed glasses. The last thing she did before putting on the glasses was to remove most of her lipstick, with a tissue she then dropped in the toilet behind her.

The smock had the name of the museum embroidered in red script on the left shoulder. Otherwise it was indistinguishable from the tunics worn by nurses. She took from the pocket a black plastic nameplate with "L. Fiocco" engraved in white letters on it, pinned it on her chest, then extracted a plain steel chain with a laminated plastic card attached. The card held her photograph, a signature — *"Luisa Fiocco"* — and a number, as well as the insignia of the museum. She put the chain around her neck, then tucked the card inside the front of her smock.

The last thing she took from the bag was a large clipboard. Then she closed the drawstring of the bag and opened the door of the stall a couple of inches. She was still alone.

The toilet was the old kind, with a seat of varnished wood, a cistern above, and a chain. By standing on the seat, the woman was just tall enough to reach behind the tank and wedge the bag between the cistern and the wall behind. She slipped down off the seat, made sure the bag could not be seen, and pulled the chain before stepping out of the cubicle.

Before leaving the *gabinetto*, the woman gave herself a quick, appraising glance in the mirror. "Disguise" was too strong a word; she looked a bit more severe, that was all. If any of the guards at the front caught a glimpse of her she would not be recognized, which was enough.

She took a deep breath and stepped back into the corridor. This bit was dangerous; the corridor was a major thoroughfare of the museum. But a few quick steps brought her to the galleries where Italian Renaissance pictures were exhibited. Beyond them was the final room, which contained the pictures of the Northern Schools from the fifteenth to the nineteenth centuries.

Seated in the doorway that separated the final two rooms was the guard.

"*'Giorno, Franco.*"

"*'Giorno, Dottoressa. Come sta?*"

Franco, the guard, turned his head and beamed. He was a great admirer of the

45

dottoressa, and not without reason. When he first saw her in the museum, she had walked up and introduced herself, telling him that she had just been appointed to the restoration department. Since then she had returned several times, stopping to chat about inconsequential matters.

What impressed Franco the most, however, was that she had discussed her work with him. Once she had even toured the two rooms with him to point out matters of restoration. Franco had learned about problems like warping and flaking and woodworms, and had been taught how a panel is cradled. When she had shown him that many of the paintings had more recent overpaint on their surfaces than original paint, he was genuinely fascinated. Until then, the pictures on the walls had been as invisible to him as he had been to the people that passed through the galleries.

Franco was a stubby little man in his mid-fifties. Most of his life was spent planted on an uncomfortable folding wooden chair staring out a window or directing visitors to the *gabinetti*. That anyone should pay him any attention at all was, to him, quite wonderful. Occasionally curators would rehang the galleries, or someone would remove a picture from exhibition, but these matters were never discussed with Franco, or even explained to him. All of a sudden, it seemed, he had a friend.

Dottoressa Fiocco went into the gallery that held the Northern pictures, and pointed to a group of three small paintings on the far wall.

"Franco, these three pictures have to go down to the lab. Could you help me take them down?"

"Of course. With pleasure."

While Franco unscrewed the tiny panels from their mounts, the woman attached the necessary documents to the wall. They were notices which said that the three works were "in restoration." They bore seals at the top and bottom and were signed by the Superintendent of Works of Art in the Province of Latium, as well as the director of the museum, and had small reproductions of the pictures themselves pasted on them.

Detaching the pictures was easy (rather too easy, as the director had pointed out shortly before). There had been talk of installing electrical alarms on the pictures, but when the talk had reached the guards, there was a loud wail followed by dark threats. As usual, the guards won.

As he placed the pictures against the wall, Franco scrutinized them. One was a portrait and two were religious scenes set in landscapes. Franco didn't know any of the names, but he recognized the microscopic details as typical of the Flemish pictures. Armed with his newly acquired information about restoration, he tried to locate the problems that needed attention. He couldn't see anything wrong with them.

"Going to put cradles on them, are you?"

His companion suppressed a smile. "No, the panels are in good condition. The varnish is a little yellow, though, and we want to cover them with a new acrylic surface that won't change color. If anyone asks about them, you can tell them they should be back in about three weeks."

"Can I help you carry them downstairs?"

"No, thanks, Franco, I can manage quite easily. You'd better stay at your post. And thanks for the help."

She took three sheets of cardboard from

her clipboard, put them between the frames, and picked them up, using the clipboard as a support. The clipboard was much larger than any of the pictures, so that when she wrapped her arms around it and hugged it against her chest, the pictures were hardly visible.

"*Ciao,* Franco. See you soon."

"*Arrivederla, Dottoressa.*"

Franco smiled as he lowered his bottom carefully onto his chair. "Acrylic surfaces," he muttered to himself. "*Benissimo!*"

When the red-haired woman returned to the toilet stall, she quickly retrieved the black leather bag. She carefully wrapped the pictures in the smock, stuffing the package into the bottom of the bag, then covering it with the clipboard, the scarf, and some books. She shook her hair free, reapplied her makeup, and suddenly realized an urgent need to remain in the stall for a minute longer.

When she left the *gabinetto,* she had to restrain herself from fleeing the building immediately. Instead, she quickly crossed the corridor to the stairs leading down to the library. The part of the plan she most dreaded was this, sitting for an hour and a half at a table carrying on the charade of doing research with over a billion lire's worth of stolen paintings sitting on the floor between her feet.

At twelve, when the museum closed, the guard in the foyer had a surprise. After a routine glance in her bag and the usual nod, he noticed that she was smiling at him. He even got a cheerful *"Arrivederci"* and a wave.

As he watched her go down the stairs, he wondered if maybe he had been wrong about that one.

PART II

New York

1

Amos Hatcher leaned against the stone basement of the subway station and gazed up at the dome of the Brooklyn Borough Hall across the street, while he lazily smoked a cigarette. He was, he realized, procrastinating. The phone call from his friend Jake Sloane had sounded urgent, or at least mysterious. Since Hatcher was an art cop and Sloane worked for an auction house, the unpleasant conclusion could be reached that Sloane had a job for him.

Pilferage was an endemic disease in the auction business. Sometimes it was the art handlers or union crew, sometimes it was the customers. If it sounded like an in-house operation, you checked out the grapevine and the inevitable stoolies, or you waited for the thieves to do something incredibly dumb, like taking the goods immediately to one of the other auction houses. (This happened, in fact, fairly regularly.) If it was a customer, the problem was stickier. A collector would simply add it to his collection and you'd never see it again, except by chance. A dealer would generally know how to fence it properly.

Sloane knew all this as well as Hatcher, and was in a better position to deal with it himself. Besides, Hatcher didn't want any jobs right now. He didn't want to worry about Sloane's problems any more than he wanted to worry about the precipitous rise in art thefts in and around Rome, although this was beginning to trouble him.

Hatcher had his own problems. One of them, at present, was the heat. Common knowledge and the forecasters both stated that the weather was supposed to start acting more like autumn about now, and as usual, both were wrong. Hatcher had lived in the city for two years now, long enough to realize that there was a clear correlation between the heat, the humidity, and the general craziness of its citizenry. They had had ten days of this pulsing, tropical awfulness, and by now nerves were stretched to the snapping point.

Shootings were up; knifings were up. Stepping on a person's toes on a subway platform, in better times merely cause for a stream of obscenities, was now a killing offense. Ten blocks from Hatcher's brownstone apartment, a twelve-year-old kid playing basketball had been killed for his sneakers. The body was dragged off the court, and the game had continued. Mugger money wasn't any insurance in this weather; they would take your money and kill you anyway. Or, if you didn't have any, just kill you.

Ten minutes before, Hatcher had been standing on a street corner waiting for the light to change. A surly-looking punk with a turned-around Yankee baseball cap had come to Hatcher, in fact, right up against Hatcher, stuck his hand in Hatcher's face, and said, "Gimme a smoke, man."

Hatcher had said, "No," through clenched teeth. He hadn't liked the tone, the hand, or the invasion of his person.

The punk had said, "Yeah," and looked at Hatcher. Hatcher knew he was making a decision.

"Yeah," the punk repeated. "Well, fuck you, man," he had added, and then wandered off. He had not pulled anything out of his pocket, but Hatcher wouldn't have been particularly surprised if he had. He found he was more upset with his own idiotic reaction than he was with the punk. He had been absurdly angry; he realized that he would not have given him a cigarette if the punk had threatened him with a howitzer. So, which of them was crazier? It was the weather, Hatcher decided.

Oddly, given this recent episode, Hatcher was also spending a good deal of time brooding about his own mortality. Partly, he had decided, this was his age; Hatcher was forty-two. It did not help any that a little over six weeks before he had lain in a puddle of water on a Hamburg dock with a bullet in his abdomen, watching the water underneath him turn a ghastly shade of pink and wondering if he were dying.

Hatcher was an investigator on permanent retainer to a consortium of dealers called the International Association of Art Dealers, or IAAD for short. As he interpreted the arrangement, his job was to investigate the more serious art thefts and to report periodically to the association on the incidence, manner, and methods of significant art crimes. If Interpol had been more effective, or more powerful, Hatcher might not have had a job. Yet the local problems of combating international commerce in stolen art were still so over-whelming that it was useful to the dealers to employ Hatcher as a sort of bounty-hunter or guerrilla.

One of Hatcher's advantages over the local police was that he could cross borders. The recent unpleasantness in Hamburg was a case in point. He was chasing a benign-looking little Frenchman who had arranged a brilliant job at the Fondation Chagall near Paris, escaping with a suite of Chagall lithographs worth hundreds of thousands of dollars.

It was a clever job; the thief was a clever man. Hatcher realized that when they stopped for customs inspection at the border and the man was asked to open his large black portfolio. Hatcher was sitting close enough to him on the train to catch a surreptitious peek at the contents of the case, which appeared to be an immaculate arrangement of overlapping wallpaper samples.

At this point Hatcher should have blown the whistle. Out of curiosity, though, he followed the colorless little man to his destination, which was Hamburg. Instead of giving the portfolio to a principal, the Frenchman gave it to a courier, a go-between. A terrific taxi chase followed; then there was a footrace, which ended with Hatcher careening around a stack of lumber to find the German facing him twenty feet away with a gun in his hand. It occurred to Hatcher, just before he was shot, that it might have been a good idea to have taken out his own pistol at some earlier point.

In the end, everyone was thoroughly disgusted. The courier was disgusted at his own bad luck. He had dropped the portfolio on the edge of a pier and jumped into a dinghy that was tethered there, immediately swamping the small boat. As it happened, he couldn't swim a stroke. He was half-drowned when the harbor patrol dragged him out of the water.

The harbor patrol and the police who found Hatcher, and narrowly saved his life, were disgusted at Hatcher for disrupting a carefully orchestrated heroin bust. The Fondation Chagall was likewise disgusted, for when the prints were returned it was discovered that some of them had been slightly water-stained. The Frenchman was as disgusted at hearing that such an elegantly conceived operation had come to such an undignified opera buffa conclusion as he was at being arrested on his return to Paris.

Hatcher was disgusted at everything. First of all, of course, at his own stupidity. Secondly, at the business of having to confront his own mortality with such suddenness, and at such close quarters. Worst of all, though, was the idea that this sacrifice was being laid on the altar of Marc Chagall's art: Hatcher loathed Chagall. When they wheeled him into surgery he was still muttering about "those fucking upside-down purple cows." The surgeon, who spoke English, assumed that the patient was hallucinating.

The business in Hamburg had certain short-term as well as long-term consequences. Medically, Hatcher was lucky. The wound was clean and the bullet had managed narrowly to miss several crucial organs. The surgeon seemed to take great delight in describing to Hatcher just what would have happened if the path of the bullet had been a centimeter higher or a half-centimeter to the left. As it was, though, the operation had left Hatcher temporarily weak, and with an occasional sharp twinge, no more. It also left him even thinner than before. His friend Sheila Woods told Hatcher that he looked mean and hungry, like Jack Palance in *Shane*. He had replied that this was a great compliment: he had always secretly wanted to look like Jack Palance in *Shane*.

Other consequences were harder to assess. Hatcher found that his mood was still dark, with periods of serious brooding. He frequently found himself evaluating his life, an activity he considered basically unhealthy, and he felt no overwhelming compulsion to get back to work. Most of all, he realized, with a new poignancy, that he was in a line of work which was already dangerous and could only get more dangerous.

As art prices became astronomical, art thefts increased geometrically. Ten years before, art crimes had generally been crimes of opportunity; if the burglar had a free hand after taking care of the jewels and money, he might grab a picture off the wall. Now stealing art was a matter for specialists. The new breed working the Upper East Side could tell at a glance whether a print was genuine or a reproduction, and quote from memory its last three auction prices. Organized crime, formerly indifferent to art, was now testing the waters. Incidents of violence were becoming more common.

The affair in Hamburg had underscored Hatcher's growing sense of frustration. It seemed that he had run out of fingers and toes and the dam was getting leakier by the hour. Legislation specifically directed at art theft was urgently needed, as were police squads trained in its detection. Moreover, public awareness of the problem was needed; but none of this seemed likely to develop. Hatcher fought his minor skirmishes, winning some, losing some, but no one seemed to notice that a war had broken out, and that the war was already in danger of being lost.

Madison Avenue galleries still put valuable pictures in their windows. The electrical tape and the sonic alarms all worked like a dream when the bricks went through the windows, but the thieves were still miles away when the cops arrived eight minutes later. A major midwestern museum was rifled of a number of valuable sculptures when someone put a sledgehammer through a window, and again the alarm system worked perfectly. It was so easy the crooks came back a week later, going through the same window the same way. At high noon, in one of the most crowded corridors of the Metropolitan Museum, someone simply wrenched the head off a valuable Cypriotic statue, put it in a bag, and walked out the front door with it. It showed up later in a locker at a bus terminal, with a heart carved in the forehead. Happy Valentine's Day.

Fun city hadn't been much fun for Hatcher recently. A large abstract marble sculpture was placed on a pedestal in front of a Madison Avenue gallery. One morning it was found torn from its base, shattered on the sidewalk. Given the size of the sculpture, the police hypothesized that the vandals must have used steel cable and a pickup truck. The sculptor rebuilt it with the aid of a restorer, at great expense; the same thing happened again. This time, the gallery gave up.

A five-day seminar on art security held the week before had not helped Hatcher's mood. The seminar had been a very posh affair, held in an expensive midtown hotel, and had a cast of international experts reading papers dealing with various aspects of the problem. The tone of the conference had been very upbeat. Members of the French *Sureté* and New Scotland Yard recounted their exploits, all of which ended with the criminals brought swiftly and dramatically to justice. Security experts talked at length about ever more complex (and expensive) electronic systems, and locksmiths demonstrated devices so fiendishly complex that any burglar would be reduced to jibbering idiocy at the mere sight of them. In Hatcher's experience, a really successful lock was one that made the thief suffer the small inconvenience of going through the wall beside it.

The last speaker before Hatcher had been a short, fat, ebullient little man who expounded on the virtues of a method that used a telephonic system connected to the police station to catch anyone trying to knock over a house. At this point in the evening Hatcher had had enough, so he had begun his talk by showing the ease with which this system could be circumvented. All you had to do, as Hatcher had pointed out, was to call the house or apartment first and then leave the telephone off the hook. The circuit would be indefinitely jammed, and the call to the police station could not go through. Better yet, call the house from a pay phone, wrench the receiver out of the box and simply throw it away. For more sophisticated devices, of course, there were more sophisticated evasions; anyone interested could simply apply for electronic instruction at one of a number of highly certified institutions — Attica, for example.

Hatcher was not well liked at the seminar. His theme was that there was no such thing as "art security." You could approximate it, perhaps, if you created a virtually airless environment, devoid of light and maintained at constant levels of temperature and humidity, which could be placed in a reinforced concrete silo half a mile down in the middle of the Mojave Desert. If art was to be seen, however, then perhaps anyone in a position of responsibility for it had better get used to being in a state of perpetual, if slight, anxiety. Hatcher then went on to elaborate on the theme of art *in*security.

He got a chilly reception. The audience,

largely composed of young, fresh-faced curatorial assistants from museums all over the country, did not want to hear about unpleasantness. In fact, as Hatcher reminded himself halfway through his talk, people who choose to work in museums frequently do so specifically to *avoid* unpleasantness. At the end of his lecture, Hatcher stated that if museums were going to survive at all, the people who worked in them were going to have to stop thinking of them as ivory towers and start thinking of them as embattled fortresses.

At the moment, though, Hatcher did not want to think about impending wars. He had been shot and evacuated to the rear, and he now wanted to enjoy the R and R as long as possible before returning to the front. There were problems in Italy; so what? They weren't his problems, at least not yet.

He took a drag on his cigarette and gazed up at the dome of Brooklyn Borough Hall. Hatcher loved domes, symbols of the celestial sphere, the dome of Heaven. He also liked the fact that domes were nonfunctional and anachronistic, merely gestures in the sky, metaphors.

This wasn't, in fact, much of a dome. It was far too small for the building, and instead of being covered with gold leaf it was covered with what looked like aluminum radiator paint. Still, it had a certain dignity. You had to take what you could get; New York is a rotten city for domes.

Hatcher flicked his cigarette away and walked down into the subway.

2

Hatcher had come to realize that he would never get used to the New York subway, or inured to it. The only defenses against it were a sort of psychic numbness carefully cultivated over a long period of time, and gallows humor.

As hot as it had been on the street, it was much hotter here. Miserable-looking people gathered together in small clots on the platform, eyeing each other in wary silence, or shuffled back and forth aimlessly. The walls of the station that were not covered with graffiti were covered with soot, and the place smelled of mildew, urine, and brimstone.

You could run, but you couldn't hide. Hatcher walked down to the end of the platform, but he had yet to find a place where the cracked and strident blast of the P.A. system wasn't hundreds of decibels louder than his ears could tolerate.

Every few minutes, the same message blared forth, telling you what would happen to you if you smoked a cigarette, kept a wallet in your back pocket, or got too close to the edge of the platform. After the last part, in which the commuter was subliminally invited to imagine himself lying across the tracks with his arms and legs amputated and his hair and eyebrows singed off by the voltage of the third rail (events that took place, in fact, with enough regularity to give the announcer credibility), the taped message ended with a hearty "Have an *especially* nice day!" Hatcher had never heard this recording without wanting to find the man who had made it and flatten him.

The P.A. announcement was, in sonic terms, a gentle interlude in comparison to the sound of a train entering the station. The polyphonic effect of hundreds of pieces of metal colliding at high speed made the harshest acid-rock assault sound almost lyrical by comparison.

Hatcher stumbled into the subway car and sat down. As usual, the air-conditioning system was off. Also as usual, the heating system was on. There was a low hum, then a sort of thunking noise, and then nothing. Hatcher had recently deciphered this particular sequence of sounds to mean that somebody had turned off the whole damned train. It also meant that he was going to sit there for a while, maybe a long while. Maybe, like Charlie in the song, forever.

There was nothing to look at except the advertisements, his fellow sufferers, and the graffiti. The few clever advertisements, such as the one for roach exterminators, Hatcher had long since memorized in both their English and Spanish versions. The graffiti were annoying and boring, random collections of abstract squiggles that were repetitive and monotonous. The people who used to to talk about graffiti as if it were creative or artistic or somehow revolutionary had long since been made to shut up, and the stuff had been finally recognized for what it was: ugly, hostile, meaningless vandalism.

What annoyed Hatcher the most was that the scribbles didn't *say* anything. The scrawled lines always seemed about to resolve themselves into some identifiable message, but they never did. They remained illegible runes. Hatcher reflected on this and decided that urban civilization was reaching the point where the phrase Fuck You could evoke the same feelings of cozy nostalgia as Kilroy Was Here.

This left Hatcher with nothing to look at except the other people in the car. Across from him sat a huge woman whose massive, static bulk reminded him of a sculpture by Barlach. She wore a print dress incongruously covered with tiny flowers that looked like baby's breath, and she had the fierce, dignified, weathered face of an Indian chief. Hatcher found himself becoming intrigued with her.

She wore a heavy gold necklace, and a number of rings on her fingers. The rings looked to Hatcher like cheap costume jewelry, but the necklace looked real. She was reading a paperback book that was thick enough to be *War and Peace*, but when Hatcher deciphered the title, it turned out to be *Love's Tender Throb*. *Love's Tender Throb* was illustrated on the cover by the painting of a girl dressed in Victorian costume standing on a hilltop in the middle of a storm, and Hatcher realized, with a slight shudder, that the pose of the girl was stolen from Gainsborough's *Pinkie*.

The reader was so engrossed in the book that she didn't notice Hatcher staring at her. She read at a furious clip, seeming to turn the page every few seconds, and while Hatcher watched her, her expression never varied from one of scowling ferocity.

To his right was a man reading the *Racing News*. The paper was folded twice, and the man was circling entries with a stubby pencil in a series of sharp, jabbing motions. He was thin and weasel-like, and wore a stained, shiny brown suit, and when he noticed Hatcher watching him he instantly recoiled. He looked so nervous and furtive that Hatcher was tempted to tell him it was okay to read the *Racing News*, even in public.

The only other people in the car were a young black woman and her two children. She was very pretty but thin, too thin and too tired, Hatcher thought. Her daughter, who might have been seven or eight, chattered away cheerfully to her mother, who nodded now and then and didn't say anything. On the other side of the mother was a little boy who must have been a year or two younger than his sister.

The little boy was fussing, kicking his feet and whining. His mother shushed him and patted his shoulder, but the boy simply writhed around on the seat and Hatcher was steeled for a full-scale tantrum when suddenly the boy stopped dead. His jaw dropped, his eyes grew wider, and he became completely still. With a certain discomfiture Hatcher realized that the object of this total, hypnotic fascination was himself.

Teach me to stare at strangers, he thought to himself, dropping his eyes to the floor.

Finally there was a click, then the hums started again. Another disembodied voice came over the intercom.

"Sorry for the delay, folks. Be movin' in just a moment. Watch the doors, please."

The doors closed, then reopened. The driver was apparently so pleased to find a part of the train that actually worked that he opened and closed the doors five or six times before closing them for good and moving the train away from the station.

The next part of the trip was the worst, at least for Hatcher. This was the seemingly interminable passage from the Borough Hall Station in Brooklyn to the Bowling Green Station in Manhattan, most of which was spent under the East River.

Hatcher had no fear of flying. The idea that anything as heavy as a fully loaded 747 could even momentarily defy the laws of gravity seemed to him so wildly preposterous that he never worried about it. A subway train passing under the East River, however, was something else again. This was not impossible, but merely improbable, and thus much more terrifying. There was the chance (however remote, given the condition of the IRT) that the thing might actually arrive. One had to worry about it, weigh the odds. Hatcher always held his breath and fought against the mounting claustrophobia.

Shortly before the train should have reached the station Hatcher realized that it wasn't going to make it. It began to go slower and slower and finally stopped with a shudder. Panicked, Hatcher went to the glass window at the front of the car and was mildly reassured to see a row of red signal-lights, followed by the moonglow of the station ahead. He sat down again.

He heard a door slam open, and saw

three adolescent punks enter the car with the stylized, arrogant swagger that meant stay clear, baby, you don't want to mess with me. They came swinging down the straps, laughing and swearing, looking, searching, saying with their eyes and gestures, hey, baby, don't mess with me — but maybe I wanna mess some with you. They juked down the length of the car until they got to the front, then turned around to see if there were any games to play with the passengers.

One of them carried a huge portable radio with a pulsing rock band blaring on it. The two who were laughing and snapping their fingers didn't bother Hatcher much, but the third one, the big one with the radio, started to bother him a lot. He bothered Hatcher when he stopped smiling, and even more when he turned off the radio.

The train still didn't move. The main lights had switched off in favor of the emergency lights, which gave the car the pallid, anemic look of one of those old World War II submarine movies.

The big punk put down the radio and leaned against the frame of the door. He swiveled his head around and looked down the length of the car, then nodded to his friends to come over. Hatcher saw him drop his head and rock back and forth on his heels, muttering to the other two.

Hatcher watched him closely. He jabbed one of the smaller punks in the ribs with an elbow, and then snapped his head sideways. The smaller one looked around, and Hatcher followed the direction of his eyes to the necklace around the fat woman's throat.

Jesus, Hatcher thought to himself, noting the size of the necklace, and wondering about the latch. Maybe the latch would break easily. Maybe it was fragile, antique, and the thing would snap right off. May not, though. Maybe when they got the necklace the head would come too.

Hatcher was in no shape for games. He was twenty pounds underweight since the operation, and he still looked more like Ichabod Crane than his former self. So that was out.

"Jesus Christ," he said out loud. The nervous little man with the *Racing News* said, "Huh? What?" edging farther away from Hatcher, and this gave Hatcher an idea. He turned to the little man, grinning from ear to ear.

"I said, 'Jesus Christ,' " Hatcher said loudly. The little man buried himself in the racing sheet and pretended he hadn't heard.

"I'm just talkin' to the Lord, Brother, just talkin' to the Lord." Hatcher was beginning to pick up steam.

"Don't you talk to the Lord? Don't you think He hears you, Brother? Don't you think He hears you, way down here under the wicked streets of Manhattan?"

He slid over on the seat toward the little man, who cringed against the armrest. He glared at Hatcher like a cornered rat.

"Hey, c'mon, gimme a break."

But Hatcher was just getting started. He jumped up out of his seat, his arms flailing, and slipped across to the fat woman.

"How about *you*, Sister? Don't you talk to the Lord? Or do you think you can find His message in that filth you're reading, that snare of the devil? Oh, I know what you're thinking. You're thinking, 'Who does this crazy man think he is?' That's what you're thinking, isn't it, Sister? But I'm talking to you about JOY!"

Hatcher was pleased to find the next

part of his congregation as disgusted with him as the first.

"Fuck off," she said tartly. But Hatcher, the spirit upon him, merely shifted into high gear.

"Do you think you can wash away your sins in the polluted waters of the East River? Oh, strait is the gate, Sister . . ."

Meanwhile, the three punks were holding a meeting. Hatcher could make out bits and pieces of dialogue punctuated by "Sheeyit," and wondered how long he could keep the ball in the air.

"As Saint Paul put it, how much harder is it, brothers and sisters, to push a camel through the eye of a needle than for a rich man to walk through the valley of the shadow of . . ."

Please start the train, Hatcher thought. He decided to play his last card.

"And *you,* my brothers. When was the last time *you* talked to the Lord?"

That did it. The big punk gave the order.

"Les split, man. Don' wan' mess w'd no f'ckin' *crazy* man, sheee-*it!*"

The big one snatched up the radio and led the others down the aisle. Just as they left the car the train started up, and ten seconds later it was in the station. Before walking through the door, Hatcher delivered the last line of his sermon.

"For Christ's sake, lady, will you please take off that damn necklace?"

3

"Terrific, Amos. I suppose she looked like Bo Derek, and was just quivering with erotic gratitude to you for saving her neck?"

"Well, more like Hermione Gingold, actually. And she looked like she wanted to sic the cops on me."

The first speaker was Jake Sloane, the painting specialist for Harriman's Auction House on East Sixty-third Street, and the two were sitting in Jake's office now. Jake's office was one of Hatcher's favorite hangouts in New York, and Jake was one of his favorite people.

"She should have called the cops. My God, Hatcher. Two years in the city and you're still acting like a tourist. You're not in West Concord, Mass., any more,

Bucko. The only thing Good Samaritans get in this town is a small article with a heavy black border on page three of the *Post.*"

"It didn't have anything to do with being a Good Samaritan; it had to do with the image. That's one of the troubles with being trained as an art historian. You visualize everything. I couldn't get rid of the image of that woman with her eyes and tongue protruding, her face a kind of mottled purple, the horrible gagging sounds . . ."

"Enough. Have some more Scotch."

No matter how overworked Sloane happened to be, and he was overworked most of the time, it seemed to Hatcher, at five o'clock the telephone went off the hook, the cheap Scotch came out of the bottom drawer and the feet went up on top of the marvelous old oak rolltop desk that was the only decent piece of furniture in Jake's office. For the next hour and a half the great Swiss collector Baron Thyssen could have pulled up to Harriman's with a Rembrandt under one arm and a Cézanne under the other and been forced to wait.

As far as the auction business went, this

was one of Jake's problems. He wasn't, as his superiors frequently reminded him, "diplomatic." By this it was understood that Jake had failed to cultivate an appropriately deferential attitude toward the rich: the unctuous sycophancy and social posturing that so much of the New York art world involves. If someone asked Jake's opinion of a picture that was patently rubbish, they would get it, unwrapped and unvarnished, regardless of who owned it or where it had come from.

This was why Sloane was at Harriman's. Harriman's was a small, old New York firm that had missed out on the great art boom of the sixties and seventies for reasons that were none too clear. People spoke about "mismanagement," and there were dark hints of malfeasance, although whose, or of what kind, never became clear. The experts at Harriman's were as good as any in the city, but the house never seemed to receive the best property or the best prices. It was not unusual for a picture or piece of furniture to be sold at Harriman's and then turn up a couple of months later at Sotheby's or Christie's to fetch twice the price it had got at the smaller auction.

Sloane had been in the art business for twenty-five years, the last ten of which had been spent at Harriman's. It was generally conceded that Sloane knew as much about pictures as anyone in New York, and had an extraordinary breadth of experience as well, since he was forced to catalogue American and modern European property as well as Old Masters. People wondered why he stayed at Harriman's. The answer was fairly simple. He was too prickly and idiosyncratic to work for anyone else, and too poor to start his own business.

There was another reason that was more subtle. There are insiders and outsiders in this world, and Jake Sloane was, by temperament and preference, an outsider. Like most bachelors who reach the age of fifty without any central emotional attachments, Sloane was a man whose habits were rigid, largely selfish, and generally misanthropic. Hatcher was easygoing enough not to mind Sloane's habitual surliness, and was usually immune to Sloane's cynicism. Sloane was largely free of the first two characteristics of most people on the New York art scene, social ambition and greed, and was thus free to concentrate all his energies on the third, which was spite.

Sloane's hatred of New York's larger auction houses was unadulterated; it burned with a sharp blue flame. It was also often extremely amusing, because Sloane could mimic the competition with scathing accuracy: this man's simpering lisp, the phony Anglicisms of another who informed people she was "going to the loo" so often that someone once sympathetically inquired if she was experiencing medical difficulties, and so on. Sloane had nasty names for all of them, which he was continually changing and refining, and nothing seemed to give him greater pleasure than to leaf through a catalogue from Sotheby's or Christie's and point out all the misattributions.

As Hatcher was carefully pouring his second round of bad Scotch into one of the paper cups Sloane had snitched from the watercooler downstairs, Sloane picked a panel off the top of the desk and handed it to Hatcher.

"Here's something for you, Amos. Take a look. Quiz time. Some poor sod took it to the Tuna, who told him it was a nineteenth-century piece of crap, so he brought it over to me. What do you think?"

The Tuna (or Charlie the Tuna) was one of the auction experts whom Sloane held in greatest contempt. He was an arrogant, incompetent European fop, whose position was predicated on the rumor that someone in his family had a significant collection of something or other, and might, if properly stroked, someday put it up for auction. As he examined the painting, however, Hatcher had the uncomfortable feeling that possibly this time the Tuna had not been entirely wrong.

The painting was small, about nine by eleven inches, but it was exquisitely painted. It was a night scene with a young girl leaning through a window, holding a candle in one hand and a lantern in the other. The girl was very young and very pretty, and her face held an expression of hopeful expectation.

Hatcher had been trained as a specialist in Dutch baroque art, and had little difficulty recognizing the type of picture as the sort popularized by a student of Rembrandt named Gerrit Dou. This was the problem. Dou had had a large following, and his paintings had been copied endlessly down to the end of the nineteenth century, when his popularity had begun to decline.

Turning the panel over, Hatcher realized that it couldn't be seventeenth-century. The back of a Dutch baroque panel was a major clue to the age of the picture, and this one was all wrong. It was oak, which was correct, but it was not beveled at the edges as it should have been, and the wood had none of the dark patina of the centuries that should have intervened. Also, the surface on the back of the panel was perfectly smooth, while that of a genuine baroque panel is rough, showing the marks of the saw in rippling serrations across the back.

Hatcher was worried. Sloane, watching him, was enjoying himself. Hatcher finally decided to take a flyer on one of the later Dutch painters working more or less in Dou's manner.

"It could be Schendel, I suppose, someone like that . . ."

"Schendel! My God, Amos, you're almost as bad as Charlie the Tuna. Look at the front, man. Don't look at the back. That's the trouble with this town. Everybody can read the back of a picture, and nobody knows how to look at the front."

"The painting looks School of Dou, but the panel looks recent."

"*So?* Honest to God, Hatcher, sometimes I wonder why I waste my good two-dollar Scotch on you."

Hatcher looked at the panel carefully with a pocket magnifier, stopping near the edge for a particularly close examination. He could see a tiny furrow or indentation a quarter of an inch from the edge, and noted that there was a thin border of paint at the edge that seemed a shade too dark. Then he understood.

"It's been transferred to another panel.'

"Bravo, Hatcher. If you look carefully, you can see why. There's a small crack that was opening at the top near the center, and someone figured if they didn't transfer it, the original panel would split. So they planed it down to the paint layer and stuck it on another panel. So, to repeat, what is it?"

"Someone close to Dou. Schalken, maybe."

"Maybe. It's a problem. I can complicate it, if you want."

Sloane leaned over and extracted a book

from under a large stack of books. Somehow, the rest of the stack remained standing. Nifty trick for supermarkets, Hatcher thought to himself.

Sloane flipped the book open to a marker and handed it to Hatcher. The painting in the black-and-white reproduction looked identical to the one Hatcher was holding. Hatcher read the legend underneath.

"Looks just like it. Are you telling me somebody knocked over the Kunsthistorisches Museum in Vienna and nobody informed me about it? Or is this a copy after Dou, like fifty thousand other copies . . ."

"It's even more complicated. The painting in Vienna was bought for the Archduke Leopold Wilhelm, probably from the artist, and was in engraved in 1661. So, there's no problem with that. The problem is this. There was another version in the De Bye collection in Leyden in 1665, certainly also by Dou, and, as far as I know, no one knows where the hell that second version is."

"Where did this come from?"

"It was exported from Czechoslovakia last year, doubtless illegally. Maybe it came from a private collection, maybe a junkshop. Who knows? There's no record of it, as far as I can tell, and whoever sold it got more money from the buyer than they would have got from the authorities. So it's clean, Hatcher. I thought you might be interested."

"I might be," Hatcher said warily, already worried about the quid pro quo.

Hatcher compared the painting with the reproduction slowly, detail by detail. Both had the same exquisite surface finish and minute treatment of the details, and in certain ways, the version he held in his hand seemed superior to the version in Vienna. Hatcher had a small, very modest collection of Dutch baroque paintings, but paintings from the Dou School had generally been beyond his price range.

"I'm putting it in the small sale in December. I'm calling it 'School of Dou' and estimating it at fifteen hundred to two thousand. I decided not to call it Dou, even though I think there's perhaps a minute chance that it is by the artist. Dou is still too much of a mess. No one's done any serious work on him in fifty years. With a break or two you could get it cheap, Amos."

Hatcher was used to getting a few "breaks" from Sloane, and appreciated them. Sloane understood that Hatcher's meager salary from the IAAD didn't allow him to compete for serious pictures, but when he found something that seemed within Hatcher's range and taste, Sloane would occasionally undercatalogue and underestimate it, and once in a while the gavel would fall just a shade too soon on a picture Hatcher wanted. This was never too blatant, and Hatcher was enough of a moral relativist not to lose sleep over the ethical ambiguities. His job involved art which was stolen, after all, not just fast-hammered.

Hatcher kept looking at the seductive smile of the girl in the window, and realized that he was being seduced. She was sweet, but not innocent. Hatcher tried to remember about candles in Dutch art. Emblems about fire, people getting burned, the flame of love . . .

"Is this why you called me this morning, Jake?"

"Yes, of course. Good painting, that. I thought you might want to see it."

Hatcher had wondered what was up. He'd detected an odd sort of urgency in

Sloane's voice, a nervousness. As he looked at the other man now, he felt the same slight irritability. Sloane stuck the painting back on the table, poured himself another shot of whiskey, and began to talk. He talked for several minutes, and Hatcher still had no idea what he was getting around to.

"Ah, the wonderful, romantic world of the auction business. People write novels about it. Did you know that, Hatcher? Actual *novels?* In the books people are always discovering Rembrandts and Picassos and Christ knows what, and flitting around in their Lear jets, or else chasing Nazis. You ever chase a Nazi, Hatcher?"

"Nope. Some pretty extreme Republicans, once . . ."

"Well. I want to write my own novel about this fascinating world some day. The glamorous world of Jake W. Sloane. Know how I spend my time? The paintings, first of all, are at least ninety-seven percent dreck. Fake Bierstadts and Ryders, hoked-up prints after Picasso, fourth-rate Old Masters that have been scrubbed so long with Clorox that all that's left is the underpaint and the canvas. School pictures, manner pictures, pictures with fake signatures and false pedigrees, pictures of somebody-or-other's grandfather painted by somebody-or-other's grandmother. Paintings on cardboard, paintings on velvet, paintings on Naugahyde; Day-Glo paintings, paint-by-number paintings, paintings you wouldn't believe. Most of what I do isn't connoisseurship, it's just birdwatching. If the painting is any damned good they send it to Slovenly's or Shiftie's. I get their mistakes, or the paintings they can't sell."

It wasn't like Jake to whine about Sotheby's and Christie's. Hatcher wondered what all this was leading up to.

"If the Iron Maiden gets a painting she really hates, she sends it to Harriman's, laughing her fool head off."

"You mean Major Barbara?"

"That was last week. This week she's the Iron Maiden. Anyway, then there are the consignors. The dealers are bad, Hatcher, but not nearly the worst. The worst are the doctors and dentists and lawyers. They wheedle and cajole and lie. They try to bribe you, and if that doesn't work, they threaten you with lawsuits. They buy paintings at auction and then refuse to pay for them. They try to con you. Then, when you get a *nice* consignor for a change — Hatcher, listen to me. There's this one man who owns a delicatessen down the street."

"He's the worst?"

"Oh, no. He's the best. Sweet guy. He smuggled some paintings out of Hungary during the fifty-six uprising and damn near got killed doing it. He came over here, knocked himself out setting up a business, worked like a dog for twenty-five years. Now he wants to retire, settle in Florida, and lead the good life. Last week he brought in his treasure: eight pictures wrapped in yellowed paper. Amos, the man was so worried about these pictures that he never even hung them on his wall. He kept them hidden under his bed. Last week was the first time the package had been unwrapped in over twenty years."

Jake sighed, put down his cup, and dropped his feet to the floor.

"What could I say, Amos? Those were eight of the worst pictures I've ever seen in my life. NSV, as we say in the trade: no salable value. Not to anyone I know, at least. I looked at them, and looked at them. Every picture has something, after all. But these had *nothing*. They weren't decorative, or colorful, or original; they didn't have historical or sociological value. I couldn't even bring myself to say they were interesting."

"I get it."

"No, I got it. I got to sentence Poppa to chopping chicken livers instead of lying on the beach for his few remaining years. I've eaten at that deli every day since 1974, and now I can't bear to go near it. There are lots of dreams in this business, all right, but the ones you remember are usually the ones you smash."

Jake crumpled up the paper cup and dropped it in the wastepaper basket, and then went over to the large semicircular window at the front of his office.

"Come here, Amos. I want to show you something."

Hatcher went over to the window. There was a black man standing on the corner three stories down and across the street. He had a piece of cardboard stuck across the top of a trash container, and some cards were lying on it. Every few seconds he'd shuffle the cards and flip them over, while he harangued the crowd in front of him.

"That's us, Hatcher, that's the art business. Three-card monte. 'Watch the red, folks, keep your eye on the red. Red you win, black you lose. That one? Nope, sorry.' And it's always the same black card that turns up, and there's always another sucker to bet on it."

Hatcher was beginning to get a little tired of this. Sensing something wrong, Sloane grabbed him by the shoulder.

"Enough of this nonsense, hey? Let's go out to eat, my treat. Then I'll tell you about *my* dreams, some of which seem about to come true."

4

"Your dreams," said Hatcher.

"Oh, yes. My dreams," said Sloane.

They were just finishing a huge platter of spare ribs washed down with a copious supply of beer, and Sloane had so far avoided any serious subject in favor of a continual stream of stories, mostly scurrilous and probaby largely fictitious, having to do with various prominent members of the art community.

Part of the pleasure of any discussion with Sloane was watching his face. Sloane had a mop of curly white hair that sat on his head like a throw rug and crawled down the sides of his face in the form of huge, bristly sideburns. His most arresting feature was a pair of eyebrows that had elegant, ornamental reverse curves, like the F-holes in a violin. His eyes were dark and beady, and became beadier as he became more excited. His complexion was bright red. Hatcher had once described Sloane's appearance as a cross between a satyr and a leprechaun.

"One of my favorite dreams is a sale. A big sale, an important sale, the kind of sale that gets splashed across the papers and winds up as a feature article in *Art and Auction* and the *Burlington Magazine*. Not big in numbers, necessarily, but choice. Important pictures, pictures so serious that when they come up to the podium there is a kind of expectant hush instead of the usual yattering. In my dream the sale has to be Old Masters. Modern and contemporary sales bring in the bucks but they're carnivals, discos, know what I mean?"

Sloane dropped the last spare rib noisily onto his plate, and wiped his fingers with a flourish.

"When was the last really important sale of Old Master pictures in New York, Hatcher? Think about it."

Hatcher thought about it.

"The Erikson Sale."

"Exactly! The Erikson Sale, about

twenty years ago. Now, take a firm grip on your beer, Hatcher. There's going to be a major sale of Old Master pictures in New York in exactly . . ." Hatcher watched Sloane's eyebrows flicker up and down. ". . . exactly seventeen days. At Harriman's."

Hatcher was confused, and wondered for a moment if Sloane was losing his grip.

"That's the October second sale? But I've seen the catalogue. There are some nice pictures, I agree, but 'major'?"

Sloane grinned his Satyr's grin.

"Forget the catalogue. The real auction, the auction I'm talking about, will only take about ten minutes, and will have its own catalogue. Not even a catalogue, probably, just five loose color plates stapled together."

"Just five?"

"Just five. Five small pictures that will blow your head clean off your shoulders. The estimate for those five pictures, conservatively, is between two and two and a half million dollars. With any luck at all, the commission will be enough to get Harriman's a nice little place closer to Madison Avenue, and Jake Sloane a nice little place far, far away from Harriman's."

Hatcher looked across the table at Sloane, who was staring at him with furious concentration. He remembered the little boy on the subway.

"I don't understand. Needless to say."

"I'll explain. Everything I'm telling you, by the way, must be absolutely confidential. It's not just a matter of money. As you'll see, a life depends on it. Literally."

Sloane gave Hatcher a minute to absorb this before he started his story.

"To begin with, Amos, how well do you know Italy?"

"Pretty well."

"I don't mean just geographically, but politically?"

"Not so well. Italian politics has always seemed fairly complicated, and Italy is obviously a country with problems, but which one isn't? Their problems are maybe a bit more bizarre than ours, but I'm not sure they're necessarily any worse. More flamboyant, maybe. Kidnappings, knee-cappings, terrorism in general."

"Okay, let's start with kidnappings. Kidnapping is a serious business in Italy. I mean that in both senses. It *is* a business, and a multimillion-dollar business, in many parts of the peninsula. In Sicily, of course, there is a centuries-long tradition of kidnap for ransom. But recently the authorities have got the clever notion of sending *mafiosi* to the North for rehabilitation, with the obvious result that a Calabrian and Sicilian brand of organized crime is breaking out in Milan and Turin. The *mafiosi* have metastasized all over Italy."

"What has this got to do with pictures?"

"You'll see. Kidnapping may seem like a sport, but it's a deadly sport. Political kidnappings have been getting a lot of headlines recently, but actually these are relatively benign. Most of the victims survive. Moro was the exception, of course, but there's a good body of opinion that claims that his death was as much the fault of the political parties as it was of the Red Brigades. The authorities refused to compromise, so Moro was shot. Still, if you're kidnapped, you're better off in the hands of political extremists than in the hands of professionals."

"You sound like you've been reading up."

"I have, and you'll see why. Two weeks ago, the nine-year-old son of a Milanese industrialist was kidnapped in broad daylight on his way to school."

"I'm beginning to understand."

"Are you? The job was highly professional. They knew exactly when the boy would be at a certain spot, they knew how to divert his guards —"

"He had *guards?*"

"Oh, yes. Every scion has guards today, or gets out of the country. So the boy was taken. His father received a message that the kidnappers wanted the equivalent of two million dollars, and fast."

"If he was an industrialist, couldn't he pay it?"

"Ordinarily he could. But he made the mistake of going to the police. Wait, Hatcher, you'll see. In general the authorities have found that when someone is kidnapped, the ransom money is paid, and the person returned. Nice for the family, nice for the kidnappers, but no so nice for the cops trying to catch them. The current criminological response to kidnapping is to pay no ransom under any circumstances. This approach seems very logical and hard-headed, but it has had one small side effect: the victim almost invariably winds up dead. Regardless of what the

100

police tell the families of victims, they have found that the families usually pay up, and the only way the cops have found around *this* one is to freeze the assets of the victim's family so they can't pay up."

"What about friends, relatives?"

"Friends and relatives as well. Do you understand now, Hatcher?"

"Which leaves paintings, works of art, and jewelry. Negotiable assets. But why you? Why Harriman's?"

Sloane smiled at this.

"You mean, aside from our international reputation and the brilliance of our experts? We, that is, I, can guarantee two things which are essential: speed and discretion. If the big auction houses touched anything like this, there'd be a diplomatic explosion within five months. The Italians would raise bloody hell if they knew pictures like these were being taken out of the country. And if they try to sell the pictures privately, they'll get maybe a third or half of their fair market value."

"Tell me about the pictures."

"Not yet. Let me tell you about the auction first."

Now that Hatcher was a captive audience, Sloane took his time. He waved over a waitress to order coffee, lit a cigarette, and gazed pensively off into space for a minute before resuming the story.

"Well, the auction won't be quite like my dream, but close enough. The things in the catalogue are pretty dreary, so we'll probably have the usual ragtag collection of sharpies and hustlers and deadbeats. But the front section of the room will be roped off, completely reserved. I'm trying to arrange to borrow fifteen or twenty Louis Quinze chairs. That's all I need, I think. Every dealer, collector, or curator who could touch these pictures will be contacted individually by me, told about the works, and sworn to secrecy. There won't be any cameras or newspeople, of course, and the whole thing will probably be over in ten minutes. But what a ten minutes!"

"If the Italian authorities find out?"

"If the Italian authorities find out, the sale could be stopped, I suppose. But the pictures will be declared at United States customs, so they will be in the country legally. And since they are not stolen, they can't be impounded and returned. At any rate, they're already in Geneva."

"Jake, you're walking a thin line. What

in hell *are* those pictures?"

"You'll see. Be at my office at — say — one-thirty tomorrow. They're coming in about then."

5

At quarter past one the next day, Hatcher leaned on the counter at Harriman's and smiled at the blond receptionist, on whom he had once had designs.

"Hi, Suzy. Could you call Jake and tell him Amos — no, wait!"

Hatcher dug around in his pocket for a black address book, pulled it out, and flipped around in it for a moment.

"Aha! Here it is. Tell Jake that Ignatz Gaugengigl is here to see him."

"Who?"

"Here. It's written down. Tell Jake."

He waited while she made the call, laughed, and put her hand over the receiver.

"He says he doesn't believe you. He says you made it up."

"Nineteenth-century American painter, swear to God. Tell him I can document it."

One of the games Hatcher played with Sloane was an ongoing search for outrageous artists' names. If one of them found a name the other couldn't top, he got a meal out of it. Hatcher started out strong with Sigmund Freudenberger, but Sloane was on a streak, with Hercules Brabazon Brabazon, Sebald Bopp, and Carducius Plantagenet Ream.

"Jake says to come on up, but he wants proof."

The route from the receptionist's desk to Sloane's office was a zigzagging minefield that snaked through stacks of rugs, piles of furniture stuck together like Chinese puzzles, and racks of paintings separated by heavy slabs of cardboard, and then up a rickety flight of stairs to a balcony. In better days the auction house had had a fine neo-Georgian interior, but it had been a long time since those better days.

When he got to the office, Hatcher found Sloane shuffling a huge stack of consignment forms. Other sheets of paper lay about on the floor in stacks, and Sloane had to pirouette from one empty spot on the floor to the next to avoid knocking them over.

"What you see about you are the next three sales at Harriman's, if I can ever find the rest of these damn forms. Put another way, there are two missed deadlines at the printers' and another imminent, so if I don't find the forms there'll be no catalogues, and with no catalogues, the sales will bomb, and if the sales bomb then all the consignors will skip off to some other house, or sue us. See what I meant about the glamour? When I write my novel about the auction business, one of the main plot lines will involve looking for bloody consignment sheets. What was that name again?"

"Ignatz Marcel Gaugengigl."

"I guess you win. The best I could come up with was Alois Heinrich Priechenfried. If you can get over to that desk, I'll give you a small preview of coming attractions."

Plotting his route carefully, Hatcher made it to the desk without substantially adding to the chaos.

"Take a look at these."

Sloane handed Hatcher a folder which

held some photographs and color transparencies. Hatcher went through them very quickly, then very slowly, holding the transparencies up to the overhead light.

"Think we can say 'Important Old Master Paintings'?"

"Hell, yes! You can say anything you want. How about 'Old Master Paintings of the Highest Importance'? Does that sound nifty enough? You're not just out of your league with these, Jake. You're out of anyone's league. Pictures like these only show up in London, and then only once in a while. You're sure they're clean?"

"They're clean. The documents will be here this afternoon."

Hatcher started through the transparencies one more time. The first one was a harbor scene with a multitude of figures, and it took Hatcher a full minute to discover the subject. The scene showed a microcosm of swarming humanity gathered on a shore, and as Hatcher strained his eyes he could identify every social condition of Renaissance Europe: beggars and lords, fishermen and cooks, farmers and charlatans, cops and robbers. In the middle of this teeming glut of humanity was a tiny figure with a halo, speaking and gesticulating.

"Christ Preaching to the Multitude?" Hatcher asked, and Sloane nodded.

"He took the business about 'multitudes' seriously, didn't he? You can find Brueghels at auction, all right, but not —"

"Not like that. Look at the landscape, Amos."

The landscape elements in the picture were as minutely detailed as the figure groups. On one side was a forest with soaring trees, and the painter had taken the trouble to depict every leaf on every branch. As the landscape receded in a sequence of rolling hills, Hatcher could see farmhouses and castles, church spires and windmills. In the farthest background the landscape became a sort of blue mirage, and you could barely see a fantastic crystal palace like something in a dream. The right-hand side was a seascape with every conceivable kind of boat from a simple fishing scow to warships and galleons, all represented with a kind of hallucinatory detail.

"God, Jake, you could climb into this

picture and not come out for ten years. How big is it?"

"About the size of the transparency you're holding. The condition of the thing seems perfect, by the way. How do you estimate something like that, Hatcher?"

Hatcher thought about it. Small flower still lifes by Brueghel had long ago passed the quarter million mark, and landscapes, good ones, had brought much more. But Hatcher had never seen anything like this on the market.

"A million, maybe?"

"A million easily. The others, who knows? That *Madonna and Child in a Landscape* is Hans Memlinc, and when did you last see a Memlinc at auction? Or a Bouts? The last Bouts was the one Simon bought for over four million in London. Granted, that was much bigger and more important, but still. Look at this."

Sloane handed Hatcher a transparency. This painting showed a bust-length portrait of a man. He wore a high felt hat shaped like a fez. His hands were clasped together in prayer and his lean, ascetic face looked out at the viewer with a gentle melancholy. In the window behind him could be seen the crenellated walls of a medieval city.

"You wonder how Flemish pictures like this ever wound up in Italy, don't you, Jake? Sure must have been a lot of them there, though, even during the Renaissance. Michelangelo had such nasty things to say about Flemish painters, you wonder if maybe he was nervous about the competition."

While Sloane was holding up another of the color transparencies and squinting into the light, Hatcher became aware that someone was standing in the doorway. He was a small man with a dark complexion and delicate features, and he looked anxious. Hatcher reached over to call Sloane's attention to the man, but when Sloane turned around, the figure was gone.

"I think some man was at the door for you, Jake."

"Aha! It must be the pictures. Merry Christmas, Amos."

Sloane bounded to the door and peered out, but it seemed that whoever had been there was gone.

"What did he look like?"

"Small and nervous."

"Oh. 'Small and nervous' must be our accountant. God knows he has a lot to be nervous about. Last week one of the union men put his foot through a twenty-thousand-dollar picture. The union men: that's another major theme of my novel, by the way. You can never tell when they wreck something whether it's clumsiness or hostility or both. My theory is that if they put Harriman's art handlers in uniform they could scrap the MX missile system. What time is it, by the way?"

"Don't you have a watch? It's about two."

"He said one-thirty. I suppose the plane could have been late. Think I should call the airport?"

"No, but perhaps you could relax a little. What are you going to do when they get here, pass out cigars?"

"Maybe. Or maybe just pass out."

"Listen, Jake. It's only half an hour late, and you're already twitching like a cat. In another half an hour you'll look like a human tuning fork. I'm not well enough yet to hang out with crazies, according to my doctor, so —"

"Hey, come on, Amos. Don't split on me."

"Look, Jake. Your Christmas present is probably stacked up over Kennedy. It could stay stacked up for the next three hours. Maybe there were problems with customs."

"My God. Don't say that."

"Look. The paintings will be here tomorrow, okay? Why don't I come by then and see them?"

"It'll be a lonely vigil, Amos."

"I have things to do. I have to see someone about a new kind of motion detector, I have to see the Burgundian miniatures at the Morgan, and there are some errands. Sheila's birthday is next week."

Jake's face took on an expression of stoic resignation.

"So go, Hatcher. Laugh and play."

"Hang on, Jake. Maybe you can find those missing consignment forms. I'll see you tomorrow, same time."

"*A domani.* If you find me hanging from the light-cord, you'll know he decided to take the pictures somewhere else."

Sloane had a stricken, how-sharper-than-a-serpent's-tooth expression on his face when Hatcher edged out the door and made his escape.

Hatcher was glad to be gone. The

weather had turned cool just as suddenly as it had turned hot the week before, and the city had the exhilarating crispness of autumn. A fresh breeze off the water had blown the smog away, and the vertical thrust of the city's architecture seemed liberating and optimistic to Hatcher, rather than dispiriting and crushing as it frequently did. Hatcher had learned, in the past two years, that there are certain days in New York City that almost make you want to forgive it all. He had also learned, though, that once you did, it immediatley fell back into its old habits, like a friend you could never bring yourself quite to trust.

As soon as he left Harriman's, Hatcher decided to forget all the projects he had mentioned to Sloane and play hooky. He was still on official medical leave from the IAAD, and still rickety enough not to feel like a malingerer.

He took a cab up to Eighty-sixth street and walked down Madison Avenue, savoring the fall fashions. The twenty blocks from there down to the high sixties were among the most fashionable in the city, and the women treated this stretch of Madison like an elegantly appointed runway, parading up and down wearing extravagant plumage and striking various poses. The most startling specimens looked like professional mannequins. Hatcher's appreciation of this display was purely visual; he felt no more lust than a child watching a parade. The look of frigid inaccessibility these denizens of the haut monde cultivated didn't bother Hatcher, who had no desire to talk to any of them, let alone touch one.

Hatcher had much the same reaction to the contemporary art in the galleries along Madison as he did to the women. Most of it seemed to him clever and chic, but also self-consciously artificial and bloodless. The bright, splashy pictures in the windows were part of the decor, part of the environment, and after a while they became indistinguishable from the bizarre displays of the fashion boutiques that were also dotted along the avenue. Here art and fashion were truly united.

After ten or twelve blocks of this, Hatcher had had enough, so he hopped another cab to his favorite delicatessen on Fifty-ninth. This was one of his great discoveries. After the appraising glance, the look of mock horror, and the inevitable "Amos, honey, you're lookin' so *thin!*" his favorite waitress rushed back to the kitchen to get him a reuben sandwich the size of a small sofa cushion. The earthy clamor and heady aromas of the restaurant were the perfect antidote to the anorexia of Madison Avenue.

After this indecent meal, Hatcher decided on a movie. He found a nearby cinema that had an old Ernst Lubitsch film. It was a story about two grown-ups who managed to fall in love with all their clothes on, and even to do it in a witty and entertaining manner.

Afterward Hatcher went back to Brooklyn. Before returning to his brownstone apartment he went down to the Promenade overlooking the East River. The night was beautiful and full of stars. Hatcher leaned against the cast-iron railing and gazed across the water at lower Manhattan. The buildings were flattened out into rectangular silhouettes that twinkled like Christmas trees. To the right was the stately and still majestic form of the Brooklyn Bridge, with its marvelous gothic piers and its exquisite tracery of rods and cables. To his left were the islands and the reassuring, matronly form of the

Statue of Liberty.

Give me your tired, your poor, thought Hatcher. How about your lonely? The night would have been perfect with someone, preferably Sheila Woods, to enjoy it with.

Hatcher sighed and began to stroll back to his apartment. He was just about to close the outer gate behind him when he noticed the police car.

6

Hatcher felt exhausted and emotionally drained. He sat slumped at the detective's desk, and slowly flipped through the photographs one more time.

There were six color Polaroids, and they all showed the same scene from different angles: Sloane, slumped in his chair, his left arm hanging down with the fingers almost touching the floor and his upper torso, head, and right arm sprawled across the desk top.

None of the photos was pleasant, but the worst was one taken from the left-hand side. The photographer must have been kneeling down to take it. Jake's blind eyes seemed fixed on the camera, his mouth was open, and you could see his tongue; his face had the blank, almost imbecilic expression common to people whose deaths are violent and unexpected. Hatcher understood the universal impulse to close the eyes and mouths of corpses. Don't look at me, don't accuse me. Most of all, don't tell me your secret.

From the back of Sloane's neck, just at the juncture of his neck and shoulders, protruded the blunt handle of a knife. There was very little blood, just a red smudge around the haft.

"Know anything about knives, Hatcher?" the captain's voice was a tired rasp. They had been going over it for four hours, and the last hour and a half had not produced anything new.

"Not much, Captain. I generally use poison darts and a blowgun myself, an old trick I picked up from an Amazon tribe."

"I already apologized and I'm not planning to apologize any more. You were there; you had the opportunity."

"I was what you had."

"Have. I wouldn't let it worry me too much if I was you. But on the other hand I wouldn't get too lippy, either. We're all tired."

Hatcher was still angry. He was angry at being pulled in as a suspect rather than a witness, angry that they hadn't told him what had happened until he was inside the station, and very angry that he had been run through ha gauntlet of news photographers. But as he told the captain, they had to have something on a case like this, and Hatcher was what they had. Ruefully, Hatcher remembered Sloane's crack about winding up on the inside pages of the *Post.*

In truth, what else beside Hatcher *did* they have? The story about the phantom consignor with the five smuggled masterpieces had sounded hollow to Hatcher the first time he had repeated it, and it still sounded hollow. To be sure, it had been at least partly corroborated. The blond receptionist had spoken to a short, dark man shortly before two o'clock. The man had told her in a fluent but heavily accented English that he had an appointment with Sloane and had been directed to Sloane's office. She was harried by other calls, so she had neglected to tell Sloane that a client was on the way up.

She couldn't describe him accurately, other than by saying that he was short, thin, and dark. She thought he might be carrying a suitcase or a briefcase, but she did not see it; it was just something about the way he moved. She thought she had seen him leave about half an hour later, but she could not be sure about this, either. Sloane's body had been discovered by the treasurer, who had gone to Sloane's office to complain about an insurance claim.

The head of the company, Alfred Harriman, was apparently the only other person with whom Sloane had discussed the consignment and prospective sale, and he had been even more secretive to Harriman than to Hatcher. He had simply outlined the situation to Harriman in very summary form and said that it would necessitate an extension on the departmental budget for, among other things, a pair of armed guards to be stationed at Sloane's office around the clock. The pair had actually arrived at five that evening, to find the place swarming with policemen.

Hatcher's description of the man who appeared briefly in Sloane's doorway was depressingly vague. He was a short, thin man, well dressed but not conspicuously so, who might have been Italian. He might also have been Greek, Spanish, or Arab. His expression had been worried, but neither desperate nor enraged. Hatcher had seen him for perhaps a second. Maybe he could sharpen his description under hypnosis, but both Hatcher and the captain tended to doubt this.

The folder with the photographs was missing. The page of Sloane's desk calendar for Thursday, September 11, was also missing. The police had ransacked Sloane's correspondence file for any sort of letter or document and found nothing. Whoever had arranged the sale of the pictures had apparently emphasized strongly the need for secrecy, and Jake Sloane, a secretive man by nature and also a man who loved conspiracies, was all too happy to oblige.

The police had been alerted at Kennedy Airport, and descriptions had been sent to Fiumicino Airport near Rome and Malpensa Airport outside Milan. Neither Hatcher nor the captain held any great hopes about this, since someone who had been this careful until now was hardly likely to do anything as idiotic as hop on the next flight bound for Italy carrying a suitcase full of paintings that could implicate him in a murder.

A Lieutenant Petrocelli had been sent

off to make some inquiries, and until they heard from him the captain and Hatcher had nothing to do but sit and kick pieces of the puzzle around. The captain was a tired man who drank too much coffee and looked as if he were in mourning for the world.

"Knives, Hatcher. Christ knows I hate knives. This kind is called a parachute knife. It's spring-loaded, like a switchblade, only the blade comes straight out from the handle instead of in arc. You just place the front of the handle against something and push the little knob and *whango,* the knife does all the work. Your Aunt Sadie could take out a three-hundred-pound tackle for the Los Angeles Rams just by pushing a little knob. You have to know where to place it, is all."

"Is this necessary?"

"It is for me. I'm a great one for M.O., for how. How it was done gives you a lot about who did it. Knives usually mean two kinds of people, sadists or technicians. Slashers are always psychotic, I mean florid psychotic, and, with multiple puncture wounds you can generally figure on a sexual angle."

The telephone rang. He answered

"okay" twice and then "thanks," and hung up the receiver.

"Where was I? Oh. Anyway, the guy who did this was a surgeon, a technician. He might have done it in hot blood or cold blood, but it was done fast and done right. Commandos and spies kill like that. That phone call was Petrocelli, by the way. He got through to Milan. There've been kidnappings recently, but none has involved the young son of an industrialist."

"Maybe it was hushed up?"

"Petrocelli asked about that. The Italian cops don't do that anymore. The current theory is to get it out in the open, put a big spotlight on it. So, where does that leave us?"

Hatcher got up and yawned, feeling his joints creak.

"Give me a little while on that, will you, Captain? Say, twenty minutes?"

"Fine. You can get out of here if you want to, take a walk around the block. Watch out for the hookers, though. They get pretty thick around here at this time of night. And don't get mugged."

Hatcher thought the captain was joking until he got outside the station. There weren't any muggers that he could see, but the hookers were out in force. Hatcher wondered if they were there because they felt safer there, or just because they had been in and out of the station so often that it felt like home to them.

Hatcher went across the street to an all-night diner and spent the next ten minutes huddled over a bowl of something alleged by the management to be beef stew. Hatcher was too hungry to care. The other denizens of the diner were spread out around the room like sullen islands of loneliness. The scene reminded Hatcher of an Edward Hopper painting.

The captain was slouched at his desk when Hatcher returned, working on another cup of coffee. He glanced at Hatcher when he came in, but his expression implied that he was not really expecting anything. Hatcher started to talk.

"Okay. I don't know how much of this is true, if any of it, but it seems to cover what we've got. To begin with, the whole story about the kidnapping was rot. There were paintings, all right. I saw the photos. But they must have been stolen. The nonsense about the ransom money was cooked up because first, they had to be moved quickly, and second, they had to be moved for cash. Sloane never mentioned this, but I'd bet it was part of the deal.

"Sloane was the perfect target. He wanted those paintings so much that he swallowed the whole story. If it had gone off, a sale like that would have opened all kinds of doors for him. He wanted it so badly that I couldn't bring myself to press him about the pictures — whose they were, where they came from. That was my fault. He knew they were smuggled, and the kidnap story was calculated to keep him away from tracking them down. I'd bet Sloane was specifically told not to contact the owner. His phone was being tapped by the police, some story like that.

"I think Sloane confided in me partly from friendship, and partly because he was afraid I'd blow the whistle on the sale. The things were certainly illegally exported from Italy, at the least. Italian export laws for art are so arbitrary and irrational I might not have given a damn anyway, but he couldn't be sure. Also, he wanted to brag."

"So far so good. Why was he killed,

then?"

At this point Hatcher wanted to leave. He wanted to trip lightly out the door, pick up five or six of the girls outside, and go whistling off into the night.

"Why was he killed, is it? Well. Maybe he was killed because of me."

"You, Hatcher?"

"Sure. I'm an art cop, right? Not what you might call a household name in the Big Apple, but reasonably respected in certain quarters. One of these quarters . . . oh, Christ."

"Yes?"

"All right. One of these quarters was Italy. Last year I recovered a Greek pot that had been smuggled out of Italy. It was a very major piece, as it happens, and I got a big play in the Italian press. I was decorated, feted, a ten-minute hero. Amos the famous."

"I see."

"Anyway, I'm known in Italy. If I'm right that the pictures were stolen, then the little man in the doorway must have done some rapid calculations. He must have assumed, first of all, that the whole scheme was blown, that Jake had spotted the hot paintings and brought me in for

126

the bust. He looked through Jake's door and saw that he'd walked into a trap."

"All right. What then?"

"I don't know if you noticed this, but the area around Jake's office is a rabbit-warren. There are storage bins, offices, viewing rooms, and so on. My assumption is that he found one of these places where he could hide while figuring out his next move, and then, when he saw me leave Jake's office, he went back. Jake probably greeted him like his long-lost brother, and the little man decided to play along with the charade, up to a certain moment."

"Still, why kill Jake?"

"Frustration, perhaps, or rage. Maybe Jake knew something he didn't tell me. He must have had a name, after all, and probably a telephone number in Italy. Possibly there was something incriminating in the file that I overlooked. Or maybe there was something that he suddenly noticed, like the name of a photographic studio stamped on the back of one of the prints. Maybe he thought he had to get the photos back at any cost. He had to move quickly, because he probably thought that I'd be back shortly, with friends."

The telephone rang. The captain picked it up, listened for a moment, muttered, "I'll be damned," and then, "Thanks, Joe," and put it back. He smiled weakly across the table.

"When something like this happens, I keep everyone up. No time-and-a-half in this business. So, for the next week or so everybody around here hates me. But the book says that if you're going to crack a homicide, you're probably going to do it in the first twenty-four hours, if at all. As usual, the book is right."

The captain picked up a pen and started doodling on a note pad. First he drew a cat, then a palm tree, then a jet plane with guns blazing. Hatcher couldn't tell, from upside down, whether it was the cat or the palm tree that was being shot down.

"That call was the lab. They found a clean print on the knife, right index finger. Isn't that nice? The print wasn't yours, by the way."

"Where did you get my prints?" Hatcher was too tired even to get mad.

"Took them off a coffee cup about an hour after you got here. Nothing illegal, just sneaky. I figured we'd better start things with you, just in case."

"Just in case. I could still be an accessory, Captain. Maybe I set up this whole deal, and maybe I set up Jake Sloane."

"And maybe Dolly Parton's a female impersonator. I wanted to get you out of it fast, Hatcher, because I thought maybe I was going to need you. I had to clear you first."

"Need me? Well, bless my soul, Captain."

Another jet fighter appeared on the pad, and a furious dogfight started. Hatcher wondered which plane was us and which was them.

"It comes down to those damn paintings. Art isn't what you might call a specialty of mine."

Hatcher was always surprised at how defensive people became about art. Twenty years ago art was supposed to be a dubious and slightly reprehensible activity involving people you wouldn't want your daughter to go out with, and now it was more popular than takeout food. Like sex, it had gone from being disreputable to being obligatory without ever being simply another option. First you shouldn't like it, now you had to. Hatcher found himself across the desk from a police captain in the New York City homicide department who was embarrassed because he didn't know anything about early Netherlandish painting. The whole thing was ridiculous.

"Stolen art is my job, Captain. The first thing I want to do is to track down the pictures. If I'm going to do that I need a free hand, and that means the reporters off my back. All of them. I don't care what you tell them, but tell them something that gets them uninterested in me. The second thing is that I need to be formally included in the investigation. I may have to go to Italy. If so, it would be good to have some kind of written authority from the NYPD, preferably something official-looking, covered with stamps, seals, and signatures. I'll probably be able to come up with something on the pictures in the next few days, and I'll be in touch."

"Fine. Go on home, get some sleep. I'll take care of that stuff."

"One more thing, Captain. What's your name?"

"Burke. Fred Burke. There's a nameplate here someplace." He rummaged around on the desk top.

"Skip it. I believe you. Good night, Captain."

"Yeah. Good night, Hatcher. Call me tomorrow."

7

The next day Hatcher awoke to a certain notoriety. He was on page one in one tabloid, page three in another, and page twenty-six in *The New York Times*. Both tabloids carried pictures of Hatcher being hustled into the station, and one even had the obligatory interviews with neighbors. "He seemed like such a nice man," they said, as they always say. Luckily Hatcher had stayed in bed until the early afternoon, so he didn't have to wait too long for the retractions in the afternoon editions. Nevertheless he felt mugged. The man in the photos was clearly guilty of something horrific.

New York is fickle. An expert at an auction house found with a knife in his neck is a fair to middling thrill, by the standards of the local papers, but certainly nothing really great. Better was the discovery of a decapitated diamond-trader stuffed into a plastic garbagecan liner, which had happened the previous day. Better yet was the woman who became convinced that her child was possessed by the devil and who decided to exorcise him by sticking him in the oven and turning it up to broil. Jake Sloane's murder was a significant item as long as Hatcher could be implicated, but as soon as he was cleared and no apparent connection could be found with the Mafia, drugs, or sex, the case began to sink out of sight. Peripheral acquaintances did not seem particularly surprised that Hatcher had been hauled into the police station on suspicion of murder. On the other hand, they weren't particularly surprised when he was cleared, either. "People do funny things" is a part of the credo of the New Yorker, and another part is, "You never know about people, know what I mean?"

In the next five days Hatcher did what he could think of to do, and so did Captain Burke. Burke seemed like a good cop. He checked the fingerprint with the Italian police and then, through Interpol, with the other countries of Europe, and finally with the FBI, and found nothing. He kept in contact with the airports and other ports of entry into Italy, but the luggage checks failed to disclose the five panels Hatcher had described. The knife proved to be an Italian copy of a German army knife, of a type made in Mestre and sold in souvenir shops from Venice to Naples, as popular as it was illegal.

Meanwhile, technical reports from a minute examination of the scene of the crime piled up on Burke's desk. The reports contained classified breakdowns and descriptions of particles of dirt, dust, pollen, fabrics, and tobacco, and they were all carefully documented, rigorously thorough, and equally irrelevant. The autopsy report, stripped of medical jargon, seemed more significant. The angle of penetration by the blade and the way the knife was turned both corroborated Burke's contention that the killer knew exactly what he was doing. Whether he had learned his technique from a manual or through long practical experience was, of course, the big question.

Hatcher's researches took him first to the Frick Art Reference Library on East

Seventy-first Street, and then to the Platt Photo Archive at Princeton University. Hatcher had been a familiar figure in both spots ever since his graduate-school days, and both made him feel a series of uncomfortable emotions ranging from nostalgia to embarrassment. At one time he had expected to devote his life to the kind of activity these places represented: the slow, reflective life of scholarship. Later, for reasons that were still not entirely clear to him, he had defected from the scholarly community. Whenever he returned to it, he felt like something of an apostate, and he almost always sensed a vague yearning to return to the well-ordered life and intellectual rigor of the academic sphere. At the same time, he could still recall the sense of suffocation and alienation he had felt while he was actually in it. He had finally reconciled himself to the fact that his feet were planted firmly in two different worlds. He often found himself playing art historian at the scene of a violent crime, or conversely, looking for a criminal in the stacks of a library.

The information Hatcher discovered about the pictures didn't seem to make any sense. Three of them, one by Dirck

Bouts, another by Hans Memlinc, and the third by Gerard David, seemed identical with works in the Museo Procacci in Rome. Yet he had received no published alert of a theft there, and when he sent a wire inquiring about any recent robberies, the answer was negative. Could the three pictures have been copies? Of course Hatcher had only seen photographs and transparencies, but even so he was inclined to doubt this. The almost microscopic exactitude of Flemish paintings, as well as certain characteristic technical subtleties such as the fine crackle pattern of the paint surface, made forgeries of them extremely difficult. And, if they *were* forgeries, why were they all works from a single museum? Hatcher fretted over these problems while the librarian made photocopies of the pictures for him.

The other two pictures were more difficult to trace. The Brueghel and Elsheimer panels were known to scholars, but the most recent literature listed them as "whereabouts unknown." One book published just after the war cited the Brueghel as "Formerly in an Italian private collection." The last resort, for Hatcher, was the art photo archive at

Princeton, which had been compiled over sixty years before by an indefatigable scholar-collector named Platt. For years, every available reproduction of every work of art Platt could find disappeared into massive leather-bound portfolios, hundreds of which now reposed in metal boxes in a room in the Princeton Fine Arts Library. The only trick to using the Platt collection lay in remembering that each metal box weighed roughly the same as a concrete cinder block. Several venerable scholars who had blithely slid one of Mr. Platt's boxes off a high shelf had nearly had their feet amputated when the box came plummeting down on them.

Hatcher finally located the remaining two pictures that he had seen in Sloane's transparencies, the magnificent Brueghel panel with Christ preaching and a small nocturnal scene by the German painter Adam Elsheimer. They were reproduced in two old sepia-toned photographs, and at the bottom both were inscribed "Caprese Collection, Rome." Still, the information was of dubious value. Hatcher had never heard of the Caprese Collection. Given his recent luck, it had probably been dispersed thirty years ago, without leaving a trace. He caught the bus back to New York with more photocopies and more questions.

Everything Hatcher could think of to do seemed to end in frustration. A lengthy wire sent to the Italian government's Department of Art Theft in Rome received a noncommittal reply: "Many thanks for the information." Hatcher was surprised at this, since he had worked closely with the head of the Italian Department of Art Theft, Roberto Anselmo. He sent Anselmo a long letter, and waited.

As Hatcher sat brooding in his apartment, the whole affair began to seem unreal: the story, the paintings, the little man standing in the doorway. All that was indisputably real was the body of Jake Sloane collapsed on his desk with a knife in the back of his neck. As time passed, Hatcher remembered Captain Burke's remark about the first twenty-four hours being crucial to the solution of a crime. Although Burke had not mentioned this, practical considerations, not theoretical ones, dictated this limit. There were too many other homicides, too many other problems. After a week, Sloane would be just another open file marked "pending."

For the newspapers, the police were "waiting for a break" or "following several leads." In point of fact, they were doing nothing.

Hatcher had glanced through the literature on recent art thefts before looking for the five paintings, but now he went through it carefully once more. There had been a surge of thefts recently in Central Italy, around Rome. These crimes seemed more elaborate, more carefully planned and sophisticated than usual. One in particular caught Hatcher's attention. Early in April, a van carrying a number of paintings for an exhibition of Caravaggio and his school had been hijacked near Rome. Since the hijackers seemed to have anticipated the route of the van, it was assumed that the robbery was an inside job, and the driver was considered a prime suspect. However, one detail of the dispatch caught Hatcher's attention. The driver had described one of the hijackers as "a small, thin man in his mid-thirties." Hatcher wondered again about the slight man in the doorway of Sloane's office.

It seemed this man knew about art. He knew what he had and what it was worth on the open market. This didn't worry Hatcher as much as the fact that he could fabricate an elaborate story for Jake Sloane and make him swallow it whole. Sloane was neither stupid nor gullible. The little man was actor enough to play the role of a Milanese businessman, or at least the agent of a Milanese businessman, and educated enough to carry it off in English. Unless there were others.

What else could this little man do?

The choice of pictures was clever. They were small and easily smuggled. They were Northern rather than Italian, which was also smart. It was Hatcher's experience that the Italians were almost as xenophobic as the French, and felt a similar contempt for the art of other countries. The Uffizi had a small but superb collection of Dutch and Flemish paintings; most of them were in storage, and the galleries that displayed the rest were often locked. A number of Northern pictures had been stolen several years before from the Pitti Palace because when the new alarm system had been installed, the rooms where the Northern pictures were hung were the last to be wired. So, if the small man had been stopped at the border with some Flemish paintings, he might have bluffed his way through with some forged papers and a thick German accent.

The little man also seemed to know about knives and how to use them. And, Hatcher reminded himself, about Hatcher. The little man seemed to know altogether too much.

Hatcher telephoned Sheila Woods, which didn't improve his mood. It was her birthday in a few days, and he had promised to spend it with her in Boston.

"I've got to go to Italy." Hatcher sounded firmer than he felt.

"What do you want me to say? If you're going, you're going. But it's only been six weeks or so since you were shot, Amos."

"I'm resilient. The Iron Man, they call me."

"Not the last time I saw you, you weren't."

"I'm rarin' to go. Just send me in, coach. Seriously, Sheila, I'm okay."

"Want me along?" Hatcher had been afraid of this question.

"Sheila, I can't ask you along on this one. For one thing, they wouldn't give me the money. I'm not sure they'll give me the money for me to go."

"Is it really the money?"

"That, and the fact that I don't know what I'm doing. I may be in way over my head, or I may get there and find that Anselmo has the whole thing wrapped up and just be in the way. And there's your Hudson River Landscape show. I can't drag you away for nothing."

"True. I'll miss it, though. I already miss you. And it's fun to play Nick and Nora Charles."

"They had lots of money, and a cute dog. And, they never got shot."

"Don't you get shot. Seriously, Amos."

"I won't. I'll eat lots of pasta. The next time you see me, I'll be fat and sassy."

"Work on the 'fat.' Forget the 'sassy.' "

The next day Hatcher went to see Max Fleischmann at his gallery on Fifty-seventh Street. Fleischmann was the president of the IAAD, and therefore Hatcher's nominal boss. A wizened man in his late seventies, Fleischmann owned a small, cluttered gallery that made no effort to impress the Park Avenue set. He had been in the same place for forty years, and had become famous for the phrase "It's not so bad."

The first thing Max had decided was

not "so bad" was art nouveau. That was in the early fifties, when Tiffany lamps were junk-shop items and nobody had heard of Alphonse Mucha. His next interest was late-nineteenth-century academic painting. When Fleischmann had decided that was not so bad, "academic" was considered a four-letter word in the critical vocabulary. Max had bought Coutures, Bouguereaus, and Alma-Tademas for next to nothing. He had made a healthy profit from the sale of his art nouveau collection, and more from the academic pictures.

Max had never stayed in one area long enough to get really rich, however. When people began to show enough interest in his current hobby to vindicate his judgment, Max, perfectly satisfied, would move on to something else. When the market in the first area continued to climb, he would get increasingly annoyed. "Two hundred thousand dollars for a Bouguereau! What is it, is everyone *meshuggah?* I said it wasn't so bad. I never said it was *great art.*"

Now Fleischmann's gallery was full of Venetian baroque paintings by artists Hatcher had never heard of.

"All right," Max had said to Hatcher one day, his arms thrust out in his habitual rhetorical shrug. "So the sixteenth century in Venice was the Golden Age, and the eighteenth century was the Silver Age. Would I argue? What does that make the seventeenth century — the Chopped Liver Age? Look at these paintings: Mazzoni, Maffei. I'm telling you, Hatcher, the Venetian *seicento*, it's not *so bad*."

It had been Max who had hired Hatcher as an investigator for the IAAD some years before, and Max who defended his expenses to the rest of the Association. Max and Amos argued a lot, and got along splendidly.

"Max, I want to go to Italy. It's about this Jake Sloane thing."

Max's eyes slowly lifted toward the ceiling, his shoulders following.

"He says he wants to go to Italy. A few weeks ago he gets shot, and now —"

"Max? Who are you talking to, Max? The only other person here is me. I have to go to Italy, and I need six or eight thousand dollars."

"Six or eight thousand dollars, he says. So where should I get —"

"Call in some markers. I pay my way

with the dealers, Max. Remind them how much I saved them on those phony graphics that were flooding the market before I nailed that guy upstate. Remind Stapleton why he still has some pictures left on his wall. Remind them —"

"Enough. Jake Sloane was a friend."

"Yes. Jake Sloane was a friend. That's the main thing."

"So, go to Italy. But don't get shot anymore. You might keep in touch a little this time. Would a few postcards hurt? I'll give you a bank draft and a letter. What else?"

"Nothing I can think of. Just make the letter as official-looking as possible. I've got one from the police department, too." Hatcher smiled, remembering the formidable documents he had taken to Italy years ago to get into private collections and the storage areas of small museums.

"Back in graduate school we used to call them 'dago dazzlers.' "

PART III

Rome

1

Vittorio Pecci, the new minister in charge of the Department of Art Theft, did not appear dazzled. In fact, he appeared hardly interested at all.

He sat across from Hatcher, behind a large, glass-topped desk on which a few objects were carefully arranged. Hatcher's portfolio of documents was open before him. He read the first few sentences of the letters, scanned the rest, and flipped them over quickly. He seemed only mildly interested in the brief résumé Hatcher had included, summarizing his career and noting several of the more important cases in which he had been involved.

"You are employed, as I understand, by a group of art dealers? As a sort of private detective?"

"The International Association of Art Dealers pays my salary, but I pick my own cases. I try to work with the police, of course."

"Of course. And Interpol?"

"I've worked closely with Interpol, and I have many connections . . ."

"But no formal status?"

Hatcher hesitated a moment, and tried to answer this in a neutral tone of voice.

"I have no formal relationship with Interpol, or with any other agency."

"You are a bit of a lone wolf, then? Like the Lone Ranger?"

Before Hatcher had a chance to weigh the insinuations behind this little joke, Pecci's telephone rang. The minister listened, murmured, *"Si, pronto,"* and asked if Signore Hatcher would please excuse him for a few minutes. Hatcher was all too happy to oblige.

In this short respite, Hatcher tried to orient himself. He knew nothing of Pecci. He had arrived in Rome three hours before, left his luggage at his *pensione,* and gone off to meet Roberto Anselmo. At the ministry he was informed that Anselmo no longer worked there; if it was absolutely necessary to speak to someone, a short meeting with the present minister could perhaps be arranged. Only, Hatcher was informed, if it was a matter of particular urgency. No explanation of Anselmo's departure was forthcoming, but Hatcher had the curious sensation that the adjutant at the desk had almost recoiled at the name.

Whoever Pecci was, he was nothing like Anselmo. Hatcher had had no qualms about arriving at the ministry looking rumpled, red-eyed, and generally disreputable since this was Anselmo's habitual condition. Pecci seemed about twenty years younger than Anselmo, and several years younger than Hatcher. His appearance was as crisp as his manner; a perfectly tailored charcoal-gray suit, delicate powder-blue shirt and sapphire tie, a gold wristwatch that looked slightly smaller and thinner than a Necco wafer, and the sort of shoes that make the best American shoes look like hiking boots bought three sizes too large. And the kind of good looks that Hatcher — craggy, balding, and weatherbeaten as he was — tended to find annoying. Early Omar Sharif. There was nothing obviously wrong with Hatcher's face, taken piece by piece. The trouble was that none of the pieces seemed to bear much relationship to any of the other pieces. "I like your face," Sheila Woods had told Hatcher once. "It's sort of eclectic." Pecci's face was remarkably homogeneous.

Pecci's office was also disconcerting. Anselmo's office, a slightly smaller cubicle in the same building, had been a crazy amalgam of art works, art historical treatises, and police records. Hellenistic terracottas and small Renaissance liturgical bronzes had been used as paperweights, and a large, exceedingly ugly black Etruscan drinking vessel had served as an ashtray. Pecci's office had no ashtrays, nor any works of art. The long wall in front of Pecci's desk was furnished with a mahogany bookcase that ran from floor to ceiling and contained mainly legal records and texts. There were a few art books, but these, like the law books, were sets, carefully arranged either historically or alphabetically. One of the short walls of the room contained a series of filing cabinets, the other held a desk with a mimeograph machine, typewriter, file trays, and a cylindrical cardboard pencil-holder covered with a floral design in bright primary colors. Hatcher appreciated this small act of rebellion, and wondered if it was Pecci's secretary or his wife that was responsible for this cheerful splash of color inserting itself into such an otherwise beige environment.

But in his inspection of the office, Hatcher didn't find what he was looking for, namely, a foothold. He was always in a delicate position with police. He needed them, and was often in the awkward situation of having to prove to them that they needed him. The trick was in convincing them that his expertise was a valid exchange for their information and facilities, which was not always the case. At best, this was a delicate transaction. With Pecci, Hatcher sensed that it might be impossible. He didn't have a gambit, and was too tired to play the game with the required subtlety.

Pecci returned to the office, and picked up the file again without speaking. He pulled out the series of photocopies Hatcher had included and dropped them on the desk. Then he regarded Hatcher with an amiable smile that Hatcher found himself distrusting. He seemed to be waiting.

"I could be wrong about the first set, but I doubt it."

"Do you know where they are from?"

"Recently, no. They were in the Caprese Collection around the late nineteen twenties or thirties, but after that they seem to have been lost, or at least lost to scholarship."

"And about the 'Caprese Collection'?"

Hatcher looked at Pecci. The smile was still there. Hatcher didn't like it, but decided he could live with it a bit longer.

"I've never heard of it."

"I see, Mr. Hatcher. And these?" Pecci tapped the other pile.

Hatcher waited before answering. He could control himself, but he hoped the smile would not get any bigger.

"There I must have been wrong. Flemish paintings follow fairly rigid conventions in the fifteenth century. I may have misidentified them, but they seem to be three panels in the Procacci Museum."

"There have been no thefts of art from the Museo Procacci, Signore, I assure you."

"As I said, I may be wrong. But they may have been copies, or fakes."

"Copies and fakes do not interest me,

154

Mr. Hatcher."

"And murders?"

Hatcher's last remark at least had the satisfying result of eliminating Pecci's smile, at least momentarily.

"We are talking of art theft at the moment. These paintings" — here Pecci tapped the pair of photos on his desk — "were indeed taken from the Caprese Collection, which still exists, although it has been maintained for several decades in secrecy. The theft of these works, which took place last March, has also been kept as secret as possible."

"Why?"

"At the request of the victim, who does not wish to become a target again. One must sympathize. I should not even discuss this with you, but — well, you have come a long way. I must ask, however, that you discuss these matters with no one."

"I came here to discuss these matters with you."

Pecci gave Hatcher a quizzical look. Hatcher gave up.

"Look. A friend of mine was murdered. He got involved with some stolen paintings and somebody drove a knife into the back of his neck, and I'd very much like to find the man who did it."

"I understand. Could you identify this man you think you saw?"

Pecci got up and went to the window. He leaned against the sill, his back to Hatcher, and looked out on the gray courtyard below. Hatcher didn't mind talking to Pecci's back. At least he didn't have to worry about the smile.

"I'm not sure. But I'm fairly certain he can identify me, which is perhaps equally valuable."

Pecci turned around, looked rather mournfully at Hatcher, sighed, and returned to his desk. He returned the photocopies to the folder, tapped it on the desk to straighten the documents inside, and pushed it across the desk. Hatcher knew what he was about to say before he opened his mouth.

"Go home, Mr. Hatcher. The man you are looking for will be caught, and the people with him. If murder can be proven, he will be extradited, of course."

"I can help you, Pecci."

"No. Not according to Italian law, and law is very important to me. This man you think you saw — we know about him, a great deal about him — but he is just one of them, and there are many others. The trick is to get all of them, without warning."

"I know a certain amount about art theft. And art smuggling. I know the routes . . ."

"You are looking for revenge, a vendetta. This is dangerous for you, and I cannot promise to protect you."

"I didn't ask for protection, I —"

"Let me finish. To find this man you are looking for, alone, would be like a surgeon removing part of a tumor. It would merely help it spread. There is much more to this situation than you know or than I can tell you. There are political aspects, serious political aspects, which make these events both dangerous and delicate."

"Delicate? In what sense?"

"That I cannot say. But I can tell you this: the man will be caught."

Hatcher raised a skeptical eyebrow.

"Perhaps the record will reassure you. In the years in which my predecessor held this job, the average number of criminals arrested for art theft was between eighty and one hundred. In the past six months

157

alone there have been over one hundred and fifty arrests, and the number of successful prosecutions has nearly doubled. We have fifteen men working for us now; before me there were seven or eight. We have a computer, we have research specialists and photographic files that never existed before. But this is not the most important thing, Hatcher. The most important thing is laws."

At this point, Hatcher wistfully recalled Pecci's earlier advice to go home.

"Laws are the key. To make art theft a serious offense, to make people understand that stealing Italy's art is stealing her past, her history, to make them understand that this is a *political* crime, a crime against the state, this is my goal. I am beginning, at least. Anselmo is gone, and with him the graft and corrupt practices of decades."

"I worked with Anselmo."

"Did you? It seems Anselmo worked with everyone, including the thieves and smugglers. I harbor no anger toward him. He was effective, in his way, but he had no respect for laws. At the end, it was just a question of whether he would end up in Regina Coeli or not. Do you know Regina

Coeli?"

" 'The Queen of Heaven.' I have always thought that was a pretty name for a prison."

"Yes. Not such a pretty place to be, though. Luckily I managed to help Signore Anselmo avoid it."

Hatcher put the folder in his attaché case and stood up somewhat shakily. His whole body ached, and he was not in any mood for the rest of Pecci's speech. He had liked Anselmo.

"Well, Signore Pecci, you don't seem to want my services in this case."

"I must regretfully decline your kind offer, Signore Hatcher."

Hatcher offered his hand, and Pecci took it in both of his.

"You will follow my advice, then?"

"About going home?"

Hatcher felt himself flush. He understood the threat behind the question, and it made him angry. Pecci still held Hatcher's hand, and Hatcher jerked it away as if stung.

"I think I might stick around for a little while. Play tourist. Maybe I'll go out to the villa at Tivoli and see the waterfalls."

"There are no waterfalls at Tivoli in

November."

"I'll bribe a guard to turn them on for me. Think I'd wind up in Regina Coeli for that? Oh, well, I'll keep myself amused somehow. *Buongiorno,* Signore Pecci."

"Mr. Hatcher."

Pecci was not smiling when Hatcher left the office.

2

"Pecci was the first person I've spoken to since I got here. You're the second. I'd expected Anselmo, and instead I get some tight-assed, double-talking bureaucrat who tells me to turn around and go home before I've even unpacked."

Luigi Landini gave a tired shrug. Hatcher had known Landini for years and had never been able to decide whether his mournful expression was an aspect of some deep-seated weltschmerz or simply a quirk of bone structure.

"Pecci is a problem, *paesano*. For us, too."

"Tell me about him."

Hatcher was still exhausted, but he felt much better after eating. The place Landini had selected was a nondescript

161

trattoria in one of the poorer parts of Rome, Trastevere, and Hatcher had thought it a curious choice until the *padrone* had arrived with the *bistecca alla fiorentina*. Hatcher could have found a steak that good in New York, but it would have been half the size and cost at least thirty dollars.

"Pecci's a bureaucrat, as you say, and in this country that means trouble. More trouble if it's an intelligent bureaucrat, and Pecci is by no means stupid."

"Scared, then?"

Landini thought about this. He was a considerate man, in both senses of the word: deliberate in his judgments, and unselfish in his concern for others.

"In a way, yes, but Pecci's not exactly a coward. I'll tell you what I know about him and you can make up your own mind. You didn't know about the business with Anselmo?"

"Nothing."

"Maybe I should start there."

Hatcher leaned back in the stool until he was resting his weight against the cool plaster wall behind him. He didn't mind the uncomfortable hardwood stool, the tiny table covered with butcher's paper

162

rather than a cloth, the suspicious glances of the other patrons, or the babble of voices in rough and largely (to him) incomprehensible Roman dialect. Landini lifted the huge fiasco of wine and refilled their glasses, and Hatcher felt fine.

They had met years ago as graduate students. Landini's father had moved his family from Rome to New York when Luigi was eight, so his education was almost entirely American. After receiving a doctorate in Italian Renaissance art from Columbia, he had discovered that immigration laws did not allow him to take a teaching position in the States. He returned to Italy to discover that his academic path was effectively blocked because of his American training, and he had been forced to take a job as researcher for an important art dealer on the Via del Babuino. After eighteen years he was still there. Tainted by his contact with "the trade," as even the most respected dealers are contemptuously referred to by their academic colleagues, Landini had little choice. Not that he was dissatisfied. He was not well paid — few people who work for dealers are — but the dealer's stock was superb, and he was able to spend most of his time on research rather than commerce. A delicate, unstated pact existed between Landini and his employer based on the mutual recognition that if Landini was paid too little, he would leave, taking a dangerous number of secrets, and perhaps clients, with him. On the other hand, if he was paid too well, he might also leave in order to start his own business. One large carrot was dangled tantalizingly before Landini's skeptical nose: the repeated promise of a small branch of the firm someday opening under Landini's supervision on Madison Avenue or Fifty-seventh Street in New York. Somehow this never quite happened. Currency regulations were tightened, the exchange rate became disadvantageous, or the market shifted. Something intervened, always. By now Luigi had a wife and two children, and it was by no means clear to Hatcher that he would take this opportunity even if it came.

Landini was not lazy, but he was slow, sedentary, and ruminative. He had devoted his life to developing his powers of observation. He was a cross between a sponge, a filing cabinet, and a delicately calibrated optical instrument. He was also perfectly bicultural, and one of the few such people in Hatcher's acquaintance who combined the virtues rather than the vices of both countries.

Luigi Landini took a long sip of his wine, and then began.

"Anselmo's troubles started about a year ago, in the newspaper. Items started to pop up here and there. Stories about graft, corruption, bribery, that kind of thing."

"Any of them true?"

"Sure. Most of them, probably, but so what? Anselmo had his own methods, some of them perhaps a little shady, but he got the job done. People didn't pay much attention to the articles at first. I don't think Anselmo himself did. Then they got sharper and nastier, and they started naming names and places. Then it became a political issue."

"Anselmo-gate?"

"Exactly. Formal investigations, boards of inquiry, the whole thing."

"Who was behind it?"

"That's a hard question to answer. There's a good possibility that it was Pecci, of course. In this country when there's a hue and cry about corruption and you want to know the source, the immediate question should be, 'Who's after whose job?' "

"I see. What were the exact charges against Anselmo?"

"Basically, aiding and abetting the smuggling of Italian art. True, as far as it went, but it didn't go far enough."

"Explain."

"Sure. Anselmo is a good, hardhearted Neapolitan realist, and he understood years ago that the job of stopping art theft and art smuggling in Italy altogether was an absurdity. Not only is there too much valuable art in a country which is largely impoverished, but the ridiculous restrictions on importing and exporting art and/ or currency make huge black-market operations inevitable. Taking the laws at face value, it is impossible for any Italian to be an international dealer of any consequence without breaking the law right and left. Technically, we're all crooks. So Anselmo worked out an angle, a *sistema*.

"Anselmo's *sistema* was basically simple: up to a certain level of quality, or artistic importance, anything went. Beyond that, nothing. Try to get out of the country with a minor Raphael school painting that can be duplicated in any half-baked museum in Italy, and that was fine.

166

He not only wouldn't stop you, he might even help you."

"But try to get out of Italy with a Raphael . . ."

"Exactly. Try to take a Raphael out of Italy, and he'd nail your balls to the highest parapet of the Castel Sant'Angelo."

"Fair enough. And the Raphaels *didn't* get out of Italy. What about export papers and the *belle arti* commission?"

"Part of the absurdity. Anything that leaves Italy has to pass the *belle arti* commission, as you know. If it is officially 'notified' — receives a *notifica* — it can't legally leave the country. This can happen on some scholar's whim. He doesn't like the dealer, he hasn't been properly bribed, whatever. There's another bind, of course. If the dealer wants to export a work, he must declare a price and allow the Italian government to buy it at that price. If his declared price is too high, he risks tipping off the gnomes in the basement of the Uffizi that it's an important piece and thus runs the risk of the *notifica*, as well as the certainty of an exorbitant export tax. If the price he quotes is too low, then the gnomes will buy it for a song, and it will wind up in the storage area of some provincial museum. So every time a dealer asks for an export license, he's playing a game that's half poker, half Russian roulette. But you know this song already.'

Hatcher smiled. "I know the whole opera. *Il commerciante collerico*, by Puccini. Tell me some more about Anselmo's *sistema*."

"Basically the way it worked was that Anselmo set himself up as a sort of one-man *belle arti* commission. It got out that if you wanted a work to leave the country, you could take it to them and go through the whole formal procedure, or you could take it to Anselmo. If Anselmo passed it, you wouldn't be nailed by his boys; if you got nailed by somebody else, of course, that was your problem"

"And the export taxes?"

"As I said, Anselmo is a Neapolitan."

"I see. Was this a racket, or just Anselmo's peculiar investigating procedure? What was the quid pro quo?"

"As far as Anselmo was concerned, information. He realized that if he had enough small-timers and middlemen in his pocket one way or another, he'd usually know what the big boys were doing. He was always, and only, after the big boys. And he got them, too."

"Funny. Pecci told me that the arrest record for art crime went up dramatically since he took over Anselmo's job."

"Pah, Pecci. Let me get us some strong coffee, and then I'll get on to Pecci."

While he waited for Landini to return with the espresso, Hatcher let his eyes wander around the room. The other diners had long since forgotten about the Americans in the corner and, indifferent to this minor intrusion, gone back to the animated theatrical performances that could only loosely be termed "conversations." The only decoration on the much-stained walls, other than the inevitable shelves of wine bottles, was an old lithograph of the Virgin. She was depicted as an adolescent, her tiny hands clasped together in prayer, her huge eyes cast passionately upward like a Madonna by Guido Reni. Her mouth was a neat little cupid's bow, and Hatcher wondered if the model had perhaps been some silent film actress like Lillian Gish or Pola Negri.

When Landini returned he brought espresso, but in large cups, not small.

"I thought you might need a bit of a

jolt, and you won't get it hearing about Vittorio Pecci."

"That bad?"

"Bad enough. So he bragged about his arrest record, did he? Well. As soon as he was installed in Anselmo's job he went after all the small-time hustlers that Anselmo had so carefully cultivated, and in a few months, managed to destroy Anselmo's whole network. Numbers make great headlines, of course, and Pecci was very quickly blathering about stopping art crimes in Italy altogether."

"Anselmo — how did he react to this?"

"Publicly, with silence and a great show of stoic resignation. Privately, he's seething, and waiting for vindication."

"And Pecci's humiliation, I assume. Napoleon on Elba. What's Pecci's story?"

"He's not just a bureaucrat, a functionary. He's also a politician with his eye on the main chance. He's from Turin originally, and was trained as a lawyer. Part of the animosity between Pecci and Anselmo is temperamental and geographical. Anselmo finds Pecci stiff, cold-blooded, and legalistic, which he is. Anselmo calls him 'Frenchy,' among other things."

"He also speaks perfect English. My mother told me never to trust a foreigner who speaks English better than I do."

"Pecci studied in England for several years. He's a great believer in English common law."

"I'll bet. So Pecci believes in the rule of law and sweet reason and computers, and I imagine Anselmo doesn't give a damn about any of them. Does Pecci know anything about art?"

"Not much. One of the ironies of the situation is that Pecci, who's always mouthing conservative pieties about 'our sacred Italian artistic heritage,' really doesn't care much about art personally. As far as I can tell, he wants to use the post as a political gambit. His only qualification for this job is an excellent record in Milan as a criminal prosecutor."

"I see. He has the manner of a criminal prosecutor. Why did he leave Milan?"

"Partly for his health, I think. At the beginning of last year he managed to secure stiff convictions against two of the leaders of the Red Brigades, and word got back that he was on a hit list. If word was needed."

"Things are like that?"

"Things are worse. Judges, prosecutors, antiterrorist groups, politicians — they're all targets. Pecci is still a target."

"You said he isn't a coward."

"Oh, no, he's a brave man, which doesn't mean he isn't scared stiff. I also said he wasn't stupid."

Hatcher rubbed his eyes, then the knot in his temple. He was completely exhausted, but he wanted to get through it once, and didn't want to lose the thread. He thought he could make it on caffeine and adrenaline, but he had to get outside. He had to get on his feet.

"You look like hell, Amos. Let me take you back."

"Okay. But I want to talk about the crime. I want to get the whole thing shaken out on the floor so I can look for patterns in the morning. I can keep going if you can."

"All right, but you really look awful."

"I got shot a while back. Nothing serious and very much my own stupid fault. Lost a lot of weight, though, so now I look like Marley's ghost when I get tired. We'd better get moving."

Hatcher was too tired to argue when Landini grabbed the bill. Luigi went into the back of the *trattoria* and a moment later reemerged with the *padrone*, a short, fierce-looking man with the creased and eroded features of a Sicilian peasant. The two men shared a joke which Hatcher couldn't understand, evidently fairly scabrous, judging from the *padrone*'s wheezing cackle, and then Hatcher was introduced. The introduction was brief but formal, and ended with a stiff handshake. From the brevity of the handshake and the scowl on the man's face, Hatcher understood that his future presence in the *trattoria* would be tolerated, if not exactly welcomed. Hatcher smiled. It wasn't much, but it was more than he had got from Pecci.

3

They found a stand-up bar in the Campo Marzio near Hatcher's *pensione*, and Hatcher told Landini about Jake Sloane's murder.

"So. The murder is tied in with the knockover of the Caprese Collection, and probably other thefts as well. I got that out of Pecci, at least. I also got the hint that Pecci was keeping the whole thing tightly lidded down, and that he didn't want anyone — me, for example — connecting the dots. Why not? And why does he want me out of town?"

Landini thought about this for a long time. Hatcher gazed across the zinc-topped bar at the forest of bottles with their reflections in the mirror behind it. Hundreds of liqueurs, most of which

Hatcher had never heard of, made a brilliant kaleidoscope which blazed and twinked in a sea of glass. He'd discovered long ago that when he got exhausted his color sense became vividly acute, while all of his other senses dulled, and now he had to wrench his gaze away to avoid being mesmerized.

"I think Pecci wants it lidded down because he suspects what every dealer on the Via del Babuino suspects; namely, that there is a well-organized and very dangerous gang of thieves operating more or less at will."

"He suggested to me that he was about to break the case."

"He would. The word on the street is that the case is more likely to break him. So far, Pecci's managed to keep most of the details out of the papers, and the news reports have treated the thefts as separate and discrete occurrences rather than the beginning of an epidemic. There's something else."

Landini hesitated, and Hatcher became alert. There was something Pecci had refused to tell him, and something Landini also seemed to be circling around.

"There's a theory going around that the

crimes are the work of terrorists."

It was Hatcher's turn to hesitate. He wanted to frame the right questions.

"Is that plausible? Is there any evidence for it?"

"What do you know about the Caprese business?"

"Very little. Pecci implied that he was covering it up to protect Caprese. I stumbled across it researching the pictures Sloane showed me, but otherwise I've never heard of Caprese, the collection, or the crime."

Landini sighed, took a sip of his cheap, raw Italian cognac, and began to speak a fraction of a second before Hatcher throttled him.

"Caprese's a wine merchant, comes from a long family of wine merchants. The wine is Chianti, but it's none too good, and Caprese was one of the ones caught a few years ago in the big adulteration scandals. Anyway, for sixty years or so the family has had a palazzo in Rome, a fantastically hokey piece of late baroque nonsense by Martino Longhi, or someone like that. Caprese's father was a bit of an odd duck, but a great art collector. In the middle of the Berenson frenzy, when

176

everyone was running around beating the bushes for goldback pictures and early Renaissance stuff, he was quietly buying up mannerist and baroque art. Nothing anyone thought of as 'major' — mostly small panels, bronzes, and decorative objects. The climax of the collection was a room which he discovered in a Florentine palace and shipped to Rome in toto. It was a little octagonal *studiolo* modeled on Cosimo de' Medici's *studiolo* in the Uffizi: small, but exquisite, encrusted with serpentine and porphyry, rather like a *pietra dura* table.

"Anyway, he spent years furnishing it with precious, ornamental works of art. This was in the twenties and thirties, when 'less is more' was the golden rule, and anybody who knew about Caprese — and not many people did — thought of him as a dotty eccentric with an expensive playpen. Caprese's collection was a small in-joke when he was assembling it and then, when he died, it was forgotten."

"Not entirely, I gather."

"Not entirely, but almost. It was an embarrassment to his son, who almost dispersed it a number of times. Then, in the late fifties and sixties, when interest in Italian mannerist and baroque art revived, the son realized he was sitting on a substantial fortune. Earlier, he had frequently denied that the collection existed for fear of mockery. Now he denied it existed for fear of theft and tax-assessors. He even began, very discreetly, to amplify the collection.''

"And still it was kept a secret? No catalogues, no guides?''

''Nobody mentioned it, and no art historians, so far as I know, got near it. A few dealers must have known about it, but they kept it a secret for obvious reasons. The rest of us only heard about it after the robbery.''

"So much for Pecci's security. What about the robbery, then?''

"The first thing that bothers people about the robbery is, simply, how did they know about the collection?''

"A dealer leak, maybe. Maybe Caprese himself. Maybe a maid, a servant — who knows? That's low on the list. What else?'

"It was a commando-style raid. They called Caprese a pig — 'Signore Porco' — and threw around a lot of radical nonsense. The whole operation looked like the Red Brigades, except there was no kidnapping

178

and no ransom attempt for the art. And there was something else, a slogan sprayed on the wall. I wrote it down somewhere."

While Landini rummaged around, found a thin leather notebook, and began to flip the pages with almost sadistic methodicalness, Hatcher finished his drink. Finally Landini found the page.

"What they wrote on the wall was *'Ti ho in culo, polizia assassina.'*"

"The thing about 'police assassins' is a left-wing formula. What's the first part again?"

"*'Ti ho in culo.'* It means 'shove it,' more or less, but no Italian would say that."

"Oh? Are you sure?"

"Almost certain. The phrase is *'va 'fanculo'* — a universal Italian insult, good from Milan to Mulberry Street in New York."

"This other thing, this —"

"*'Ti ho in culo.'*"

"Could that be dialect?"

"No, I've tried that. It's just wrong, just nonsense. As if an American said, 'Place it up your ass.' He might say 'shove it,' 'cram it,' or 'stuff it,' but never 'place it.'"

"That's strange as hell. If it isn't an idiom or dialect, then it's someone who doesn't speak the language perfectly, and we're up a very different kind of creek. Let me copy that down."

While Hatcher wrote down the phrase, Landini continued the train of thought. "That's my suspicion. For example, it's possible that Germans were involved."

"Germans? Are you serious?"

"That's what's going around the galleries. That's what has the dealers scared, and maybe what has Pecci scared, too. There's been a theory for years that the Red Brigades are being supported in part by West German terrorists, fragments of the old Baader-Meinhof gang. There was a lot of talk about that when Aldo Moro was kidnapped, and just enough evidence to keep the talk going."

Suddenly Hatcher had had enough. The alcohol which he had been using to keep going was beginning to hit him, and he was too tired to fight it off. He leaned against the bar with his right hand and tried to untie the knots in the back of his neck with his left. When he glanced up, the kaleidoscope of bottles was beginning to vibrate and swirl.

"I don't want any of that stuff, Lou. I don't want any goddam Red Brigades or any crazy Germans or any Pecci or any political horseshit. Just a man, one man. Just one man."

"Okay, Amos, It may not be that simple."

"Why not? Why's everything so fucking complicated in this country? There's a man stole some paintings, killed someone — friend of mine, matter of fact — I want to find him, that's all. Get him. What's everybody so goddamn *scared of?*"

Landini smiled a brief, tight smile, but didn't answer the question. While Hatcher glared at him, he pulled out his wallet, went over to the counter, and paid for the drinks. Hatcher was still glaring when Landini returned.

"I'll drive you back to your *pensione.* Maybe I can point out a couple of things on the way."

Landini's car was a tiny, battered Fiat with a loose muffler, and while Landini jerked it through a series of narrow alleys and sharp curves, Hatcher felt as if he were in a bumper car at an amusement park. The streets were dark and empty, and the massive faces of the buildings, heavy and oppressive at night, seemed sinister and unreal.

After a couple of minutes the Fiat turned onto a wide avenue Hatcher recognized as the Via del Plebiscito, and a moment later Landini stopped the car at the entrance of a large square dominated by the massive facade of a church.

"You know this, of course."

"Sure. God, I taught it often enough. That's the Gesù, by Vignola and della Porta."

"I don't mean the church. Across from it, the palazzo."

Hatcher looked. It was a large building with an odd trapezoidal shape, the short segment facing the square serving as the facade. There were flags and a cartouche over a narrow entranceway leading into the central court. Still thinking of architecture, it took Hatcher a fraction of a second to realize that Landini wasn't looking at the building, but at a small knot of figures standing near the portal.

Hatcher knew by the uniforms that they were military, not police. As he watched them the knot broke apart and began to fan out. Each of the men held a machine gun at his waist, the left hand on the barrel, the right hand around the throat, the right index finger hooked around the back of the trigger-guard.

"That's the headquarters of the Christian Democrats, the DC, Italy's largest political party."

"Why the soldiers? Was there a bomb threat?"

Landini smiled. "There have been many bomb threats. And many bombs, too. The soldiers are there for a simple, practical reason: the Christian Democrats don't want to show up in the morning and find a hole in the ground where their headquarters used to be. You get used to soldiers, by the way. You'll see them all over."

Landini started the Fiat, drove across the piazza and down a curving street flanking the Christian Democrats' palazzo.

"Don't want to sit there for more than a minute, or they'll start a computer check on the car. A waste of time usually. They never seem to get the right car."

Landini turned right onto the ancient street known as the Via delle Botteghe Oscure, the Street of the Dark Shops, and pulled to a stop at the entrance of a narrow alley.

"This is the Via Caetani. One of the cars they missed a few years ago was a red Renault. It was parked about ten meters ahead of us, with the body of Aldo Moro wedged in the back under a blanket. The Red Brigades had pumped about ten shots into him. There, you can see the plaque on the wall."

Landini pointed to the left, and Hatcher could indeed make out a bronze plaque. Underneath it, a few wilted bouquets of flowers were propped up against the plaster wall.

"Moro had been prime minister five times. He was perhaps the most important political figure in Italy. When they kidnapped him, they killed a carload of guards, all heavily armed."

"Trying to scare me, Lou?"

"Yes, maybe. Tell you, anyway. Warn you."

A few minutes later they arrived at Hatcher's lodgings, an old and relatively modest *pensione* near the Pantheon in the old part of the city. Landini seemed reluctant to let Hatcher go.

"Look, Amos, if this is a terrorist thing maybe you ought to think about it."

"What do you mean?"

"Think about Pecci's advice."

"You mean get out?"

Landini nodded. He looked as tired as Hatcher.

"Can't do that, Lou."

Landini slowly nodded again.

"Oh, by the way. There's an article you should read about the art thefts." He reached into his coat pocket and slid out a rolled-up magazine, which he handed to Hatcher. Hatcher unrolled it; it was called *Marforio* and had a nude woman on the cover.

"The article is full of cheap cynicism, but then maybe he's right. Let me know what you think. Keep in touch."

"*Buona notte,* Lou."

"*Buona notte,* Amos. Oh — and *benvenuto a Roma.*"

Hatcher was too tired to laugh.

4

Hatcher slept until half past eleven the next morning and awoke with a start, feeling marvelous — alert, taut, all his senses sharp. He often experienced this sensation while traveling: a sense of regeneration, a sudden injection of energy and adrenaline. He understood that this nervous overdrive could be counted on for about a week before the inevitable crash.

He went over to the washbasin in the corner of the room, threw some cold water on his face, and looked out the window. The building across the street was being restored. An elaborate structure of metal pipes and wooden planks covered the lower stories where workmen fought to overcome the effects of decades of blackening and corrosive chemical fumes.

Above this curious, fragile-looking cage of pipes and sticks stood a dome.

It was the dome of Sant'Ivo della Sapienza, and it was one of the reasons Hatcher had chosen this room in this *pensione*. Admiring it, Hatcher wondered if "dome" were the right word; it wasn't a regular hemisphere at all, but a witty and brilliant architectural invention which managed to orchestrate bits and pieces of classical architecture with strangely oriental details in a completely original and whimsical way. In a whole city of domes, dominated by Michelangelo's magnificent cupola of Saint Peter's, the "dome" of Sant'Ivo stood out like a Chinese pagoda.

Francesco Borromini, Sant'Ivo's designer, was Hatcher's favorite architect. In a place where, for two thousand years, men had built structures intended to be grand and solemn, Borromini taught the Romans that architecture could leap and cavort and crack jokes. Capitals could be turned upside down, the front of a building could undulate like a snake, straight lines could be bent into fantastic abstract patterns. So Borromini went about not just breaking the rules, but turning them inside out, dressing them up in funny costumes, and laughing at them. And of course, paying the price for his iconoclasm in the form of declining commissions, increasing artistic isolation, bitterness, and finally suicide.

Hatcher continued to think about Borromini while he shaved and dressed. He felt a curious empathy with the architect that he had difficulty identifying. It was not Borromini's creative genius — Hatcher had no illusions about himself on that score. Nor was it even the architect's iconoclasm. Hatcher had known plenty of "rebels" of one sort or another, and generally found them infantile, self-advertising bores. There was something else about Borromini, his status as an outsider, as a kind of stranger in his own society, that Hatcher found sympathetic.

Hatcher realized, without any particular pang of self-pity, that he was an outsider himself, as were most of his friends. An outsider in America, since most of his interests were European; but even more of an outsider in Europe, where his clothes, manners, diction, and gestures immediately marked him as a foreigner. In fact, Hatcher was a New England Yankee and vaguely proud of it. He spoke foreign languages badly. Even Italian, one of the easier ones he had to use, was a problem. Hatcher's Italian had none of the lilting, mellifluous rhythms characteristic of the spoken language, but tended to come out of his mouth in a jerky series of spasmodic phrases. Hatcher's command of grammar was equally unsteady, and he tried to steer every conversation into the calm waters of the present tense, keeping a fierce lookout against unsuspected reefs and shoals such as subjunctives and conditionals.

Jake Sloane had been an outsider, too. Independent, crusty, and self-protective, Sloane had befriended Hatcher with the tacit understanding that his privacy was more important to him than the need for intimacy. Hatcher understood and respected this reticence; "good fences make good neighbors," as Robert Frost had put it.

Sloane's murderer — had he been an outsider or an insider? If he were indeed a terrorist, Hatcher thought, he was probably a dangerous and volatile mixture of both. An outsider, of course, since he was literally an outlaw; but also an insider, since he was presumably a member of a gang, and thus committed to a rigidly organized social hierarchy with its own absolute laws and proscriptions. In Hatcher's experience the members of cults, whether religious or political, defined themselves socially. They were either leaders or followers, charismatic visionaries or weak-willed, ego-damaged victims eager to unburden themselves of the unpleasant responsibilities of their own identities and fates. Charlie Manson and his lost crew of forlorn, waiflike murderesses; the Reverend Jim Jones, ranting his crazy vision of the Apocalypse over a bullhorn in the South American jungle while his followers lined up for their poisoned Kool-Aid like dutiful children. Except in degree, were political terrorists that different?

Hatcher put on his best suit, a slightly sub-Brooks Brothers blue pinstripe that made him look presentable if not particularly prosperous, a narrow silk tie with tiny silver diamonds on a sapphire background of which he was rather proud, and a pair of comfortable, ugly brown shoes that had been with him through many campaigns, and looked it. Then he pulled down the cuffs of his shirt, straightened the knot on his tie, squared his shoulders, examined himself critically in the mirror on the door of the armoire, and decided that he looked exactly like an American tourist.

He quickly unpacked the rest of his luggage, put his clothes in the armoire, and locked it, pocketing the key. At the last minute he remembered the magazine Landini had given him the night before. He found it next to the bed, unrolled it, and put it in his case. Then he threw his trench coat over the crook of an arm, closed the shutters of his window, and left the room. After dropping his key off at the desk, Hatcher bought several telephone *gettoni* from the manager, and used one of the tokens to make a call to an attaché at the American Embassy.

The telephone call left an odd taste in Hatcher's mouth, but he shrugged it off, and had virtually forgotten it when, a few moments later, he walked out the front door of the *pensione* into the Roman sun.

Hatcher headed for the nearby Piazza di Sant'Eustachio and realized, as he craned his neck, gawked around corners, and peered up alleys for familiar sights, that the image in the mirror was accurate; he was a tourist. He felt the same surge of excitement that he had experienced on his first trip to Italy twenty years before, when he had gone through the streets of Rome, drunk on the riches of history.

What amazed him then and now, more than anything else, was the way everything seemed to endure in this chaotic slag-heap of a city. His *pensione* was on the Via dei Sediari — the Street of the Chairmakers — known by that name time out of mind. They were still there. Every day a truck would pull up to a little *bottego* and be piled high with the heavy, simple oak ladderback chairs that had been crafted the same way for hundreds of years.

The municipal insignia stamped on manhole covers today was the same one that had been stamped on the lead pipes of the ancient Roman aqueducts: SPQR, Senatus Populusque Romanus, the Senate and People of Rome. The water systems constructed by the Romans two thousand years before still supplied the city, after having been destroyed by Goths and Vandals and then laboriously reexcavated by a succession of Renaissance and baroque popes.

There was no way to escape the past in Rome. Hatcher went to the Piazza di Sant'Eustachio for coffee because it was known to have the best cappuccino in town. Pressed for the reason, a Roman might have mentioned the water. For the water at Sant'Eustachio came from the Acqua Vergine — "Virgin Water" — the softest and purest in the city. This was true today and had been true for two thousand years.

Agrippa had finished constructing the aqueduct in 19 B.C. The ancient Romans had called it the "Aqua Virgo" because of a legend that a young maiden had led a group of soldiers to its source in the hills just northeast of the city. The whole quarter of Rome then called the Campus Martius depended on the Aqua Virgo; during the Middle Ages and early Renaissance, when this water supply was interrupted, and the inhabitants had to get their water from wells and the Tiber, the quarter had degenerated into a slum, only to be resurrected when the aqueduct was reopened by Pope Nicholas V in the middle of the fifteenth century. Then, in the seventeenth century, Pope Urban VIII . . .

It went on and on. To follow a single strand of Roman history was to disappear into a maze of past and present, reality and illusion, fact and legend. Hatcher sat in the bar sipping his cappuccino and feeling like Swann with his *madeleine*.

The city was like a drug, and Hatcher understood the dangers. Friends of his had come to Rome on obscure and slightly pedantic scholarly missions, never to return. Years later they would still be here, impoverished, apparently happy, leading aimless lives with no goal other than to maintain a marginal existence in the city. They led tours, they took part-time jobs in English-speaking bookstores and hotels, they leeched off their friends; nothing seemed to bother them very much.

Dolce far niente, "sweet doing nothing." But Hatcher had things to do. After breakfast, he began by reading the article Landini had given him.

5

Hatcher read around in *Marforio* for a while before the appropriateness of the name began to dawn on him.

"Marforio" and "Pasquino" were the popular names given to two antique statues in Rome, the "speaking statues." Sometime during the Renaissance the custom arose of covering the bases of the statues, both of which stood in public squares in the old city, with satiric comments — puns, lampoons, even short political tracts. Frequently these comments were witty and memorable; often they were scandalous or even scabrous. Eventually "Pasquino," the battered torso of Menelaus that still stands in the little Roman piazza which bears its name, became so famous that the word *pasquinade* entered the language as the generic term for sharp, epigrammatic satire. And before it was hauled away from its original site to the Capitol at the end of the sixteenth century, the Roman river god nicknamed "Marforio" was equally famous, and the poems affixed to the two statues' bases comprised a vitriolic dialogue that kept most of the city amused.

Most, but not all. Periodically the authorities tried to silence the "speaking statues." One Renaissance pope wanted the two of them smashed and thrown in the Tiber, and they were rescued only by the personal intervention of the poet Tasso. As late as 1727 an edict appeared threatening the authors (as well as publishers, editors, and printers) of "such pieces of the character of pasquinades" with execution.

Reading *Marforio,* Hatcher wondered whether the magazine's critics had not been tempted at one time or another to smash the presses, drop the pieces in the Tiber, and possibly also string up the editors. The magazine seemed to contain scathing political and anticlerical satire, semipornographic photos, and radical political propaganda in about equal

196

measure. Perhaps in the spirit of fair play, the fascists seemed to be given equal time with the Communists, and the tone of the writing oscillated between weary cynicism and violent ranting.

The article on art theft fell on the side of cynicism. It was entitled *"Ciao, Bella"* — "So long, Beautiful" — and was illustrated by a photograph of a gallery that had recently been robbed. The thieves had not even bothered to remove the paintings from the wall; the frames still hung, mostly at crazy angles, and jagged fragments of canvas protruded from the edges of the frames where the pictures had been slashed out with razor-blades or knives. Hatcher realized at once that the photo had nothing to do with the recent crimes in Rome. This theft was clearly the work of greedy amateurs, and the photo chosen simply for shock value, like the title above it.

The author of the article recounted the recent history of crimes in Rome in much the same way as Landini had, and with many of the same assumptions, with the result that Hatcher found himself wondering whether they had a common source of information, or whether Landini was simply parroting the article. The article assumed, for example, that the crimes were all committed by a single band; that the impulse was political; and that terrorists were involved. The author also had a "foreign devils" theory, mentioning the possibility that the thefts were orchestrated by an outside organization such as West German's Red Army Faction.

Hatcher was more intrigued by the author's tone and bias. He defended the thieves, who emerged in the course of the article more or less as heroes. The masterpieces of Italian art were seen as legitimate targets of opportunity in a political war, since they represented in tangible form the oppressive forces that had governed Italian life for a thousand years — the twin tyrannies of the rich aristocracy and the Catholic church.

It was equally clear that Italy's artistic patrimony held, for the writer, an even more insidious implication involving the tyranny of the past over the present. As long as Italy remained chained to two thousand years of history, the country would be nothing but a gigantic museum inhabited by custodians and tour guides, alienated from its own present, and without any vision of the future. Back in the teens, the article pointed out, the writers and painters of the Futurist movement had reached the same conclusions. "Burn the Louvre" had been their battle cry. This was fine as far as it went, the journalist remarked, but it didn't go far enough. Besides, the Louvre was in France. Instead they should burn the Uffizi, the Pitti, the Brera, ten or fifteen other major museums, and then start in on the churches.

Failing such large-scale conflagrations, theft would do, he continued. In fact, art theft has had a long and glorious history in Italy, stretching back to antiquity. Since the art of ancient Rome was literally as well as figuratively stolen from the Greeks, modern art thieves continued a vast historical tradition. The great aristocratic families habitually had stolen art from each other, and the popes had stolen it from the aristocrats. Every conqueror ever to enter the Italian peninsula walked off with Italian art, from Attila to Napoleon to Goering. Such people should not be considered as thieves but as liberators, the article went on to state. One of Italy's oldest problems has been her art. However, the author concluded, one should not be overly pessimistic. At the current rate of attrition, Italy would not have to worry about this burden much longer.

Hatcher was moderately surprised to realize that the author of this article, a certain Burton Crelly, was not Italian. However, the name rang a distant bell. Hatcher tried to dredge a memory up into his consciousness, failed, and made a note to save one of his *gettoni* to call the editorial offices of *Marforio*.

Half an hour after sticking the magazine back into his briefcase, Hatcher found the seedy bar two blocks from the train station where he was scheduled to meet with the embassy aide.

The aide's last name was Stanbush. Hatcher couldn't remember his first name. A year before, when Hatcher had been something of a hero for returning the stolen Greek pot, Stanbush had been assigned to him by the embassy as the Official American (as Hatcher thought of him), or as an American Official (as he was designated in various newspapers). His job, apparently, had consisted largely of throwing a meaty arm over Hatcher's shoulders and smiling broadly whenever anyone approached them with a camera. Hatcher didn't remember much about Stanbush later, except for his crewcut, the extraordinary number of very small, very even, and very white teeth he possessed, and the impact of his arm across his, Hatcher's, back. Hatcher had had trouble shrugging his shoulders for a week afterward.

Stanbush had agreed to meet Hatcher at "fourteen-hundred hours" at the cheap bar, and had referred to the meeting as a "rendezvous." The meeting seemed to make Stanbush nervous. He had actually whispered the name of the bar over the phone, and when Hatcher had inquired about its location, started to give a set of coordinates, until Hatcher told him he did not know what he was talking about. All Hatcher wanted was a pistol, after all. He didn't want to borrow a nuclear warhead.

Stanbush kept Hatcher waiting for twenty minutes. When he came through the door of the bar, he stopped, peered around the room for moment, and went scurrying over to Hatcher's table. He slid into a chair, dropped his briefcase on the floor, and furtively glanced around the room again. He could not have been any more conspicuous if he had been wearing a grass skirt.

"Did you bring the letters of transit?" Hatcher asked.

Stanbush looked blank. Apparently he had missed *Casablanca*.

"Did you bring what I asked for?"

Stanbush waited a beat before answering, and when he spoke it was in a toneless half-whisper.

"Roger. Keep it down, Hatcher."

Hatcher could not tell if Stanbush really was nervous, or was just trying to look nervous, or was acting that way out of force of habit.

"We don't want any trouble, Hatcher. We don't want any waves. You've got a license for this, of course."

"Of course," Hatcher lied.

"Won't do any good here. The dagos are really nuts on the subject of guns, so if they catch you, you're in trouble."

Then, Hatcher was tempted to say, why the hell did you ask me about it in the first place?

Hatcher sighed. Airport X-ray machines and metal detectors made it impossible to travel freely with a gun. Previously Hatcher had asked an Alitalia pilot he knew to bring the pistol over for him, but he had not been able to reach him this time. Anselmo could have gotten him one, but now Anselmo was off the scene. This left Stanbush. Hatcher had the impression that Stanbush had been a bad idea after talking to him on the telephone, and when he saw him come through the door of the bar, he *knew* Stanbush had been a bad idea.

Stanbush reached over into his briefcase and extracted a crumpled paper bag which he slid across the table to Hatcher. Hatcher was about to open it when Stanbush hissed at him again behind his hand.

"For *Christ's* sake, will you just put it away, Hatcher?"

Hatcher shrugged, and then stuck the bag in his case. Anyone with even a minimal imagination, witnessing the scene, would have been justified in assuming the bag contained a set of counterfeit plates or a kilo of pure heroin at the very least. In fact, no one seemed even slightly interested in the pair. There was a much more interesting scene taking place in a back corner of the bar, where two tough-looking kids were trying to beat a pinball machine. The one at the side helped out with an occasional slap or kick, a loud stream of epithets and general moral support, while his mute friend hit the flippers and the back corners of the set with sudden darting movements while dancing and lunging at the machine like Muhammad Ali doing his shuffle.

"It's a Cobra thirty-eight with the numbers filed off, so it's dirty as hell. If they catch you with it, don't call us — we never heard of you. There's six rounds in the cylinder and six rounds taped to a piece of cardboard underneath. Damned if I know why I'm doing this for you, Hatcher."

"Auld lang syne. I was a hero, remember?"

"That was then. The embassy got a call about you yesterday."

"Oh?"

"Guy named Pecci. It seems he wants you out of his hair."

"Pecci wants me 'out of his hair'? Christ, Stanbush, I'm not in his hair, he's in my face. I'm looking for a killer, somebody who put a knife in a friend of mine in the middle of Manhattan.''

"He says he doesn't want you interfering with his investigation.''

"What 'investigation'? He doesn't act
like a cop running an investigation. He
acts like a politico trying to keep his image
bright and shiny while he figures out how
to stuff the ballot boxes.''

"It's his turf, Hatcher.''

"Yeah. And my friend.''

"Well, don't get into any trouble. If they
declare you *persona non grata* there's not
a damn thing we can do about it.''

"Noted. Thanks for the gun. I'll have
the numbers carved back on it before I
drop it off at the embassy.''

An hour and a half later Hatcher used
his second *gettone.*

"Pronto!"

"My name is Signore Hatcher, and I
would like to speak to Minister Pecci.''

"I am afraid the minister is occupied.
Would it be possible —''

"Please be so kind as to inform Minister
Pecci that it is a matter of the most grave
urgency.''

The last phrase Hatcher had learned by
rote. He had found it useful over the years
dealing with minor annoyances in Italy,

such as noisy hotel rooms, mistakes in addition in restaurant bills, and the like. He hoped it was strong enough for a genuine emergency.

Apparently it was. A minute later, Pecci was on the line.

"What is it, Hatcher?"

"Do you have a pen and a pad of paper?"

"Yes, but —"

"Good. Listen carefully. I'm in the lobby of the Procacci Museum. Three paintings have been stolen."

"*What?*"

"The three I mentioned to you. A portrait by Dirck Bouts, a *Rest on the Flight into Egypt* by Gerard David, and a *Madonna and Child in a Landscape* by Hans Memlinc."

"Impossible!"

"Quite possible, apparently. When you get here, I suggest that you speak to the guard in the Flemish room, one Franco Grasso. He will tell you that late last spring the nice red-headed *dottoressa* took the paintings down to the restoration laboratory. Franco doesn't understand why the *dottoressa* doesn't come around anymore; he'd thought she was his friend."

"The restoration laboratory — what do they say?"

"There is a *dottoressa,* but not Franco's. Franco's is apparently a redhead and *molto bella.* She told Franco that the pictures would be back in a few weeks, but that doesn't bother him. Pictures frequently stay in the lab for months, even years. What bothers him is that he hasn't seen the *dottoressa* for months."

"This Franco Grasso . . ."

"He has nothing to do with it. He never suspected a thing. It was a neat job, very professionally planned. Take a careful look at the restoration notices on the wall. You'll see."

There was a pause in the conversation in which Hatcher amused himself by trying to imagine Pecci's expression.

"Signore Hatcher, you will recall my suggestion the last time we met. I repeat it now."

"About leaving? Fine. I just have a few little things to do, a few 'odds and ends,' as we say."

"What?"

"Oh, you know. Visit the pope, go to Alfredo's for some fettucine Alfredo, toss a coin in the Trevi Fountain. That sort of thing. Then it's '*Arrivederci,* Roma.' "

"Listen, Hatcher —"

"*Arrivederci,* Pecci."

6

"Pecci! That *stupidone*, that *figlio di buona donna* . . . what is it for you, *figlio di buona donna?*"

Hatcher smiled. Literally, the phrase meant "son of a good woman."

"We say 'son of a bitch.' "

"Ah, good, 'son of a bitch.' Pecci is some big son of a bitch, is it not so? My God, Hatcher, look what they do to me! Look at me!"

In fact, Anselmo looked terrific, even with his eyes rolled up to heaven and his face set in an expression of anguished martyrdom. He looked a good ten years younger than his age. He had a face which was both aristocratically handsome and marvelously expressive, a splendid mane of carefully tended silver hair, and the lithe, athletic body of a dancer or mime. Disgrace or not, Anselmo cut a *bella figura*. The rumpled appearance Hatcher was accustomed to was gone.

" 'Corruption,' Hatcher, *corruzione* — that is what they say. It is a joke, eh? For thirty years I keep the *capolavori* of Italian art safe — safe from the Nazis, safe from the Americans, from the Mafia, from criminals and crazy people and *terroristi*, and then they have the face of bronze to speak to me of corruption. How many millions of lire have I paid — *of my own lire* — to keep the art of Italy in Italy? They speak of 'bribery.' What is this nonsense? Of course there is bribery. How else? And whose money? I give my little birds money and they sing to me. Why not?"

Hatcher said nothing, but nodded sympathetically. He did not want to interrupt the performance.

"For years I have taken care of my little birds, my — what is it, *piccioni da richiamo?*"

"Stool pigeons. 'Stoolies' for short."

"Ah. 'Stoolies,' you say. Pigeons. I use them. I use them, but they are my friends, do you understand? I use the little fish to catch the big fish, but they are also my friends. They eat with me, they ask for things and I give them. I am the *padrone*, I am like an uncle to them, *capisc'?*"

"*Si, capito.*"

"*Bene*. So Pecci, that . . . that Milanese idiot, puts all my birds in a cage. Nobody sings to Pecci. You understand?"

"Yes."

Anselmo paused for a moment and strode to the railing of the roof garden. When he turned toward Hatcher, the whole city of Rome spread out behind him like a tapestry.

"To catch an art thief, one must know art, one must be an artist, is that not so? What does Pecci know of these things? *Niente!* And of people? Again, *niente.* Listen to me, Hatcher."

Anselmo walked over next to Hatcher and dropped his voice conspiratorially.

"To get someone by the *coglioni* — 'cullions,' is it not . . . ?"

"Shakespeare said 'cullions.' We say 'balls.' "

"To get them by the balls, then — this is the easy part. Knowing how to squeeze — this is the hard part."

Anselmo held out his hand, palm up,

211

with his fingers extended like claws.

"Do you know *Tosca?*"

Hatcher nodded. He knew *Tosca*. He also knew Anselmo well enough not to worry about the non sequitur.

"If you want one kind of song, you squeeze very gently."

Anselmo drew his fingers together slightly, at the same time launching into one of Scarpia's arias from the second act of Puccini's opera. Anselmo had a nice bass, and managed to impart a fine aura of malevolence to the fragment of the song. After a couple of lines, he broke off abruptly.

"Of course, sometimes one must squeeze harder."

He drew his hand more tightly together, bursting into the great tenor aria *"O dolci bacci."* Not bad, Hatcher decided, but not Pavarotti either.

"Or even harder." The fingers were closed in a circle now, and Hatcher cringed — not out of sympathy for the imaginary testicles, but from fear of the vocal accompaniment. He hoped it wouldn't be *"Vissi d'arte,"* one of his favorite arias.

"Vi-issi d'a-arte," sang Anselmo in a horrible falsetto, mercifully stopping after

the first line. Hatcher had by now got the point.

"But, Hatcher," Anselmo said, dropping his voice to a hoarse whisper, "if you squeeze *too* hard, you get nothing. *Silenzio.* The Milanese idiot, he always squeezes too hard." Anselmo's hand was a fist now, and he shook it twice under Hatcher's nose.

"I understand that, Roberto. I've been squeezed."

"Too hard, eh?"

"Hard enough. He wants me out of Italy."

Anselmo shrugged, smiled, and raised his eyebrows in a manner that suggested, in translation, that one must not tempt the gods.

"*Bene.* Go, then. These thefts are not my problem, why should they be your problem? Let us see the great genius of Signore Pecci . . ."

"No. It's not just the paintings. A friend of mine was murdered."

Anselmo looked shocked, and his manner immediately became grave. Hatcher was relieved to find that there was no elaboration or explanation needed, that Anselmo immediately understood the implication of this simple fact. A friend was murdered; there could be no question of evasion, or of shifting responsibility, or of who had to do what. There were no options for Hatcher. Anselmo understood this.

He listened to Hatcher tell the story of Jake Sloane's murder, and followed intently while he outlined his theories about the rash of art thefts that had taken place recently in Italy. Occasionally Anselmo nodded or interjected a question. Otherwise he simply sat and listened. At the end, he waited a long time before speaking.

"I am very sorry about your friend, Amos. For many reasons. I think this is a very dangerous game. You are right that it is all one group, and that it is a political problem. But I am frightened. They are very good, these people. But that is not what I am afraid of. What I am afraid of is this: I don't know them at all. No one knows them. Not me, not Pecci, not the *carabinieri,* and not my pigeons.

"Until now, this pleases me. Should I be ashamed to say this? Pecci is the big trombone now; we will see what kind of music he makes. In what — six weeks?

214

Six months, perhaps, they will all come to Anselmo. *'Prego, Signore Anselmo, per favore aiuto* — help us, Signore Anselmo!' And this will be very beautiful to me. The disgrace will be forgotten, the newspaper stories, the legal threats, all of this will be like smoke in the wind. My country is blessed with a very short memory. But now there is you, and your friend."

"My problem, not yours. I don't want to drag you into it."

"What can I do, then?"

"I need reports, if I can get them. Behind Pecci's back. The police reports of art thefts for the past six or eight months, I think, no more than that."

Anselmo excused himself briefly, and disappeared into his bedroom. When he returned ten minutes later, he was carrying a large brown file which he handed to Hatcher without comment. Hatcher opened it and found a series of folders, chronologically arranged, of laboratory reports, depositions, and police descriptions of art thefts that had taken place in Rome during the past year.

While Hatcher looked at him in amazement, Anselmo shrugged. "Perhaps there are one or two people who have not entirely forgotten me. But I must ask that you return this soon."

"I gather from these files that you're not planning a very long retirement."

Anselmo laughed. "One must be active. One cannot spend one's life simply admiring the view."

Looking out over the railing of Anselmo's balcony, Hatcher was not sure about that. The view was spectacular. Craning his neck, he could see the marvelous curves and countercurves of the Spanish Steps as they descended in an elegant, lilting rhythm down to Bernini's fountain in the Piazza di Spagna. From the great basilica of Santa Maria Maggiore at the extreme left to the Villa Medici at the right, the splendid panoply of Rome stretched out before him. Domes glinted in the late afternoon sun, columns and obelisks and pediments punctuated the horizon-line, and two thousand years of architectural wonders clamored for attention. Looking down from the top of the Pincian Hill on a city built by Caesars, popes, and princes, Hatcher felt his spirit expand and breathe, breaking the shackles and constraints of Manhattan. New York suddenly seemed mean and greedy to him:

a city built by committees, by and for corporations. Bigness without grandeur: form without meaning.

"Many great writers have lived here, or near here. Byron, Shelley, Goethe, d'Annunzio. There is the house where Keats died. There, you can see the plaque. Artists, too: Claude Lorraine, Salvator Rosa, Ingres. The French Academy was over there."

Looking at the squinting, smiling face of his host, Hatcher had the impression that this view had never lost its magic for Anselmo.

"I bought this apartment just after the war, when such things were possible. My family had some money. We come from near Napoli, so, 'How do they have money?' they ask. 'Of course. They must be *collaboratori, mafiosi*. Maybe in the black market.' Today, how do I live in such an apartment? 'Bribery, corruption. *Ecco*, perhaps Anselmo steals the art himself!' So simple, so obvious."

Anselmo sighed theatrically, and then shrugged. Hatcher had long understood that the shrug was the universal Italian gesture. Things are never so bad, it seemed to imply, that they cannot go worse, or won't. Particularly in Rome, the Italian soul seemed steeped in some ancient fatalism, girded about with skepticism and suspicion. Of course there were compensations, great compensations: good food and wine, the dazzling beauty of the country and her people, and always the refined art of living well. Anselmo might well rail against the world's injustice, sitting with an aperitif in his hand on a balcony overlooking the splendid panorama of the city spread out below him. Hatcher began to find the situation comical. Anselmo, perhaps sensing this, smiled and clapped his hands.

"Enough of this. You will stay for supper? Angela will be back from market soon, and she is not a bad cook, as you may remember. She would love to see you again."

"Please convey my regrets. I would love to stay, as you know, but there is someone else I must see. Another time?"

"Another time, then."

As Hatcher descended the Spanish Steps a few minutes later he started to laugh. Since arriving in Rome, he had not done anything or discovered anything crucial about the case at all, yet somehow he found himself caught up in a labyrinth of cross-purposes. Pecci wanted him out because of his associations with Anselmo. Anselmo wanted him out, although he was too polite to insist, because he wanted the pleasure of watching Pecci fall dramatically (and publicly) on his face. People at the American Embassy wanted him out to please Pecci, and Landini wanted him out because he was convinced that Hatcher was going to get himself shot. This didn't seem like an auspicious beginning.

7

Hatcher located Burton Crelly in an *osteria* beside the ancient Baths of Diocletian, and he was surprised to find that the restaurant incorporated parts of the original masonry of the baths themselves. Crelly was at a corner table, precisely where they had said he would be. They had also warned him that Crelly would not want to see him.

Crelly was a huge bear of a man with eyes like small black marbles, a wild beard and mustache which screened his mouth, and small tufts of wiry hair which covered the backs of his hands and the first two joints of his fingers. He was dressed in a heavy red and black plaid shirt and dirty jeans which, with the heavy boots, made him look like a misplaced lumberjack.

There was a huge bottle of Chianti in front of him, and as he filled his water glass with the wine, Hatcher noticed that the bottle was about half empty. There was nothing else on the table but a ball-point pen and a notebook and Crelly's massive arms, terminating in fists like hams. Hatcher went over to him, resisting a strong impulse to tiptoe quietly off into the night.

"Mr. Crelly? Burton Crelly?"

At first, Crelly did not react at all. Hatcher wondered just how drunk he was. When he finally spoke, he did not raise his head or acknowledge Hatcher in any way.

"Yeah?"

"Mr. Crelly, my name is Amos Hatcher. I'd like to ask you some questions about an article you wrote."

Crelly sighed, and cocked his head up at Hatcher. Nothing in his expression indicated that he was delighted to make Hatcher's acquaintance.

" 'Wrote,' Hatcher. 'Wrote' is the past tense. The only article I give a damn about is the one that's due next Thursday. Now, if you have any particularly nifty suggestions concerning the subject of that article, preferably something sensational, scandalous, or just dirty, I'd be happy to hear about it. Otherwise, piss off."

Hatcher waited a beat before answering this.

"Mr. Crelly, I've only been in Italy two days, and already four people have told me to piss off. After the last time, I promised myself that I'd slug the next person that suggested it."

"Want to slug *me*, Hatcher?" The tone of voice was quizzical, amused.

Amos looked across the table at Crelly. The line that ran from his fist through his arm, his massive shoulders, and down to his other fist was a broad, continuous, curved plane.

"Not if it would make you angry."

It seemed to Hatcher that the pause before Crelly started to laugh was a fraction of a second too long, but at least he laughed.

"Christ! Oh, all right. Sit down, stop looming over me like that. Make it short. Who are you and what do you want?"

Hatcher sat down quickly, lest the offer be withdrawn.

"A few weeks ago, you wrote an article in *Marforio* about a series of art thefts in

Italy."

"Old news, Hatcher."

"Not to me. Some of the stolen pictures were taken to New York and peddled to a friend of mine in an auction house. My friend was murdered. I think it was the head of the ring that did it. From your article I assume you know something about the ring, that you didn't just make it up. I need to know about your sources."

Crelly was amused at this, which was all right with Hatcher, who assumed that he would be allowed to talk to Crelly as long as Crelly found him amusing. Or until the alcohol started to hit Crelly the wrong way, which was something Hatcher had found he was never able to predict.

" 'Sources,' Hatcher? What the hell do you mean, 'sources'? What do you think *Marforio* is, anyway, the goddamn *New York Times?* Christ, man, it isn't even the *Post.* Sometimes it prints the truth, but usually this is just an oversight by the copy editor. *This* is my main source, in fact my only reliable source. Want some?"

Crelly refilled his glass, then snapped his fingers, bringing a shapely waitress quickly to the table. He called her *"Cara,"* and sent her on her way with a light slap on the rump.

"I should also tell you that I'm an art cop by trade, so this is not just a matter of friendship. I read your article closely, and most of your ideas make sense. You didn't just pour them out of a Chianti bottle."

Crelly smiled warily at Hatcher, who decided that it had to be done carefully, one step at a time, if it was going to be done at all.

"What ideas are you referring to?" Suddenly Crelly sounded cold, stone sober.

"For example, the idea that the thefts are part of a political conspiracy."

Crelly looked at Hatcher for a moment, then threw back his head and roared with laughter.

"My God, are you kidding? In this town, everything is a political conspiracy; the fucking *weather* is a political conspiracy. Let me tell you a little story, Sonny. There's a shortage of change in this country. Nobody has enough coins. It's not so bad now but a couple of years ago you didn't get change from anyone. Buy something with a thousand-lire note, you'd get a couple of pieces of candy in change. Of course, as soon as that happened, everybody panicked and started hoarding their change, so it got worse. Little local banks started *printing* change, on what looked and acted like American toilet paper. The stuff was probably worthless and it tended to fall apart in your pocket, but what the hell, anything was better than spending precious *spiccioli*. So all the Italians who were nervously keeping their hoards of coins in socks and bowls and piggy banks and trunks got together three times a day at the local bar to discuss this mysterious disappearance of the coins, and do you know what they decided? It was a conspiracy, of course. My landlady explained it to me. You know who was behind it? The *Japanese*. Thousands of innocent-looking tourists were being sent over here by the Japanese government to corner the market on Italian coins, which were then smuggled back to Japan. Why? I asked the landlady. Were they melting them down and making cameras out of them? My landlady didn't know why, wasn't interested in why; she was satisfied as soon as she heard about the Great Japanese Conspiracy."

Hatcher decided it was worth trying to keep Crelly on the hook, but had very little confidence in being able to do it.

"That's a lovely story, but it doesn't answer the question."

Crelly smiled at Hatcher and shook his head.

"Nobody loves a hard-ass, Hatcher, but okay. Conspiracy stories are a dime a dozen here. They're my stock in trade. If I wrote a story about Italy's problems that didn't involve a conspiracy, I probably couldn't get it published. And if I *could* get it published, no one would read it. And if they read it, they wouldn't believe it. *Capisc'?*"

Hatcher sighed, and dug in for a long haul.

"You mentioned the Red Brigades in the article, and Baader-Meinhof."

"Good copy. Better, of course, if I could have got the CIA into it somehow. Every Italian believes that the CIA is behind at least half of Italy's problems. God, would this country be disappointed if they ever found out how incompetent the CIA is!"

"No. You had reasons. Let's stop pretending I take your article more seriously than you do."

Crelly took a long sip of wine and smiled across the table at Hatcher. "Nicely done. Neat trick, insulting and flattering someone in the same sentence. Let me see. What do you know about the Red Brigades?"

"Not enough."

"Nobody does. That's why they're still around. Every once in a while they nail a few of them and the government announces that they've 'broken the back' of the Red Brigades, but this is a lot of crap, 'light at the end of the tunnel' kind of nonsense. Anyway, they're still around, and they need money badly, so they're into crime: bank robbery, hijacking, art theft, anything."

"Is that all?"

"No. The knockover of the Caprese Collection had all the earmarks of the Red Brigades: the organization, the random violence, the ranting and political slogans . . ."

"How did you know about the Caprese theft?"

Crelly laughed.

"Well, how about that? I must have some sources after all."

"On which side?"

227

Crelly stopped laughing.

"Are you kidding, or crazy? Do you think I know who did it? Christ, Hatcher, these are dangerous people. If I knew who did it, if they even suspected I knew who did it, I'd either be on the run or dead. Didn't it occur to you that maybe the people telling you to piss off were doing you a favor?"

Hatcher nodded.

"Fine. Do *me* a favor, then. Piss off."

Hatcher waited a moment to see if Crelly meant it.

"Look, Hatcher. These aren't my office hours. This is just a little place I like to hang out, a home away from home, as it were. They understand me here. They let me sit here all alone and scribble illegible notes to myself. They don't mind if I get drunk, and they don't mind if I pinch the waitress's ass once in a while, but I'm not sure that they don't mind you. And I'm not sure I don't mind you."

Hatcher got up quickly.

"Thanks for your time, Crelly. We'll get along. *Arrivederci.*"

"*Arrivederci.* Not any too goddamn soon, though."

8

The next day Hatcher awoke to find Rome in the grips of the sirocco, the hot wind from the south, with its cargo of sand from the Sahara and its famous side effects of discomfort and nervous irritability in everyone it touched. By noon a desultory rain was falling. It got stronger during the day, and by evening the city looked gray and funereal. That night the rain lifted, but clouds still hung ominously over the city. Hatcher had spent enough time in Rome to know that he could expect a spate of miserable weather that would not change until the fresh northern breeze, the *tramontana*, came down from the Alps.

His work didn't help his mood. Police reports are reasonably cryptic in any country, but Hatcher found the files

Anselmo had given him virtually indecipherable. Trivialities were discussed in long-winded detail, but anything interesting tended either to be couched in the most elaborate technical jargon, or reduced to abbreviations that left Hatcher quivering in frustrated rage. At one point he even found himself on the verge of calling up Pecci and demanding to know why the hell nobody in his department could write a simple declarative sentence. Later he realized his mood was partly the result of the sirocco, which made people crazy anyway, even without Pecci's reports.

In the afternoon Hatcher found a photocopy machine and reproduced a number of reports. Then he returned the originals to Anselmo. After that, he shoehorned himself back on the No. 95 bus and returned to his neighborhood just in time to catch someone in the Roman Archives. Hatcher had a simple question; remarkably, the professor he hunted down had a simple answer to it. The day's work left him with one answer and a whole stack of bright, shiny new problems, so he decided to contact Landini. Landini was still in the gallery, luckily, and agreed to meet

Hatcher after supper in one of the sidewalk cafés in the Piazza Navona.

Food had become a very serious matter to Hatcher since his arrival in Rome. Particularly pasta. With the justification that he still needed to put on weight after the recent unpleasantness in Germany, Hatcher had decided to get heavily involved in pasta, not just physically, but spiritually. He was convinced that if he could ever master the distinctions between the hundreds of different kinds of pasta he would somehow understand Italy and the Italians, just as he was convinced that the key to the French soul was hidden in the hundreds of different kinds of cheese produced by that country. Why did the same stuff become totally different depending on whether it was shaped into strings or tubes or ribbons or butterfly wings or flat leaves? Why was fettucine as different from spaghetti as Mozart from Brahms? Why did the pasta in the cheapest Roman dive make the pasta in fancy Manhattan restaurants seem like soggy cardboard? Hatcher was pondering these matters over a cup of cappuccino in the Piazza Navona when Landini arrived and dropped into the chair next to him.

For a while, the two simply sat and watched the theatrical spectacle of the characters in the piazza. It was a show that had been running continuously for about four hundred years, always changing but always amusing. Then they talked about the art market. Landini wanted to hear how things were going in the States, so Hatcher told him. With the dollar suddenly stronger against the European currencies, and with the combination of high interest rates and low inflation, all the funny money that had kept sales prices surging forward in the past two years had suddenly dried up. Speculators had stopped buying art at auction.

In one way, this was a healthy thing. The people buying now were more likely to be art lovers than commercial investors trading in paintings as if they were pork-belly futures. On the other hand, serious dealers who had had to pay outrageous prices in the recent past just to maintain an inventory were now seeing their stock devalued at auction after auction. But this was an old story. Hatcher reminded Landini of the bankruptcy sale of Rembrandt's private collection, where the aging artist had had to watch the treasures meticulously assembled over a lifetime disappear at a fraction of their value.

Finally, Hatcher brought the conversation around to the case.

"It's a little like packing a drawer, or a suitcase. You throw everything into it and then try to close it. Usually something or other sticks out. Then you have to pull everything out and start all over again. If it still doesn't close, you concentrate on whatever the hell keeps sticking out. It took me years to realize that you can't force it; you can't just chop off whatever is hanging out, or break it, or jam it in any which way. If it *still* won't close, you have to go out and buy another suitcase."

"What are you thinking of?"

"Well, one thing that doesn't seem to want to fit is that damned phrase left on the wall of the Palazzo Caprese. *'Ti ho in culo.'* I got an idea about that yesterday, talking to Anselmo. He thought the translation for *coglioni* was 'cullions.' Now, 'cullions' is a perfectly good Elizabethan word, but no one would use it now. This gave me an idea about *'ti ho in culo.'* I checked it out with an archivist at the Spaienza today, and he told me that *'ti ho in culo'* is an idiomatic insult in seventeenth-century Roman slang."

"Interesting detail."

"Very. Pretty intellectual kind of joke for a bunch of terrorist thugs. I still don't get the punch line, exactly, but I think that when I do a lot of other things will fall into place. Then there is the problem of the pictures that were stolen from that truck."

"They were from the Caravaggio show, weren't they?"

"Caravaggio and his followers."

"I don't see the problem. Caravaggesque painters are very valuable, very commercial."

"Okay, there are a number of problems. The first is notoriety. The show was very popular. It had a huge, comprehensive catalogue. Every picture was illustrated, and most of them shown with details. In fact, that catalogue will probably serve as the standard scholarly treatise on Caravaggio's followers for years. Anyone interested in that kind of picture will be familiar with the book, so any painting in that show would be immediately identifiable to a specialist. If the thieves tried to move those paintings to a dealer or auction house, the mark would immediately go to the catalogue and spot it. Especially in Italy."

"But outside of Italy . . ."

"That's another problem. One of the cardinal rules of art theft is, take something small. Those paintings are big. Huge, some of them. It would be very difficult to get them out of Italy without cutting them up. And this brings me to the strangest part of all. The pictures they stole weren't particularly valuable."

"Are you sure?"

"Quite sure. The paintings in the truck were mostly by minor artists: Lionello Spada, Baglione, people like that."

"I remember now. I assumed at the time that they'd made a mistake, that they thought they were getting Caravaggios."

"That's what the police thought, and that's what I thought when I first saw the list. That's what I meant about the suitcase: it's easier to bust something in half and cram it in than to buy a new suitcase. Put it another way, if something continues to make no sense at all, you'd better take a look at what you mean by 'sense.'"

"Look. Knocking over the truck was no picnic. They had to know the exact route it was taking, which meant — probably —

that they had museum informers. The placing and timing of the theft were carefully worked out, the charade that made the driver get out of his cab was beautifully rehearsed. Nothing about the crime seems casual or extemporaneous at all. They wouldn't have gone to that trouble if they didn't know exactly what they were getting, and if they didn't consider it worth the danger.

"So, how does this add up? Paintings which are not particularly valuable stolen at great risk; paintings which are unimportant but nevertheless extremely hot, since they've just been exhibited and published, and which are too large to be easily portable, stolen. *For what reason?* To be sold? How, and to whom? The other obvious motive, blackmail, doesn't make sense either. And, anyway, that's a moot point since no one was ever contacted about the pictures. So this leaves the most improbable motives. The people who stole the pictures either wanted to keep them, or they simply wanted to *have them stolen.*

"None of this fits into the same suitcase with the Caprese job, which was a classic art theft. Look at it. The paintings were small, incredibly valuable, yet ice-cold, since they hadn't been seen in decades. They were easy to move and relatively easy to fence, given their value. But I'm convinced that both jobs were done by the same bunch."

"You're assuming that whoever planned these things knows a lot about art."

"A hell of a lot. If you had to choose a group of paintings to steal from the Caprese Collection and the Procacci Museum you could hardly do better than the ones they snatched, which is another thing that doesn't fit with the Caravaggio school pieces."

Hatcher finished his coffee, and when he glanced up, he noticed an expression of wry amusement on his friend's face.

"Does this sound like I'm chasing my own tail around in circles?"

Landini nodded, still smiling. "A little."

"More than a little. I feel like I'm fencing with shadows. This is the point in the story when somebody's supposed to come barreling around the corner with guns blazing, just to break the monotony. That, or I dream up a fantastically clever scheme to bring everybody out into the open. But I don't have the slightest idea who I'm supposed to be after. And tell me, Lou, how the hell can that *be?* The son of a bitch is brilliant, he's multilingual, he's an expert in Renaissance and baroque art, and he's mixed up with terrorists — how many people like that are there? Why doesn't Anselmo know him? Why don't *you* know him? This is somebody rare we're looking for, somebody very special; it's not Sam the Old Accordion Man, for Christ's sake."

"I've wondered about that. The trouble with the art trade is that fantastic rumors are a dime a dozen. If I heard a description of someone like the one you just gave me, I'd assume it was just another Via del Babuino fairy tale. Maybe I should pay more attention to gossip."

"Maybe so. Anyway, if you find out that your cleaning lady is a transsexual spy working for the KGB, be sure to let me know. I could use a suspicious character or two about now."

"No such luck. She's a grandmother, and a Christian Democrat."

"Too bad. Meanwhile, I want to see some more of Crelly. I had a short session with him that left me feeling like I'd been led around by the nose, and I don't quite know why. I also want to hook up with the people who organized the Caravaggio show."

"The curators at the museum?"

"No. Aldo Bruni and Richard Blake, the pair that did the catalogue. Maybe I'll try the museum later. I have to stay away from Pecci, though, so I'd better approach the museum crowd carefully."

"I see. Then what?"

"God knows, Lou. I'm running out of gambits. If nothing else works, I could always come barreling around the corner with guns blazing myself. If I kept it up for a while, I'd have to hit something, wouldn't I?"

9

After leaving Landini, Hatcher found himself with a vague mental tic. He liked to talk about cases, going over them again and again before any captive audience he could manage to dredge up, because he often found himself describing patterns and making connections that he had only been half aware of before. This process was as useful to Hatcher as it often was boring to his friends.

What bothered him now had something to do with police reports, Caravaggio, and the phrase *"ti ho in culo."* That was as far as Hatcher could get with it. In his teaching days he had been over Caravaggio's paintings many times, and he recalled that a good deal of the artist's biography had been culled from the police records of the time. Maybe this was just a coincidence. Or maybe it was a delusion, a trick of the sirocco. At any rate, the three elements lay tantalizingly just over the horizon line of Hatcher's consciousness and refused to be coaxed any closer.

After a bad night offset by a good breakfast Hatcher arrived at one of his favorite libraries, the Biblioteca Herziana. The Herziana was located in a tiny palazzo designed by the mannerist painter Federico Zuccaro for himself at the end of the sixteenth century. The central bay of the facade was sculpted in the witty form of a huge giant's face, with the gaping mouth forming the entrance portal.

In contrast to the mock ferocity of the stone demon outside, the people inside the Herziana were notably polite and obliging. It was one of the best and most smoothly run art historical libraries in the world, and in a relatively short time Hatcher had most of the books he needed.

He started with Walter Friedlaender's monumental *Caravaggio Studies*. Half an hour later Hatcher had what he was looking for. He silently thanked the great scholar's shade for providing all the Caravaggio documents, and also gave thanks to the anonymous officials who, centuries before, had demanded legible reports from the Roman constabulary.

The document Hatcher discovered was a police record for November 18, 1604. It recorded the incidents of an encounter between the painter Caravaggio and a police sergeant near a notorious sewer in downtown Rome. The painter had been halted by some of the sergeant's men, who had noticed that Caravaggio was carrying a sword and dagger. The police had demanded to see Caravaggio's license to bear arms; the artist had produced the license. The men were satisfied and preparing to go on their way, when the officer had offered the painter a conciliatory *"buono notte"* — "good evening, sir." That was when Caravaggio had told the sergeant loudly to shove it up his ass: *"Ti ho in culo."*

The policeman must have been almost as shocked at the phrase as Hatcher. In Hatcher's experience it was not such a good idea to tell an Italian cop to shove it. Caravaggio didn't stop there, however. In case the first time didn't take, he broadened his invitation to include the others, suggesting that all of the men who were with the sergeant could shove it as well. That was when he had been arrested.

Following the painter's arrest for insulting the officer, he had been thrown into the infamous medieval dungeon beside the Tiber River called the Tor di Nona. This tower had had a long and bloody history, and Caravaggio had been by no means its only famous denizen. The sculptor Benvenuto Cellini had spent time there, and the philosopher Giordano Bruno had been incarcerated there briefly before his execution for heresy in 1600. Beside the tower was a spot designated for public executions. The lucky were hanged; the unlucky were tortured before being drawn and quartered.

Hatcher continued to read. During his brief and chaotic life, Caravaggio must have become familiar not only with the Tor di Nona, but with most of the other prisons in Rome as well. From the first days of his growing artistic success, the painter seemed inexorably drawn by some dark force toward his own destruction. Some of the police records were almost comical. In one minor fracas, Caravaggio had been dragged before the authorities for flinging a plate of artichokes at a waiter's head. Most of the citations, however, were more serious, involving weapons and violence. An incident in 1600, for example, in which a certain Gerolamo Spampa got into an argument with Caravaggio, began with sticks and ended with swords. Spampa had parried the painter's thrust with his cloak, and produced the cloak in evidence later, presumably thankful that the gash went through his garment rather than himself. Others were not so lucky: a Mariano Pasqualone was ambushed by Caravaggio in the Piazza Navona one night, and the back of his head laid open by a slash of the painter's sword. There had been an argument about a certain "Lena," a girl who hung out in the piazza.

Just as the shadows in Caravaggio's paintings grew heavier and more tragic, as his career progressed, so the episodes of willful aggression and violent behavior became more common. Finally, almost inevitably, they ended in homicide. On the twenty-ninth of May, 1606, a fight broke out over a ball game in the Campo Marzio near the Piazza Navona. Four men were involved; two were killed. Caravaggio survived, barely, but as a fugitive wanted for the murder of one Ranuccio

Tomassoni.

The artist fled — to Naples, to Malta, then to Sicily, and then back to Naples. Everywhere, success was followed by trouble. Everything Caravaggio could do with his brush, he could undo with his behavior. He won such renown for his portrait of the Grand Duke of the Knights of Malta that he was received into the order and presented with a gold chain and Turkish slaves. Soon after that there was another violent argument, and the artist was back in prison, thrown there by the same people who had just knighted him. With a Byronic flourish, Caravaggio escaped. He ran to Messina, then back to Naples, still followed by the agents of the Maltese Knights. In Naples he was seriously beaten and jailed — ironically, mistaken for someone else. Then he was released from prison, just in time to see the boat bearing all his possessions leaving for Rome without him. In a blind fury the artist had stumbled along the shore, railing at the boat, the gods, his fate. Several days later he was dead from a malignant fever. He was thirty-seven years old. One critic, quoting Hobbes, aptly characterized the painter's life as "nasty, brutish, and short."

Hatcher wondered about the sword Caravaggio had left in Ranuccio Tomassoni, and remembered the photo of Jake Sloane slumped over in his chair, the ugly, black knife handle protruding from the back of his neck. He wondered why anyone would want to quote an obscene insult that hadn't achieved much more than a day or two in a barbaric prison the first time it had been used, and he wondered who, if anyone, was supposed to get the joke. He decided that he needed to think a bit more about Caravaggio. He also concluded that the next phase of his research had better take place in less genteel surroundings: surroundings, that is, where he could drink, swear, and throw things, if necessary.

Since the Herziana was a noncirculating library, it took several hours for Hatcher, scouring the bookstores, to find the material he needed. Six books on Caravaggio, including Friedlaender's monograph, some picture books without text, and a particularly lurid novel based on Caravaggio's life formed the main haul. Luckily, Rizzoli's still had one copy left of the exhibition catalogue of the show of Caravaggio and his followers.

Hatcher left the packages at his *pensione* and went hunting for provisions at a nearby market. He found bread and cheese, some delicious chicken liver paté with truffles, and bought a bag full of ripe figs and melons. Nothing fancy, but then — as he reminded himself — he wasn't planning a banquet, but a siege. The final item was a large flask of Orvieto wine. He couldn't manage the espresso he knew he would need himself, but the bar a few doors down from his *pensione* stayed open late.

By half-past eight he was back to work.

10

Hatcher sat cross-legged on the floor of his room, his eyes riveted to the reproduction of Caravaggio's *David and Goliath* taped to the wall in front of him.

The figure in the picture was surrounded by darkness. This was a new kind of shadow in painting: not a natural element, a simple absence of light, but an all-encompassing blackness which was sinister and corrosive, eating away the solid forms of the objects in the composition.

At the lower right-hand corner, suspended by his hair and isolated by the surrounding gloom, was the severed head of the artist. Even when it was painted, critics had been aware that the brooding, heavy, and carnal features of the shocking trophy thrust out at the viewer in Caravaggio's work belonged to the painter himself.

Looking at the reproduction, Hatcher felt that the drama had just been completed. Blood still poured from the stump of the neck; the open mouth was no longer a mouth, but an aperture that had suddenly fallen slack, exposing a crooked row of ragged teeth. The glance of the wide, staring eyes was unfocused, and the eyes themselves seemed to be glazed over as if with cataracts. The skin was no longer flesh-colored but a livid gray-green. The head was depicted with a brutal, unblinking realism that reminded Hatcher of Caravaggio's alleged belief that what was not real was not worth painting.

As he examined the picture, more and more details seemed strange to Hatcher. The focus of the picture was wrong, and the meaning curiously ambivalent. David was supposed to be a hero, the savior of his people. But there was nothing triumphant or heroic about Caravaggio's David, an adolescent who seemed to look down on his grisly prize with a mixture of revulsion and melancholy, as if suddenly stricken with remorse. It was not a painting about victory and liberation, but about violence and death.

Under the plate of *David and Goliath*, Hatcher had taped a reproduction of Caravaggio's *Martyrdom of Saint Matthew*. Here, at least, the drama was depicted before its bloody climax. Sprawled in front of the altar, the saint was shown throwing his hand up to protect himself against the stark, looming figure of the assassin. The assassin was grabbing the saint's wrist with his left hand, about to twist Matthew's arm away while preparing to pivot and thrust the sword into his target. Following the diagonal line of the swordblade, Hatcher could discern, among a welter of figures, the face of a fleeing onlooker. Was it anguish or guilt that marked this character's expression? What impulse made him, at the last moment, turn to view the scene he was so intent on escaping? There were no answers to these questions. One thing, however, was certain: the swarthy face with its heavy, blunt features was again a self-portrait of the artist.

Hatcher continued to tape illustrations on the wall, grouping them in several rough categories. To the left of the bureau went what Hatcher thought of as the blood-lust group: *David and Goliath, Medusa, Judith Beheading Holofernes, The Sacrifice of Isaac,* and several others. Many of these pictures were so clinical and sadistic that Hatcher still found the details shocking. The way the beautiful, ice-cold Judith wrenched the head of Holofernes toward the viewer as her sword severed his head from his body was so deftly cinematic that Hatcher was mildly surprised that Judith did not look a bit more like Joan Crawford.

These subjects were not titillating attempts to shock, as they later became in the hands of Caravaggio's followers, but the expression of a black strain in the painter's soul. There were too many swords and daggers in the artist's life, mirroring the arsenal in his work. There was too much blood, and too much pathological rage.

Not all of the artist's works reflected this dark mood. With relief, Hatcher turned to the early works. He cut the reproductions from one of the picture books, arranged them on the wall, and poured himself some wine.

Some of the early paintings had a lyrical, almost idyllic quality which Hatcher had always found curious in the light of the later works. A *Rest on the Flight into Egypt,* for example, showed the Holy Family peacefully arrayed against an ideal landscape. The colors were rich and silvery, and the lines of the composition had a grace and elegance that showed Caravaggio could be as serenely poetic as Giorgione when he chose.

A picture of Mary Magdalene projected the same poetic charm. Dressed in rich brocades, the subject seemed neither a saint nor a sinner but simply a beautiful young woman caught in a manner of repose. Beside her on the floor was a still life of gold jewelry, pearls, and an ointment jar that formed a casual piece of virtuoso naturalism. The picture looked like a love poem. Again Hatcher found himself wondering about the correspondences of art and life. Who was the model? Could it have been the woman over whom Caravaggio had fought in the Piazza Navona?

Next to the *Mary Magdalene* Hatcher put the reproduction of Caravaggio's *Bacchus* from the Uffizi. In some ways the paintings were similar. There were the same light, clear colors in the *Bacchus,* the same elegant, linear rhythms, and another magnificent still life, this composed of a flagon of wine and a bowl of fruit. But the figure of Bacchus himself was disturbing and became more disturbing as Hatcher looked at him.

He was no god, but a fleshy, feminine-looking adolescent dressed up to play a part. In his wig, rouge, and mascara, the round-faced youth looked like a geisha. Smiling indolently, he toyed with the knot of his robe with one hand, while delicately holding a glass of wine out to the viewer with the other. The erotic overtones of both the gestures and the expression were unmistakable. "First the wine," he seemed to say, "then perhaps some fruit. Then me."

The painting had been done for a certain Cardinal del Monte, Hatcher remembered, a corrupt sophisticate who had enjoyed giving transvestite parties as a young man. There were other paintings by Caravaggio with similar subjects: young boys with baskets of fruit, young boys dressed as musicians, suggesting, in ways that were not necessarily subtle, that music was indeed "the food of love." In fact, there were altogether too many pretty young men in Caravaggio's early pictures to allow any evasion of the fact that the artist had shared the same tendencies as his patron.

So what? Plenty of great artists had been homosexual, or bisexual, and what difference did it make? But as Hatcher looked at the face in the picture he realized that it was the expression and gestures of the model that were shocking, not his sex. The painting would have been equally depraved if it had been of a young girl. More so, perhaps, since the average viewer would be quicker to reach the conclusion that he was looking at a whore.

A final grouping of pictures was pinned to the front doors of Hatcher's armoire. These were so different in mood, style, and subject from the others that they seemed to have been painted by another artist. They were the austere, monumental religious paintings that occupied the last ten years of the artist's short life.

There was very little about these works that could be called pretty or charming. The brilliant surface realism was gone. Most of the color was gone as well, leaving the late pictures dark and monochromatic. Detail and anecdote were stripped away, leaving large areas of empty space that seemed to engulf the figures in a vast, murky void.

The mood of the painting was stark and tragic. Saint Peter, crucified, did not accept his fate with a smile on his lips, but twisted his body painfully on his cross to stare with rage at his tormentors. The Virgin Mary in Caravaggio's *Death of the Virgin* was not shown dying, as was the custom, but dead. Worse than dead: a bloated corpse resting on a crude bed in a nondescript cellar. There were no choirs of angels carrying her soul heavenward, either: simply a group of rough-looking peasants, Caravaggio's Apostles, standing in frozen attitudes of mute grief. Strong enough today, it was too strong for the people who commissioned it. Like many of Caravaggio's greatest works, it was rejected.

Rejection had been a common theme in Caravaggio's career. His figures were said to be vulgar peasants, without beauty or grace; he had no sense of artistic decorum; worst of all, he had no sense of artistic imagination. All he was capable of depicting, his critics claimed, was what was in front of him. The chorus swelled, fed by the painter's enemies. He could not draw; he had no mastery of perspective or anatomy; he did not follow "the rules." The shadows in his pictures were not viewed as a revolutionary dramatic device, but simply as a cheap trick to cover up his inadequacy as a draftsman. He did not study the antique, or the great painters before him. Thus the greatest revolutionary since Michelangelo was hounded and ridiculed, and had to watch the best commissions of his day go to hacks and sycophants.

Hatcher sat on the floor, surrounded by books. He leaned against the side of his bed and took another sip of the Orvieto. Then he glared at Caravaggio's Saint Peter, who glared back at him.

It occurred to him that he had very little idea of what he was looking for. The old axiom stated that if you didn't know what the hell you were doing, you might consider not doing it anymore. You might even consider doing something else.

Hatcher decided to go see Burton Crelly.

11

It was late that night when Hatcher reached the *osteria,* and he was pleasantly surprised to find Crelly still at his battle station. The waterline on the wine flask was distinctly lower than on the previous occasion, so he was even more surprised when Crelly seemed glad to see him.

"Hatcher, you old son of a bitch. Pull up a chair. I'll get another glass."

"Why the sudden bonhomie?"

"Decided maybe you were okay, Hatcher. In fact, I figured maybe there was a story in you."

Hatcher looked dubious.

"Make you a hero. Hatcher the Art Cop. Young Lochinvar come out of the West, bringing all of Italy's stolen treasures back to her, that kind of thing."

Hatcher looked more dubious.

"Look, Crelly, I don't want to be a spoilsport, but I know about your heroes. I've read your stuff. You're looking for the Horse's Ass of the Week."

Crelly looked hurt.

"Ah, you don't understand. Fame, notoriety, it's all the same. The main thing is, get your name out there! Be seen! I can tell your story, make you a household word."

"I don't want my story told. And 'herpes' is a household word."

"Can't turn your nose up at the world's honors, Son."

"It would certainly be an honor. Yes, indeed. I could wear it proudly, right next to the medal for good citizenship given me by the Ayatollah Khomeini. Right now, anonymity suits me just fine."

Crelly shrugged. It was a good Roman shrug, meant to indicate that the rest of the world was mad.

"Well, just to satisfy my own curiosity, then, maybe I could ask you a few questions."

"Off the record?"

Crelly laughed. "Of course. What record? I told you, I make up most of what I write anyway."

"I'm serious. No stories."

"Natural modesty, Hatcher. It becomes you."

"A natural desire to stay alive. The odds on this are a lot better if the person I'm looking for isn't looking for me at the same time."

Crelly sighed, filled a glass, and pushed it across the table to Hatcher.

"What made me curious about this whole thing, I mean about you, is this business about being an 'art cop.' I thought about that, the other night. I mean, Jesus, that's a weird thing to be, an art cop, so I got to wondering why the hell anybody would want to do that for a living."

"No stories, Crelly?"

"I told you. What do you want, an affidavit?"

"A promise is fine. Just like my promise to you that if you print anything I'll be coming after you with an ax."

Hatcher took a long drink of wine and waited for Crelly to say something. Crelly was waiting for Hatcher.

"Was that a serious question?"

"Sure, why not?"

"I like art."

"That's a stupid answer."

"It was a stupid question. In my experience, if you ask a cop why he does what he does, you'll get a stupid answer ten times out of ten. Or a lie."

Crelly smiled. It didn't seem to Hatcher that Crelly was going to let him off the hook.

"Forget *me,* Hatcher. What answer do you give yourself to that question?"

Hatcher knit his brows together in mock seriousness.

" 'Down these mean streets a man must go . . .' "

Crelly's smile did not move. Hatcher decided to try again. He dropped his voice.

"A man's gotta do what a man's gotta do." The smile was still there. Hatcher dropped his voice lower.

"It's a dirty job, but someone . . ."

"Cut the crap, Hatcher." Crelly was really angry now, and Hatcher felt a little sheepish for assuming that it had been a loaded question.

"All right, then. You should have taken the first answer. It's more than that, I suppose. I really love art."

Crelly relaxed, which made Hatcher

nervous.

"You're an art-lover, then. Is that all?"

Hatcher thought for a moment before answering.

"No. People who steal art enrage me. It seems like a desecration to me, a personal insult. I've always reacted the same way to the destruction of art, reading about the idiotic bonfires in Florence under Savonarola, or the rampages of the iconoclasts during the Reformation, or the destruction of Gothic sculpture during the French Revolution. Wars, too, of course. I get sick thinking about Dresden, Monte Cassino, Coventry, and all the rest."

"You're an art-lover and a cop."

"A conservationist. 'Save the Whales,' but with me it's 'Save the Pictures.' "

"For what? For posterity?"

"Screw posterity. For me. I'm very selfish. There's nothing noble about it."

"Ah, but you really mean it. You're an aesthete, Hatcher."

Hatcher grinned. "Wow. And I thought there weren't any dirty words left to call people anymore."

"You're a real old-school aesthete. I like that, Hatcher. It has a nice quaint ring to it, sort of fin de siècle. What was that

Gilbert and Sullivan line — 'As you walk down Piccadilly, with a poppy or a lily'?''

"Is that what you think I am, some overbred intellectual fop? Terrific. You think I'm Algernon Swinburne, Pecci thinks I'm Billy the Kid. I seem to have an image problem. Well, what about you, Crelly? You're a muckraker, a cheap-shot artist."

"You forgot scandalmonger."

"Sorry. Scandalmonger."

"Only on the surface, Hatcher. Actually, I'm a historian and a philosopher. I'm also a millenarian. Here, have some more wine."

"Thank you. What was that third thing?"

"Millenarian? Someone who believes the world will come to a crashing close at the end of a thousand-year period. Remember all the loopy-looking characters in those old *New Yorker* cartoons? The ones with the sandwich boards saying 'The end of the world is at hand'? They were right. In the year 999, people were hunkering down all over Europe. Must have felt pretty foolish when the year 1000 passed, and they were all still there. There was nothing the matter with the general theory, they just got their dates wrong. It's 2000, not 1000. And it won't be the trumpets of the Lord sounding, either, it'll probably be a small nuclear indiscretion by one of the senile delinquents in Washington or Moscow. Think of it, Hatcher. The whole world will be one ground zero. Want to know something else? When it happens, no one will be particularly surprised, because by the time it happens, there won't be anything much worth saving. And in that fraction of a second between the flash and the thermal pulse that turns everybody to vapor, you know what we will all be feeling? I swear to you, Hatcher, you know I'm right: not shock, not even fear, but *relief*."

Hatcher looked at Crelly. Crelly's eyes were red and his shoulders were slumped, but he wasn't slurring his words or rambling. He was a big man, so it would take a lot of alcohol to bring him down. Still, it was Hatcher's feeling that Crelly had reached that magical stage of alcoholism where it seems that you can drink forever with very little effect.

Hatcher had heard lots of excuses for drinking before, but Armageddon was a new one. He did not have many illusions about the state of civilization in the late twentieth century, but suspected that it probably was in somewhat better shape than Crelly's liver. He did not know if he could get the conversation back on the track, but decided to give it a try.

"Before the Big Bang, though, we've all got to keep moving, eh? Got to keep the old rent money coming in somehow. You have to keep churning out nasty stories, for example."

"For instance, the nasty story about the art thefts?"

"For instance."

"You'll have to excuse me for a minute. When I get back, I'll talk to you about that."

When he was gone, Hatcher realized that Crelly had got under his skin. He could not figure him out. Was the cynicism real, or just some kind of sophomoric pose useful in his trade? Hatcher always felt vulnerable to the Crellys of the world. He always seemed to wind up as the straight man. But at least Crelly's trip to the lavatory gave him a chance to work out a new line of attack. When Crelly returned, Hatcher understood from his broad grin and the way he clapped his hands together that he was prepared to close in for the kill.

"Art, Hatcher. That's one of the biggest problems with this lousy country."

"Oh?" This was not, Hatcher decided, one of his snappier rejoinders.

"There's too damn much of it."

"No such thing."

"Oh? You don't think so? Try living here for six or eight years, then you'll understand. Was it Stendhal or Byron who said that Italy had 'a fatal gift of beauty'? I thought that line was clever and ironic when I first heard it, but it's the flat truth. 'Fatal' is the word."

"Care to explain that?"

"Sure. Italy's in bad trouble, Hatcher. You don't see it, because you're a tourist, but almost nothing in this country works, from the postal system to the government to the economy. Look at the hospitals and the schools. Go to Naples, get a whiff of the poverty. Or further south, to the Abruzzi. In fact, the only part of Italy that really works is tourist Italy, which is a gigantic illusion, a huge facade that's been carefully constructed over a thousand years' time. And the Italians lead you by the hand, and show you the facade, and note your gasps of admiration and murmur *'che bella, che bella,'* and wait for their tips. But they don't let you get behind the facade, because there's nothing there. And they hate you, and themselves, and the whole damned show."

"Do you really believe that?"

"Sure. Let me tell you a story, Hatcher. A few years ago, during the floods, people realized that the joke about Venice sinking back into the Adriatic wasn't funny anymore. It was about to happen. The city was crumbling, the *vaporetti* were weakening the foundations of the buildings with their wakes, and so on and so forth. Big hue and cry. Foundations sprang up right and left like mushrooms. 'Save Venice,' everybody screamed, and millions of dollars poured in. Know what happened to the money, Hatcher? Huge amounts of it simply disappeared, went up in smoke. People were shocked. Tourists, like you, were shocked because the money was siphoned off into food and clothing instead of being used to restore the marble filigree on some damned palazzo."

"You think it was 'food and clothing'? How about television sets, cars, and transistor radios, or maybe Scotch and women and numbered accounts in Swiss banks?"

"Okay, why not? It doesn't change the argument. My point is this, Hatcher. The people in this country have been carting more than two thousand years of art and history around with them and they're sick of it. They're tired of being custodians of the past, they're tired of living in a goddamn museum. Look at the Venetians. They're leaving Venice by the thousands, like rats leaving a sinking ship. Know where they're going, a lot of them? *Mestre.* Now, Mestre is a little industrial horror with smokestacks and air pollution, and it's about as scenic as Trenton, New Jersey. But it has one priceless advantage, and do you know what that is? *No art.* No museums, no palaces, no Roman temples, no tourists, and no past."

"Ah. So your solution to Italy's problems is, get rid of the art."

"Part of it. That's not the whole answer, of course, but it might help. Besides, stealing art is historically one of Italy's major industries. They're good at it. They've been doing it for a long time. You should read Cicero on Gaius Verres."

"I have. Verres was a rapacious monster. He should have been hung up by his thumbs."

"He was a man of his times. The emperors stole all the art they could find, and what they couldn't steal, they had copied or faked."

"Right. And if they hadn't we wouldn't know a hell of a lot about Greek sculpture, would we?"

Crelly grinned and looked pleased with himself. It took Hatcher a moment to realize that his own remark was not only pompous, but it put him on the wrong side of the argument.

"Just out of curiosity, Crelly, if you believe half of what you've been saying about Italy, why the hell are you here?"

A short shrug.

"The wine is cheap, and the women are easy."

"As cheap and easy as that crack?"

Crelly laughed, threw a wad of bills on the table, and got up.

"Not bad, Hatcher. You're improving. Come back and see me again sometime."

12

The small man suddenly stopped drumming his fingers on the tabletop and became absolutely still. The woman with him felt a sharp pang. He scared her when he got this way, so quiet and cold. It was as if he was retreating far inside himself, to some secret place she could never find or reach.

His voice, when he finally spoke, was more of a hiss than a whisper. If she had not heard it before, she could not have identified it as his.

"Lena, listen. That man over there — the tall one with the brown jacket, talking to the other man. Have you ever seen him before?"

"There? At the front table? I've seen him before. Here, at the café, I mean."

"Who is he?"

"How would I know? He comes here at night. I think I've seen him a few times."

"Alone?"

"Sometimes, sometimes not. I suppose he's a tourist of some kind. English or German, I think. I forget what I've heard him speak, but I think it was one of those."

"Is that all?"

Lena shrugged. With anyone else, she would have known what it was: fear, anger, jealousy even.

"What is it?"

He didn't seem to hear the question.

"Listen carefully. I want you to stay here. Have another cappuc' or some brandy, or whatever you want. Watch that man. Don't stare, just watch. Then meet me at Giorgio's over by the Pantheon. I'll be in the back. Meet me in about forty minutes."

Then he was gone. Lena looked across at the man seated several tables away, which only deepened the mystery. There was no way she could imagine the tall, angular figure as dangerous in any way. She thought he was comical, with his white, bony ankles and wrists sticking out,

270

his drab clothes and the awkward jerky gestures he made when he spoke to his companion. A couple of nights before he had recognized her, and nodded and smiled as he sat down at his table. It had been easy, she remembered, to smile back. He was just another *straniero*. Typical.

Hatcher was seated with Landini. It had become something of a habit with him to come to the Piazza Navona after supper. He always picked the same café, where he could watch the lights at the bottom of the pool dancing around the sprawling stone giants of Bernini's fountain of the Four Rivers, framed in the background by the front of Borromini's Church of Sant'Agnese. Neither the church nor the fountain had existed in 1605, when Caravaggio had attacked Mariano Pasqualone in the piazza with his sword. Hatcher had tried to imagine what the Piazza Navona had looked like then, and failed. He assumed it had been a marketplace then, as now. But then the hawkers would have been selling farm produce and cheap religious items. Today the many commercial activities had to do with bad tourist art: sloppy watercolors of the piazza, hideous caricatures, and the like. There was also a brisk trade in pirated tapes of American rock music, lighted yo-yos, and dope. It had slipped a bit since the great days of the eighteenth century, when, in high summer, the whole piazza was flooded with water and the Roman aristocracy would splash around in gilded carriages with fireworks blazing in the sky overhead.

"I had another chat with Crelly."

"What do you think of him?"

"He's a cynic. A real price-of-everything-value-of-nothing type. There's always a kind of seductiveness to those people. It's not the cynicism that bothers me so much as my own reactions to it. They make you play their games. I find myself becoming a wise guy, a peddler of one-liners and cheap comebacks."

"He's clever, though. A lot of people read his stuff."

"Ingenious, maybe. I get the feeling that there's never more than a half-truth in anything he writes."

This brought a wry smile from Landini.

"There's a big market for half-truths here. And cynicism. It's always the same question: 'What's wrong with Italy?' We all spend our time asking that question, and providing half-baked answers to it. This question is our real national pastime. Soccer and politics are way behind it. Most of our literature is just singing the same old song, from the satires of Juvenal to the latest novel by Moravia. Ever heard of Alberto Arbasino, by the way?"

"No, I don't think so."

"He recently wrote a book of essays called 'A Country Without.' It begins with a list: 'A country without memory, a country without history, a country without a past, a country without experience' — and so on, like a litany, for about half a page. It was a best-seller here. Naturally."

"What about the Red Brigades?"

Landini waited a full minute before answering. Hatcher appreciated the pause; it meant that Landini was giving the question full consideration.

"I assume you know the general outline of the story. It's almost a cliché in Europe by now: a small group of university intellectuals who feel alienated and disaffected band together to fight 'society' and 'the establishment' — whatever they may be — on behalf of 'the people' and 'the workers,' whoever *they* may be. In Italy it gets a little more complicated since we already have a Communist party. In fact, the Red Brigades hate the Communists, whom they consider to be hypocritical tools of the corrupt bourgeoisie.

"Like most student uprisings, the Red Brigades started with pamphlets and speeches and talk about Marxist-Leninist dialects. Then, talk gave way to guns. At first, the main targets were the fat-cat industrialists. They were more often kidnapped than murdered, and then usually dragged before so-called peoples' courts to sign bogus confessions for propaganda purposes.

"It didn't take long for the situation to escalate. Violence went from being a means to being an end, and the list of targets broadened. 'Enemies of the People' became a euphemism for enemies of the Red Brigades. Judges were intimidated or shot, any prosecutor in charge of a case involving the Brigades became a marked man. Pecci is a case in point, by the way. In any event, as the campaign of terror widened, the alleged constituency of the Red Brigades shrank. The 'workers,' whose rights the Red Brigades claimed to be defending, had very little use for them, of course. They've always distrusted intellectuals anyway, and they weren't interested in a new set of problems. The Communists, already nervous about their tenuous position politically, disavowed the Brigades from the beginning. As the whole notion that the Red Brigades were in business to 'liberate' anyone began to seem like more and more of a charade, the goals of the terrorists became more overtly revolutionary. Any violent act against the government, or even the governmental bureaucracy, was condoned.

"The turning point was probably the Moro affair. Any popular support the terrorists had had began to sour from then on. Even the students became disillusioned. Then last year, when the police broke the case of the kidnapping of General Dozier, big chunks of the Red Brigades' organization got knocked off with it."

"Are you optimistic about the situation right now?"

"Yes and no. In the sense that the terrorists are weakened and on the run, yes, I'm optimistic. At the same time we are in a very delicate and dangerous position. Look: the government has been labeled brutal and repressive by the Red Brigades, and their only hope of gaining credibility is to make the government seem as fascistic as they've always claimed it to be. So their tactic is to increase the violence, and the level of provocation, in the hope of creating some kind of Draconian overreaction. They also need money badly, so they've turned to crime."

"They don't sound like starry-eyed adolescents to me."

"Hardly. And that's another problem. As more and more of them have been caught and thrown in jail, they've discovered a new constituency among hard-core criminals. In prison they found what they were looking for: real rage, real hatred of the system, not some half-baked phrases from Mao's *Little Red Book* or Ché Guevera. The real thing. Another point: the career criminal has practical experience. He's a professional, not an amateur. He may also be a psychopath, but they don't worry too much about that. They need all the help they can get."

"It sounds as if they would take anybody with a grudge, anybody with an urge to destroy, for whatever reason."

"Probably. I have the feeling that the

war has already been lost, and that the Red Brigades know it. This makes them more unpredictable, and more dangerous. Declaring war on the system in this country is not necessarily wrong, Amos, it's just silly. It's like invading Russia. You go charging across the border, and what do you find? Snow. Hundreds of thousands of miles of it. It's a ridiculous goal to bring down the Italian government. What the hell, give it a couple of weeks and it will bring itself down. Why waste the effort?"

"So you think the Red Brigades will be defeated?"

"No, not exactly defeated, but outlasted. Endured, and ultimately survived. They will have killed a lot of people in the meantime, though."

"I see."

The men sat quietly for a moment. The crowd in the piazza was thinning out, and the artists were closing up their cardboard portfolios, folding their easels and stealing away like gypsies.

"So, Amos. How is the case going?"

"Don't know, Lou. I have an idea."

"Want to talk about it?"

"Not yet. Maybe in a couple of days,

okay? I have some appointments tomorrow, and I think that after I see the people I'll have a better idea whether I'm on the right track. Maybe I'm just pissing into the wind."

He felt discouraged. He scanned the café, but the redhead didn't seem to be there tonight. What the hell, thought Hatcher, maybe she's like me: a tourist. It had angered him when Crelly had called him that, but Crelly had been right. He was just another tourist.

Several minutes after Hatcher and Landini had left, the small, thin man ran into the piazza. He stopped at the café for a moment, noted the vacant table, then veered into the center of the square, and raced from the Fountain of the Four Rivers to the Fountain of the Moor at the south end. He clipped two people and knocked over one man, who swore and shook his fist. The thin man didn't seem to notice. When he got to the Fountain of the Moor, he climbed up on the basin of the fountain and craned his neck around the square.

As soon as he caught his breath he began to swear.

13

By the time Hatcher found himself on Bus No. 75 on his way across the Tiber, through Trastevere and up the shoulder of the Janiculum, it was late afternoon. Siesta time, he remembered, relishing the idea. He was hot, tired, and more discouraged than he had been the night before.

The interview with *Dottore* Bruni, one of the scholars who had organized the Caravaggio show, had been a disaster. Hatcher had tried to prepare himself for the occasion by reading some of Bruni's articles, and had considered them brilliant and subtle. One of them, entitled "Realism and Reality in the Art of Caravaggio," had dealt at great length with the nature and function of the curious distortions found in Caravaggio's pictures. With what struck Hatcher as a daring stroke of perception, Bruni argued that these apparent "mistakes" were not accidental but quite intentional, a clue intended to shock the viewer out of interpreting the paintings as simple transcriptions of visual reality. When Hatcher finished the article, he was still not sure that he bought Bruni's thesis in its entirety, but he was at least provoked into looking at the artist's paintings again from a novel point of view.

None of the qualities Hatcher had sensed in Bruni's scholarship had been obvious in the scholar himself. Bruni was a short, voluble man of about fifty, who seemed unable to express himself except in superlatives, punctuated with flamboyant outbursts of passion. The pictures in the exhibition were "so beautiful, you would not believe." The theft of the pictures was "the greatest tragedy of my life — my God, how I weep for them!" The "assassins" who stole the paintings must be found and executed, "a lesson to the world." Who, Hatcher inquired, did the *dottore* think they might be? "Those bastards of the *Brigate Rosse*, the Red Brigades, there can be no doubt." But maybe also the neofascists, the *Prima*

Linea. Maybe they worked together. They were organized by foreigners, of course; what Italian would do such a terrible thing?

When Hatcher had excused himself, Bruni was weighing the relative possibilities of the CIA and the KGB as the real masterminds of the operation. Bruni was clearly enjoying his own performance, but Hatcher had had enough. By the time he succeeded in making his escape, he had been tempted to give Bruni a box of flashing yo-yos and send him to the Piazza Navona.

Richard Blake met Hatcher in his apartment at the American Academy. Both in looks and in manner, the contrast between Bruni and Blake was dramatic. Blake was tall and gaunt with a shock of white hair that fell down over his forehead. His eyes and eyebrows were both black, and his gaze had a searing quality. He invited Hatcher in with a brusqueness that implied that he did not want him there, and would be rid of him as soon as he could conveniently manage it.

"I'm in charge of a Caravaggio symposium that's supposed to take place in exactly ten days. I say 'supposed to,' because, as usual, none of the people concerned with the conference have done a damned thing to help. If it comes off at all, it'll be a miracle. So I'd appreciate it if you could be brief."

"It's a fairly complicated business, but I'll try."

"Then try."

"I'm trying to find the people who stole the pictures from the Caravaggio show you organized. I think they're also responsible for a number of other thefts, and at least one murder. The murdered man was a friend of mine."

"I see, then. Well, you might as well take a seat. Want a drink? Dubonnet, Campari soda? I may still have some Scotch . . ."

"Just soda, thanks."

"Right. I'll be back in a minute."

Blake's apartment, what Hatcher could see of it, was more of a library or study than a place to relax. The furniture was largely Renaissance or baroque: long oak refectory tables and Savonarola chairs, as handsome as they were uncomfortable. Bookcases ran floor to ceiling, and the only decorations on the walls were prints and a few posters. In its austerity, Blake's apartment reminded Hatcher a little of the monks' cells in Renaissance depictions of Saint Jerome in his study.

In a short time Blake returned with the drinks.

"I'm afraid I can't help you, Mr. Hatcher. I can only repeat what I told that man Pecci. I don't have any idea who stole the paintings, or why. It must have been some kind of mistake."

"No mistake, I think. The hijacking was too elaborate and too carefully planned. The problem is that the pictures were by very minor artists."

Blake shrugged. He did not seem especially interested.

"I wouldn't expect a gang of thieves to be particularly knowledgeable about the art market. What the hell, it was a fairly big show, they would have assumed that the paintings were valuable. Must have been an unpleasant surprise when they discovered they weren't."

"You don't seem very excited by the whole thing."

This brought a curt, sardonic laugh from Blake.

"Not particularly. I'm a little too busy to play cops and robbers right now. If you

283

want righteous indignation, hysterics, and all the rest, you should speak to Aldo Bruni."

"I have."

"Then I should be a pleasant relief. I don't give much of a damn about the paintings, and I don't have an idea in the world who stole them."

"I find your reaction more curious than Bruni's."

"Oh? As an art historian, you —"

"Ex-art historian."

"Ex-art historian, then, I'd think you would understand. They weren't great paintings, they were a series of interesting problems. I worked on them for a long time. Some I found I could answer, some escaped me, but by the time I finished the catalogue I was fairly sick of the damn pictures. I have an excellent set of photographs. If the paintings are found in shreds at the bottom of the Tiber, it would make very little difference to anyone, least of all me. I'm sorry if I've wasted your time."

At least Blake was not the sort that required anyone to be delicate or oblique, and for this Hatcher was grateful. He decided to try a frontal charge, bayonet fixed.

"If you're not interested in the crime, you might be interested in the criminal."

"I doubt it."

"Don't be too sure. He's multilingual, sophisticated, and has a profound knowledge of the history of art. More than that, he knows the art market inside out, and has contacts in Italian museums. He's connected with left-wing terrorists, probably the Red Brigades, and has a particular fascination with Caravaggio."

"That's crazy, Hatcher. It's someone's fabrication, someone's fantasy. Who invented this monster — you?"

It struck Hatcher that Blake was furious. He wondered why.

"Stealing some weak Caravaggio school pieces doesn't prove a knowledge of art history *or* a 'fascination with Caravaggio.' Rather the opposite, it seems to me. As for the rest —"

"Does the phrase *'ti ho in culo'* mean anything to you?"

Blake reacted sharply to that.

"It's an insult. An obscenity. What about it?"

"Caravaggio said it to a cop in 1604, and got thrown in jail for it."

"So what?"

"The same phrase was spray-painted on the walls of the Palazzo Caprese by a gang of art thieves earlier this year."

"So what? A common insult, a simple coincidence."

"No. It was a 'common insult' in the seventeenth century, perhaps, but not today."

Blake laughed again. It was an unpleasant sound, nervous and sarcastic.

"The Italian language is riddled with archaisms. They may not say that in Rome, but I'm sure there are villages in the south where you can hear that expression. My God, a dictionary of Italian insults would have to be thousands of pages long. I know most of the Caravaggio scholars, Hatcher. Let me reassure you: very few of them are left-wing terrorists."

It was Hatcher's turn to laugh, equally humorlessly.

"It's a silly idea, isn't it? Maybe not entirely, though."

Hatcher finished his soda and put the glass down. He turned his chair slightly toward Blake, making sure he had his attention.

"It's possible, just possible, to interpret Caravaggio's painting in a sort of Marxist light, isn't it? The rejection of the supernatural, the emphasis on rough, plebeian figures, the predominance of commissions for churches with largely poor and working-class congregations — all this has a slightly left-wing flavor, if I'm not mistaken."

"I've heard this nonsense before. It's oversimplified, romantic twaddle."

"You think that's all it is? Take a look at the Russian literature on Caravaggio and his followers. Russian art historians interpret Caravaggio as an 'artist of the people,' and 'artist of the common man' who rejected courtly sophistication and 'aristocratic' refinements in favor of a direct, powerful realism comprehensible to everyone. They love him in Russia."

"This is so much crap."

"Not entirely. Caravaggio was pilloried in his own time for his devotion to the common and ordinary, for his preoccupation with crude peasant types and his refusal to idealize."

"So was Rembrandt, so were a lot of painters. These are matters of artistic convention, not politics, for God's sake. I'm sick of this ridiculous business of trying to turn Caravaggio into some kind of seventeenth-century pinko. In fact, if you want to hear my ideas about Caravaggio-the-proto-Marxist, come to the symposium and listen to my lecture."

"It sounds as if you've heard this very argument before."

"It's a common fallacy."

Hatcher sensed a certain wariness in Blake.

"Perhaps my notion of a left-wing terrorist with an interest in Caravaggio isn't totally absurd."

Blake shrugged. He seemed suddenly bored with the conversation, or perhaps just annoyed.

"It sounds to me as if you're tilting at windmills, Mr. Hatcher. Now I'm afraid you'll have to excuse me. I've got to get back to work."

Five minutes later Hatcher was strolling down the Janiculum, feeling fine. Something was bothering Blake other than the conference. Hatcher had irritated him: so far, so good. He decided to give whatever it was a few days to fester before going back and irritating him some more.

14

The little man stood in front of the screen, which was not really a screen at all but simply a sheet tacked up against the wall. He would have preferred a real screen and good carousel projectors with remote controls, so that he could give his little group a professional performance. Still, he could make do; in ten days, two weeks at the most, there would be plenty of money for such things.

The image projected on the sheet was the floor plan of a church. The *Capo* was reaching the end of his lecture.

"So you see, it should all be quite easy. Alberto should have no trouble securing the equipment, and after that's done, we should meet once more to discuss traffic patterns, routes, and any possible contingencies. Oh, one more thing. If any of you have any lingering superstitions about desecrating a holy place" — here he paused — "you might remember this chapel. It was reserved for the use of the whore of Cesare Borgia, one of the most corrupt and sadistic men who ever lived."

The *Capo*'s speech was over. He enjoyed giving these little talks, and he always tried to make sure there was something for everyone. Mario was the easiest to please, satisfied with the slightest hint of potential violence. For Alberto there was always a slogan or two, some glib paraphrase of radical doctrine. The redhead was equally political, but less interested in dogma than in the human ramifications of perceived injustices. Perhaps for this reason, she was the only one with whom the *Capo* felt any real bond.

After the others were gone and the *Capo* had begun clearing away the empty paper cups and wine bottles, he noticed the figure of Alberto nervously hovering near the door. He looked like a student anxiously trying to decide whether or not to approach his professor about a grade.

"Alberto?"

"I have a couple of questions. Can we talk?"

"Of course. Why not?"

Alberto dropped his coat over the back of a chair and began fussing with his cigarette lighter. He was clearly upset.

"The painting you want to steal. Is it very valuable?"

The *Capo* laughed.

"Priceless. Why do you ask?"

"After we get it, what then? What happens to it?"

"Nothing. It comes back here and goes in that bin over there."

The *Capo* gestured to a corner of the small apartment, where crude storage racks had been hammered together out of pine boards. The structure was covered with a cheap plastic shower curtain.

"But you said it was priceless . . ."

"It is. It's also worthless. Anyone would recognize it immediately, and therefore it's unsalable."

"Then why steal it?"

The small man smiled before answering.

"It's for me, Alberto. For my collection."

The *Capo* kept smiling, while the other man exploded.

291

"*Your* collection? Good Christ, man, are you working for the Red Brigades, or are the Red Brigades working for you?"

"Both."

"We need money, lots of money, and fast. You know that. This isn't a game we're playing."

"Calm yourself, Alberto. In about two weeks there will be a man from Switzerland with a great deal of money. He'll take everything in the bin except the paintings we stole from that museum van and the altarpiece. Those will stay. They are my fee."

"Why do you want them?"

"Personal reasons. Don't look so glum, Alberto. If it helps, just think of me as a mercenary. Every army has mercenaries, after all."

"You promised us money. So far, there's been nothing."

The *Capo* sighed. He was beginning to find Alberto tiresome.

"Money was part of it. I also promised you Pecci. The Brigades, as usual, wanted him shot, which would have provided the government with another hero, another martyr. That was a stupid idea. First you must ruin him, make a buffoon of him, and then if he's shot later it won't make any difference. The same trick works with the government, but on a larger scale. As the works we steal become more important, the authorities are made to seem more frustrated and impotent. If they can't protect Italian art, what *can* they protect? All of this is important, you see, much more important than the money you keep whining about. If you didn't have the soul of a petty shopkeeper you would realize that."

"At least I *have* a soul, and some beliefs."

"Oh? What are your 'beliefs,' Alberto?"

"That materialism is evil. That when the means of production are placed in the hands of the people —"

The *Capo* started to laugh. Alberto got angrier, his face reddening.

"Those aren't beliefs, they're phrases. Formulas. People like you were talking the same shit in the 1780s in Paris, and again in 1917 in Moscow — and what did they produce? A beautiful new world of freedom and equality, where all men were brothers, working together for the common good? Don't be silly. They produced the guillotine and the Reign of

Terror and Stalin's extermination squads. And you, even if you succeed, what do you think *you'll* get? Something different? Some hero like Garibaldi to lead us out of the wilderness? If you're lucky, you'll probably get a Mussolini. At least he made the trains run on time."

"If you believe that, why are you with us?"

"I have some private matters to take care of."

"That's all? What happens then?"

"I don't really care. I did, at one time. Come over here. I want to show you something."

The two men stood by the window. The *Capo* pointed to a small building across the street.

"Do you see that? That building with the yellow and black stains was a beautiful little baroque villa until about fifty years ago. It had a marble facing with lovely carved details. Look at it now, an ugly wreck. The marble has soaked up so many chemicals that it's as soft as sandstone, and if you run your hand across it, it crumbles and turns to powder. It has crevices six or eight centimeters deep, and such wide cracks that they needed iron clamps to keep it from collapsing altogether. Every time it rains, it rains nitric and sulfuric acid, and the fissures get a little deeper. When it rains, all the buildings and all the statues in Rome weep and melt. In a few years the sculptures on the Ponte Sant'Angelo won't even be recognizable as angels. They'll stand there like rows of broken and rotting teeth. Such things bothered me once, but now I don't really care."

"What *do* you care about?"

"Settling a few debts. Other than that, very little."

15

"It is by Gianlorenzo Bernini. It is called the Fountain of the Four Rivers."

She was sitting at the table next to his. Hatcher was taken by surprise. He had not noticed her arrival at all.

"I know. I was trying to remember which figure goes with which river."

This was a lie, since the subject of his brooding had nothing to do with the fountain he was staring at, but he wanted to continue the conversation.

"Let me see. I used to know them, when I was little. The man on the corner with the beard and the great pole is the Ganges, I think, and the one on the other side is . . . how stupid I am. I forget. It is the Danube, perhaps."

"No, the Nile. He has a palm tree beside

him, and he is pulling his shirt over his head to hide, because the source of the Nile was hidden for so long."

"So he is hiding too; now I remember."

She laughed, and swept the fan of red hair off her forehead with a brush of her hand. He had never heard her speak before; her voice was darker and huskier than he had expected. She might have been about twenty-eight years old.

"Would you care to join me?"

"Oh, don't let me interrupt your work!"

Hatcher quickly closed the notebook, stood up, and gestured to the seat beside him.

"Please. My work isn't very serious, and perhaps you can help me with it."

She nodded, smiling, and stepped over to Hatcher's table. As he pushed her chair in for her, the scent of her perfume almost made his knees buckle. It had been a long time for Hatcher.

"So, we have the Nile and the Ganges on this side, and on the other side is the Danube and the fourth one, whose name I forget."

"He is my favorite, the black man. He is the Rio della Plata, with his wonderful animal and his funny gesture. Perhaps you

297

know about Bernini and his joke?"

Hatcher knew the story, but pretended not to. The figure perched on one ledge of the fountain seemed to be recoiling in horror, with his left arm thrown up over his head for protection. In front of him rose the facade of Borromini's Church of Sant'Agnese. Bernini and Borromini were bitter rivals, and the story developed that the gesture of the figure on the fountain was expressing Bernini's shock at Borromini's architecture. Since the church was finished after the fountain, the story could not be true, a fact which never stopped anyone from telling it.

". . . so the black man seems to be saying '*aiuto*, help,' because he thinks the front of the church might fall down on him! It is true, you must look at him. Come, I will show you."

Hatcher allowed himself to be led around to the front of the fountain, and tried to react with appropriate surprise to Bernini's figure representing the Rio della Plata. In fact, the sprawling giant *did* seem to be recoiling from Boromini's facade. The "wonderful animal" crawling out of a crevice in the rock underneath him was Bernini's idea of an armadillo. Knowing very little about armadillos, the sculptor had come up with a marvelous invention: part crocodile, part Chinese dragon, and part Gila monster.

As they walked around the basin of the fountain, Hatcher's companion pointed out details of the sculpture that particularly delighted her.

"When I was a child, I played here every day. We would climb into the fountain and try to crawl up on the river gods, and the police would come and pull us out and yell at us. We laughed at them — why not? Once I even got into the big cave in the middle and climbed up on the horse — it was very exciting and frightening. For a moment I thought the horse would come alive and carry me off forever."

"And did he?"

She laughed again. "Only in my dreams."

They sat on the lip of the basin. Hatcher felt the spray from the jets of water brush his skin, and watched the aquamarine light dance over the face of the beautiful redhead beside him.

It was all an illusion, like Bernini's galloping horse. Hatcher knew himself too well, and he also knew Rome too well.

Things like this didn't happen. But for a moment the fantasy was almost perfect. He had the impulse to throw his arms around her just to see what would happen. Maybe they would both burst spontaneously into an old Nelson Eddy–Jeanette MacDonald duet, and all the people in the piazza would suddenly start dancing. "Places, everyone. Quiet on the set." But as they strolled back to the café, Hatcher admitted to himself that despite the temptation, disbelief could not be suspended indefinitely. At some point he had to figure out what was going on.

"My name is Maddalena Antelami — why are you smiling?"

"Nothing. A coincidence. You remind me of a Maddalena I saw in a painting recently. She had red hair, like yours."

"Oh, I hate my name. My friends all call me Lena."

"Why? Maddalena is lovely."

"No, it is ugly. Maria Maddalena: a horrid old woman wandering around in the desert to pay for her life of sin. How silly!"

"The one I saw in the picture was beautiful, not horrid. And young."

"Call me Lena, anyway. And you?"

"My name is Harry Jackson."

"Oh? You are here on vacation?"

Hatcher couldn't tell if there were any reaction to the name or not. As much as he hated to do it, he knew it had to be played this way.

"Not really. I'm here on an assignment. I write articles for travel magazines."

"I see. And you are writing about Rome?"

"Not exactly. I'm doing an article on piazzas in Italy. Actually, great public squares all over Europe. I'm going to include this one, of course, and the Piazza San Marco in Venice, and Piazza della Signoria in Florence."

"All the famous ones; all so boring and predictable. Besides, you didn't include the most beautiful piazza of all."

"Oh? Which is that?"

"The one in Siena, the Piazza del Campo, where they race the horses. The Town Hall is a beautiful old medieval building made out of brick, with a bell tower next to it. All the buildings are delicate and graceful, not like the ones in Florence. Florence gives me a headache with its big ugly blocks of stone. You should sit in the piazza in Siena late in the afternoon and watch the colors change from orange to red. The people are beautiful, too. Even the language is more graceful there."

"As graceful as your English? Really, you speak it perfectly."

"I studied it for years, and then when I was twenty I spent a year in the States as an exchange student."

"You could work as a translator."

"I have, from time to time. My field is political science, though. In a year I shall finish my degree at the university, and then I shall teach."

"Lena, there are many things I would like to discuss with you. A drink is too short a time. Have you eaten tonight?"

"No, but —"

"Then listen. Whenever I come to Italy, I treat myself to one great meal. The rest of the time I'm happy with a little minestrone and pasta, but there must be that one great self-indulgence, that one four-star, five-course, no-holds-barred culinary extravaganza. Be my guest tonight. It's a terrible waste if I have to enjoy it alone."

"But I don't know you."

"True, but that's one of the magical things about a great meal. Afterward we will know each other much better. Besides, if I don't run up my expense account, my magazine gets suspicious. They don't think I'm doing my job."

"I don't know."

"I'll make a deal with you. Let me go inside the café and make a telephone call for a reservation for two. When I return, I'll tell you the name of the restaurant, and then you can make up your mind. Okay? *D'accordo?*"

"*D'accordo.*"

Before going back to make the telephone call, Hatcher arranged a little test. Instead of carrying his notebook with him he left it on the table, with one of the bottom corners just touching the circular rim of the tabletop. The notebook contained the photocopies of Pecci's police records that Hatcher had obtained from Anselmo. When he returned, he knew one of three things would have happened.

He was serious about the meal, and pleasantly surprised to find that he was able to make a reservation on such short notice. After hanging up the receiver, he forced himself to loiter in the back of the café for a minute or so to give her plenty of time.

She was still there when he returned. The bottom of the notebook was now projecting out over the edge of the table by about half an inch.

"Success! I have a reservation for two for nine o'clock tonight at the Osteria dell'Orso. What do you say?"

"*Dio!* What *can* I say? That is one of the best restaurants in Rome!"

"Good. I was hoping that you'd consider it an offer you couldn't refuse."

16

Hatcher woke up with a start, opened his eyes, and immediately closed them again. He made himself lie there absolutely inert, took quick, shallow breaths, and tried to concentrate on an image of the waves rolling in on the beach at Waikiki.

It didn't work. He was awake; there was nothing he could do about it. Waking brought consciousness, and there was nothing he could do about that, either. Sooner or later he would have to open his eyes and look around, and maybe even think.

Seeing no viable alternative, Hatcher got up, stumbled over to the sink, and splashed water on his face. He looked at the haggard apparition with the bloodshot eyes staring at him in the mirror for a long masochistic moment before addressing his reflection.

"You stupid bastard. Good morning, you bloody idiot. Hope you had a swell time on the town last night, you miserable, self-deluded, oversexed, bungling moron."

He looked around the room while he dried his face with a towel. The woman was gone. Oh well, Hatcher thought, it was just one of those things. Easy come, easy go. Then it occurred to him to wonder if she had taken something with her, some little trinket or souvenir. For example, his wallet.

He went over to his jacket and quickly checked its pockets. It was all in order, the whole cache: wallet and traveler's checks. He wasn't surprised, just a little disappointed. In a perverse way he might have felt better if he had discovered that he had been rolled.

She had been through the drawers of the armoire, which was all right with Hatcher, and the piles of books on the dresser were disarranged, which was less all right. What was missing was the notebook with the police reports. The pistol and bullets were safe, still taped to the back of the armoire. As far as he could tell, it was just the notebook that was gone.

"Oh, Lena, Lena. After that dinner, too, not to mention the postprandial entertainment." With a groan Hatcher dropped back on the bed.

It had been, he realized, one of his cardinal mistakes to bring her back to the *pensione*. There had been nothing to be done about that, since his passport was there, and there was no way to book a room anywhere else without it. Then when they had returned, Hatcher had formulated a vague scheme involving feigning sleep, a little covert surveillance, and then tailing her when she left.

It had been an endurance contest, which Hatcher counted as mistakes number three through six. Hey, how about me, he had wanted to shout after the third time they had made love. Forty-two years old, and still the Bull of the Woods.

After the fourth time, Hatcher had felt a mild urge to visit the *gabinetto* just across the hall. He had swung his legs out of bed and gripped the sides of the mattress with his hands. His shoulders ached, and he was still gasping for breath. Suddenly the bathroom seemed very far away. To reach it, Hatcher reasoned, he would have to walk across the room. Miles and miles, and all by himself, too. Not only that, he would first have to stand up. Nothing to it, Hatcher jauntily decided, but maybe it would be easier if he had a nap first, just for a minute or so. Pleased with this compromise, Hatcher had slid back onto the bed. That was the last he had seen of Lena.

"Lena!" Hatcher said aloud, slapping his forehead and jumping up from the bed. He grabbed one of the books off the dresser and furiously started to turn the pages. When he found what he wanted, he slammed the book shut and started to laugh, a hoarse croak.

He had suddenly remembered. The fight in which Caravaggio had assaulted Mariano Pasqualone had been over a girl: "a girl called Lena who is to be found at the Piazza Navona," the document had stated.

Hatcher looked at his watch. It said half-past ten. He decided it was time to get moving, and fast.

Before packing, Hatcher went out to speak to the manager in the lobby of the *pensione*. He was a mournful-looking man who shrugged apologetically when Hatcher accosted him.

"I am sorry, Signore Hatcher, the *signorina* —"

"I know. What time did she leave?"

"Perhaps eight-thiry, perhaps nine."

"I see." Long enough, Hatcher thought "Listen, Claudio. I'll be leaving now. Please make up my bill, and put an extra two days on it. I may have to ask a favor from you. I'll be back in fifteen minutes to pay, but in the meantime, if anyone calls for me or comes to the *pensione*, tell them I have left and say that you don't know where I've gone, or when I'll be back. Do you understand?"

"Of course, Signore."

When he got back to his room, Hatcher opened the shutters very carefully and looked down through the crack. He could see people milling around down below, which didn't mean anything one way or another. In films this scene always takes place at night, thought Hatcher. There should be a street light stronger than a klieg, and two thugs in trench coats standing right underneath it peering up at me.

Hatcher threw everything he could find

into the suitcase except for three things: a Chianti bottle and two glasses. These he treated carefully. The glasses he covered with tissue paper and shoved into a pair of socks; the bottle he wrapped in a towel. Then he packed the three objects in a plastic shoulder bag. The room looked like hell when he left, so he put a ten-thousand-lire note on the dresser in hopes of appeasing the chambermaid.

He dropped his suitcase off at the front desk, paid his bill, and asked the manager if he could arrange to have the suitcase delivered to him later by someone from the *pensione*. With the added incentive of two more ten-thousand-lire notes, the manager was happy to oblige. If he thought Hatcher's behavior was a little odd, he didn't say anything.

He probably expects the "signorina's" father to show up presently — or her husband, Hatcher thought to himself. Or maybe he just assumes that all Americans are nuts.

17

Hatcher stood inside the doorway of the *pensione* and wondered what to do. There was no exit in back and no other way out of the courtyard, just that one doorway. Half-hidden by a column, he peered out into the narrow street and waited for his eyes to adjust to the sunlight.

Across the street, hidden in the shadow of the elaborate scaffolding that covered the front of the building, another man waited for him.

As his vision adjusted, Hatcher began to make out the particular actors in the typical commotion outside. Workmen in overalls laughed and punched one another on the arm, businessmen with attaché cases strode along with grave, distracted faces, and occasionally a student hurried past on the way to class. In fact, what Hatcher could make out framed by the rectangle of the doorway was so prosaic, so ordinary, that he began to feel foolish about his nervousness.

He leaned farther out from behind the column and saw the small man standing under the scaffolding. From what Hatcher could see, the man was wearing a gray suit rather than workman's clothes. It took Hatcher a moment to react, to realize that that was an odd place to stop to read a newspaper. Strange, since there was a coffee-bar next door; unless he was waiting for someone.

The man did not lower his newspaper when he spotted Hatcher inside the doorway. He took one long drag on his cigarette, inhaled deeply, and dropped it on the pavement in front of him, grinding it out with his shoe. Still holding the newspaper in front of him, he reached into the inner pocket of his jacket with his left hand. He did not need the gun, at least not yet, but he wanted to feel it once more before he used it.

It was not until the moment after this, when he finally folded his newspaper fastidiously and placed it in his jacket pocket that Hatcher knew for certain who the smiling man just emerging from the shadows of the scaffolding and walking toward him was.

At that moment a gray van appeared from the left. It was open in back, fully loaded with simple wicker and hardwood chairs from the shop next to the *pensione*. Just as it cut off Hatcher's view of the man across the street, there was a squeal of brakes, and the van seemed to lurch drunkenly to one side. Then Hatcher heard the snap of a rope and tremendous clatter as the Chinese puzzle of chairs burst asunder and began to fall and break on the cobblestone below.

A young man on a bicycle had precipitated the accident by cutting in front of the van. Now, lying in the middle of the street beside the mangled remains of his ten-speed, he began to scream obscenities at the driver with such gusto and dramatic flair that nobody — least of all the young man himself — seemed even vaguely curious whether or not he had suffered a serious injury. It was clearly a situation with great theatrical potential, and the crowd of bystanders which had suddenly materialized had already chosen up sides when the truck driver, livid with rage, emerged from his van.

By the time the little man in the gray suit had fought his way through the chaos of chairs and people Hatcher was gone. The man made a quick decision and started to run. It was the natural assumption that Hatcher would head for the major thoroughfare — the Corso del Rinascimento. Then he could either cross it to the Piazza Navona, or follow it to the Corso Vittorio Emanuele. Anticipating this train of thought, Hatcher had taken off in the opposite direction. Two minutes later he was in the Piazza San Eustachio, where (miracle of miracles) he immediately found a taxi to carry him across town.

Hatcher picked a hotel on the Esquiline Hill across from the huge basilica of Santa Maria Maggiore, and just a few streets from the central train station. This was not where Hatcher wanted to be, but where he felt he was least likely to be found, either by Pecci or the little man in the gray suit. He knew from hard experience that his height made him an easy tail; in Italy his eyes and complexion as well as his craggy features made him even more conspicuous. The big, modern Stazione

Termini and the cluttered square in front of it were ideal for shaking off the most professional surveillance, which made the area as useful for Hatcher as it was for the hordes of petty thieves who traditionally hung around it. Alternatively, there was the cavernous space of Santa Maria Maggiore itself, with its myriad chapels, tabernacles, and sculptural adornments. A marvelous place for hide-and-seek. Even the terrorists had, as far as Hatcher knew, drawn the line at gunning people down in church.

To quiet his jangled nerves, Hatcher decided to treat himself. He got a large room with a bath and French doors leading out onto a balcony overlooking the piazza. After admiring the view for a couple of minutes he kicked off his shoes, sprawled on the bed, and picked up the telephone. The first call was to his *pensione*, directing them where to send his luggage. The second was to room service. It was too late for breakfast, so Hatcher asked for a pot of coffee, a couple of grilled ham and cheese sandwiches, and a large bottle of mineral water.

Before drawing his bath, Hatcher went to find the manager of the hotel. After informing him that his bags would be arriving shortly and requesting that they be taken to his room, Hatcher asked if he could borrow some large sheets of white paper and an ink pad. The manager complied with these requests with a Jeeves-like insouciance. Hatcher, self-conscious about the heavy stubble on his face and the black smudges under his eyes, was tempted to reassure the man that he was not really the desperate criminal that he appeared, and that he would not be causing any trouble in the future, but he doubted that this would be believed. Hatcher did not seem to be doing too well with hotel managers on this trip.

18

It took Hatcher a good deal of scrubbing to get the ink off his fingertips. Then he dried them, went over to the desk, and reread his letter:

Pecci:

The set of fingerprints at the bottom of this sheet of paper are mine. Unless they have been carefully wiped, which I doubt, the bottle and glasses you will find in the bag will have a number of the same prints on them, and you can forget them.

The other prints you find belong to the woman in this sketch. The sketch is not perfect, by any means; there is something wrong with the mouth. But I have tried to get the proportions of the face as accurate as possible. The beauty is no exaggeration.

Show the drawing to the driver of the hijacked van, and see if it doesn't remind him of the woman in the car by the side of the road. Show it also to the guard at the Procacci Museum, and ask him if it looks like his "Dottoressa."

On the back of the drawing is a physical description. The height is probably accurate, the weight is just a guess. She said her name was Maddalena — or Lena — Antelami, but I am virtually certain she was lying.

I met her in the Piazza Navona. She said she was a graduate student in political science at the university. Another lie, I assume, though she may have been there at one time. She speaks English perfectly and claimed to have studied in the United States, which I believe.

I have no idea where she lives, but I would imagine it is somewhere in or near the Campo Marzio since I saw her several times in the Piazza Navona. She frequented the café directly across from Bernini's Fontana dei Fiumi. *I do not think she will be seen near there again. She is not stupid, and she knows she is a target, but perhaps it is still worth a try.*

If I can remember any other relevant information I will let you know.

Hatcher wrote "A Friend" at the bottom, folded the two sheets of paper, and put them in the plastic shoulder bag with the bottle and the glasses.

He went by taxi to the ministry and left the bag with the guard at the door, telling him only that it was for Vittorio Pecci. Hatcher was back in the cab before the guard could stop him. As the cab drove away, Hatcher wondered if this had been such a good idea. Pecci would not accept his little present from Hatcher in quite the same magnanimous spirit in which it had been meant if he had to call out the bomb squad first. From what Hatcher had seen, Pecci's sense of humor had distinct boundaries.

Hatcher was drained by the time he got back to his room. The breakout from the *pensione* had been a useful antidote to the night before, providing a quick jolt of adrenaline, a healthy shock of fear to clear

319

the cobwebs and focus the mind. The material he had left off for Pecci was meant to complete the exorcism, reducing "Lena" to a set of statistics, a boring compound of physical characteristics.

The drawing had been the problem. Hatcher had found it impossible to emulate the hard, ugly style of police portraits. He discovered, almost against his will, that he had spent most of his time recreating the soft texture of her skin and flesh, the sensuous curve of her mouth, and the limpid clarity of her eyes. As much as he tried to suppress it, the face emerging under Hatcher's pencil had revealed as much about the draftsman as about his model.

Hatcher's mind swarmed with images. He remembered the childlike abandon of her laugh, the ferocity of her appetites, both at table and later in bed. Who was she, *what* was she? What bothered Hatcher was the fact that she did not seem mysterious at all, but almost ingenuous. He had been easy to lie to, easy to manipulate, had cheerfully acquiesced in the fraud. Well, what the hell, he was telling his own lies, wasn't he? Had it just been another lie when he felt her shudder and gasp, when she had muffled her cries in his shoulder and her body had been racked with spasms? A performance, then? Some performance. All right, what about him? What about that fourth time? And now, if she walked through the door of his room, handed Hatcher his notebook, and said, "Forgive me, there's been a terrible mistake," would he grin and try to tumble her onto his bed, just for old time's sake?

That night he tried to explain it to Landini over dinner.

"I really thought I was going to win. I mean, I had a pretty good plan. Seems I forgot about it somewhere along the line, however."

"Why torture yourself? There was no harm done. Actually, you *may* have won, if there are any prints for Pecci."

"No harm, except that she could have killed me. Quite easily, actually. There were times in the course of the evening when I would have died happily, smiling from ear to ear. Christ, Lou, I'm forty-two. That means I've had almost twenty-five years to get over being eighteen."

"It never happens. There's an old Yiddish proverb I picked up in New York: *Ven der putz shteht, ligt der sechel in*

321

drerd. Translation: When the prick stands up, the brains get buried in the ground."

"Swell, Lou. What I want to know is, how far down? How long do I have to dig to get them out again? Who knows, I may need them sometime in the near future."

"I don't know. I never saw the lady."

"Lucky man. As long as you're spouting Talmudic wisdom, maybe I could ask you another question."

"Buy low, sell high."

"That won't help."

"Then you'll have to settle for Italian proverbs."

"I'll settle for anything I can get. Okay, Lou. Here's the question. If you were going to steal a Caravaggio painting in Rome, which one would you steal?"

"Is this a serious question?"

"Deadly. It hasn't happened yet, but I'm convinced it will. The man I'm after has a personal obsession with Caravaggio. I don't mean that he's a psychotic who thinks he *is* Caravaggio, but he is fascinated with the artist in some way, and perhaps identifies with him to a degree. Don't look so skeptical, Rabbi. I have lots of evidence."

"Care to run through it?"

"Take it on faith for now. Aside from personal reasons, the theft of a picture by Caravaggio would be tempting strategically. First, it would be a dramatic escalation. It would be the biggest prize they'd ever gone after. There's another incentive as well."

"The Caravaggio symposium?"

"Exactly. The thefts so far have only attracted local interest. If he stole a Caravaggio on the eve of a big international conference on the artist, it would be hot news. It would be a major humiliation for Pecci, and perhaps even for the government."

"Yes. But could it be done?"

"Not easily."

Hatcher fished a piece of paper out of his pocket and handed it to Landini.

"Here's the shopping list. Twenty-four reasonably certain Caravaggios are in Rome, leaving aside disputed works and marginal pictures, but they are all located in only eleven or so places. Some of them we can tentatively write off: the Vatican Museum, the Capitoline, and the Borghese Gallery are all very tight. I think the Corsini and the Barberini collections are also secure. They're the national collections; they damn well better be."

"Fairly secure."

"Fairly is enough. That takes care of eleven pictures right there."

"How about the Doria?"

"The Doria-Pamphili Collection probably looks easier than it is. The three pictures are all large. Can you imagine people trying to wrestle Carravaggio's *Rest on the Flight into Egypt* down those narrow stairs, then stumbling out with it into the Piazza del Collegio Romano while trying to be inconspicuous?"

"Sure. Harold Lloyd carrying the front end, and Buster Keaton the back."

"Precisely. So, let's look at the churches."

"You have Sant'Agostino down on the list."

"The *Madonna of Loreto.*"

"You can scratch it off. I just heard that the picture's in restoration."

"Oh? When did that happen?"

Landini shrugged.

"Somebody mentioned it in the gallery. Yesterday, I think."

Hatcher continued down the list, but he found himself fighting back a growing suspicion. He remembered the blank spaces on the walls of the Procacci Museum, with the restoration notices tacked up where the paintings should have been. He also recalled seeing the *Madonna of Loreto* six years before, and thinking what a beautiful job the restorers had done with it. That was too recent. You never clean a painting unless you have to, unless it is too dirty to be seen properly.

He did not mention any of this to Landini. Landini had done enough. He had listened to Hatcher for hours on end, allowed himself to be dragged away from home and family, and had been exceedingly helpful and sympathetic. From here on out it was Hatcher's problem.

An hour later, back at the hotel, Hatcher sat at the desk in his room. He had a map of Rome and a reproduction of the *Madonna of Loreto* in front of him. As his mind raced back and forth between the two, he began to feel a growing certainty.

The place was right. The Church of Sant'Agostino was near the center of Campo Marzio, yet set off from it in its own little backwater a block or two away from the Piazza Navona. It seemed to inhabit an odd niche in the honeycomb of streets in the heart of the district. A big church tucked into an incongruously small space, surrounded by a maze of short, twisting streets.

Somehow the picture felt right, too. The gravely beautiful Madonna stood framed in a doorway, holding the Christ Child. Kneeling in front of her were two peasants, a man and a woman, their gnarled hands clasped in prayer, gazing up in dumb amazement. The Christ Child, his face largely sunk in shadows, reached out in a gesture of blessing.

The mood of the altarpiece was, however, anything but joyful. The Madonna's robe was not the traditional blue, but black. The tattered white cloth which Mary pressed against the Christ Child did not look like swaddling clothes, but the winding sheet on which the dead Christ would ultimately be placed. Even the staves of the pilgrims looked sinister, like spears.

As he stared at the small group of figures fixed against the crumbling, nondescript doorway by a lurid shaft of light, Hatcher realized that Caravaggio's altarpiece was no cheerful vignette, no Christmas card, but a brooding drama redolent of tragedy.

19

After a fitful sleep, Hatcher woke to a gray day. He had a continental breakfast sent to his room, and while he ate it he glared morosely at the rain spitting against the panes of the French doors.

He had no hat and no umbrella. He never thought about rain when he packed for Italy, and usually regretted it later. He took the gun out of his suitcase, loaded it, checked the safety catch, and then put it back in his suitcase. He was just going to church; no need for a gun in church. It would probably bring bad luck. Besides, the painting was either there or not there, and a gun would not make any difference one way or the other. This was, in retrospect, his first mistake.

He stood for a while in the Piazza

dell'Esquilino waiting for a cab. By the time Hatcher had admitted the futility of this scheme and slogged the four blocks to the train station, he was already wet and miserable. For a horrible moment he was afraid that there was a taxi strike when he saw the dreaded word *sciopero* on a wall poster, but it turned out to be prostitutes who were striking, not drivers. Reading the fine print, Hatcher discovered that the prostitutes were calling a strike to protest legal restrictions against transsexuals. Hatcher considered this a touching gesture of solidarity, and wondered if Crelly were doing a story about it.

It took almost an hour from the time Hatcher found a cab to fight through the rush-hour traffic to the little Piazza Sant'Agostino, and for most of the trip he had to endure a harangue about a new series of tariff restrictions being considered by the government, restrictions that would cause untold misery and suffering to the driver, to the driver's beloved wife, Carlotta (who had not been well recently, and now this), to the driver's no-good children, to his sainted mother in Viterbo (they would take the crust of bread from her mouth, those turds), and they call themselves *Christian* Democrats. It was a virtuoso performance such as Hatcher had not had to endure, even in New York, since the golden days of Lindsay's mayoralty.

When they reached the church, Hatcher considered, for a moment, asking the driver to wait for him. Faced with the prospect of another hour-long monologue, however, Hatcher quickly paid the man and made his escape. This was his second mistake.

The facade of the church was broad and undecorated. It was made of travertine, the coarse, porous limestone so common in Rome. Like most travertine buildings, this one had a dark, ugly patina of soot, with long light-gray streaks running down it like tears. It seemed drab and uninteresting to Hatcher, who found it hard to imagine that the greatest scholars and wits of Renaissance Rome had congregated there.

Hatcher entered the church through the right-hand doorway, bowed toward the main altar, and crossed himself. The great church was nearly empty. An old woman in black knelt before a marble sculpture of the Madonna and Child. Her lined face reminded Hatcher of the peasant woman in Caravaggio's painting, as did her expression of patient acceptance and intense faith. Hatcher envied her. Was there anything he accepted with such certainty, any dimension of his life where devotion, fidelity, or belief had any meaning? Art, perhaps. He could not think of much else.

He stood in the shadow of a pier and gazed across the nave at the chapel where the *Madonna of Loreto* was supposed to be. The chapel was screened off. A wooden framework had been erected and covered with canvas, like a theater flat, with a flimsy door in the middle. Attached to the door was a large sign saying *chiuso,* "closed," and underneath that was a sheet of paper with assorted seals on it. Hatcher had seen the same kind of notice on the wall of the Procacci Museum.

As he stared at the closed-off chapel, he thought he heard muffled sounds: people moving around, and a light tapping. He tried to focus on them, but he could not be sure of their source. They seemed to come and go. The acoustics of an old church are too complicated, Hatcher thought to himself. In some a sneeze sounded like a thunderclap and echoed for minutes, while in others a loud noise might be muffled and lost.

Hatcher decided to circle the church to the other side. He walked down the right aisle, crossed the nave, and started up the left aisle. The Caravaggio chapel was at the end, next to the left-hand portal of the church itself. The chapels of Sant'Agostino were shallow hemispheres with only one entrance, at the front. Hatcher knew that when he got there, he would have to go through that door.

As he drew close to the chapel, three women entered the church. They were talking loudly, and Hatcher ducked behind one of the large square piers of the nave and waited for their voices to die as the trio moved toward the altar at the front of the church. One of them started to cough. It sounded like pistol shots.

Hatcher stopped in front of the canvas door. He stepped close to it, and peered at the crack. He could not see anything. He reached out and put his hand against it.

"No-no-no-no-no!" Hatcher's head snapped around, and he saw the sacristan coming toward him. He was a short, seedy-looking, energetic gnome of about sixty or sixty-five, and as he walked up to Hatcher he was waggling his index finger back and forth in that infuriating Italian gesture of rebuke which nobody else would use except to a naughty child.

"*Prego, Signore! Questa capella è chiusa; leggi la notifica!*"

"*Scusi, ma —*"

"You are tourist?"

That's me, thought Hatcher. You got it.

"I came to see the Caravaggio, the *Madonna . . .*"

"Ah, no-no-no."

Wag that finger at me one more time, and I'll bite it off, Hatcher thought.

"The Caravaggio, no. Is in restoring, the Caravaggio. But the church have most beautiful other things. *Parla Italiano?*"

"*Un po'.*"

"*Bravo! Vieni*, you come, I show you. The great Raffaello, he makes a painting *anche più bella di* Caravaggio. Come."

No way out, thought Hatcher. He had to get away from the chapel now, and he had to figure out how to get around the sacristan later. He realized he had better sign up for the tour or leave, and he did not want to leave.

As he was led around from painting to painting, and from one chapel to the next, Hatcher's anger faded. The sacristan was not the usual shill, and when he realized that Hatcher knew something about art he stopped treating every work they looked at as the greatest thing since the Lascaux caves and started making some interesting observations. Raphael's *Isaiah* was certainly magnificent, but perhaps not as great as Michelangelo's prophets in the Sistine Chapel, which Raphael was trying so hard to emulate. Sansovino's *Madonna del Parto* was certainly a superb piece of Renaissance sculpture, but the sacristan had always found it a bit chilly and classical for his taste. Did the Signore prefer the baroque, then? Everyone came to see the Caravaggio, but they forgot the magnificent Guercinos, and the Lanfranco.

As they walked through the church, Hatcher was treated to large chunks of its history. This was where Cesare Borgia's mistress had had her chapel; that was where the famous prostitute Beatrici Pareggi was buried — illegally, of course. Did the Signore know that this was the favorite church of the great humanists Castiglione, Pietro Bembo, and Raphael himself?

When they reached the sacristy, Hatcher thanked the sacristan warmly and gave him a thousand-lire tip.

"I must now ask a favor. I am a scholar, as you are, and it is very important for me to see the Caravaggio chapel. It is a matter of the gravest urgency."

"It is impossible."

Hatcher added a five-thousand-lire note to the other one.

"My friend, all things are possible."

The sacristan looked skeptically at Hatcher for a moment, then shrugged.

"Wait here."

When the sacristan returned, he was smiling warmly. The favor had been granted, the money honestly earned. At the door to the sacristy he thanked Hatcher again, and Hatcher realized that he was not going to accompany him. A moment later, the gnome had disappeared through a door at the back of the sacristy, and Hatcher found himself alone in the church.

So much for surprise, Hatcher thought as he crossed the nave toward the chapel.

The only sound he could hear echoing in the cavernous space was the sound of his own footsteps. Maybe this was all silly. Maybe the door to the chapel would open to reveal a team of legitimate restorers hard at work with cotton swabs, removing a minor stain or spot of mildew that had suddenly appeared. In fact, as Hatcher came through the door he had a moment of relief when he saw the white linen coat on the figure inside. Then he saw his face. And his gun.

"Come in, Mr. Hatcher. Don't make a sound or I will shoot you dead."

His voice was calm. He seemed younger than Hatcher had expected, and his face was more delicate than he had remembered. His eyes were cold and his mouth looked cruel. As Hatcher stepped inside the chapel the door closed behind him. Hatcher instinctively started to turn his head.

"No. Don't turn around. There is nothing behind you but another man with another pistol. The good sacristan has told me that you wish to see Caravaggio's *Madonna di Loreto*. Very well. You may look at it. A very beautiful and a very tragic painting, is it not?"

The large canvas had been detached from the niche over the altar, and was now leaning against the wall. Next to it was a wooden drum about four feet high that looked like a giant spool. A pile of blankets, a coil of rope, and a switchblade sat on the altar table, and a toolbox lay open on the floor in front of it.

"Don't worry, Hatcher. We will take great care with the painting. But now we must take care of you. You and I will go first, then my friend Mario. Quickly. The door of the church is just a few steps to the right. Then down the staircase; turn right again into the alley next to the stairs. The auto is directly there. It is the blue Fiat 128 station wagon. You will get into the back with Mario. One more thing: if we meet the sacristan on the way out you will wave and smile, no more. Don't forget the pistols."

The small man took off his white smock. For a fraction of a second, when his arms were trapped in the sleeves of his coat, Hatcher realized that now there was only one man with a pistol.

The small man smiled. "Don't even think of it."

He dropped his coat over his right arm,

concealing the gun, and nodded toward the door.

"Go. Now."

There wasn't anyone near them when the three men stepped out of the chapel and into the body of the church. A few steps later, and they were outside. Hatcher had a brief illusion of freedom as he saw the square open up in front of him, and felt the wind and rain on his face, but he was no less trapped than when they had been in the chapel.

Hatcher never saw Mario until the hulking figure stepped around to open the car door for him. One look convinced Hatcher that the odds were pretty strong that he would go wherever they wanted to take him. Looking at Mario's companion, he decided that he did not want to go anywhere with either of them, and that he had better come up with another alternative fast.

As Mario climbed onto the seat next to him, Hatcher had the terrifying sensation, for a fraction of a second, that the huge man was simply going to lunge forward and crush him. Instead he sat down with a heavy grunt, wedging Hatcher into the corner and pinning his right arm against his body.

"*Bene*, Mario?"

The other man was twisted around in the driver's seat. Hatcher was looking at Mario and wondering what you do about someone who weighs around two hundred and sixty pounds and whose eyebrows grow together when the man in the front seat swung his pistol.

Because of the awkward position of the small man who delivered it, the blow had no real weight behind it. Still, it was enough. Hatcher had time to turn his head a couple of inches so that the pistol did not catch him flush, but the blow still knocked him unconscious.

He woke to a terrible throbbing pain accompanied by waves of nausea. He was surprised to find himself in a car, and it took a moment to remember where he was and how he had got there. The car was not moving. Opening his eyes halfway, letting his head loll back on his shoulders, Hatcher saw that they were in the middle of Roman traffic.

He felt a heavy weight in his lap. Letting his head fall forward, he noticed that his wrists were tied together with a plastic-wrapped bicycle chain. There was no sensation in his hands, so the chain was pulled tight enough to cut off his circulation.

He made his head loll back on his shoulders again, which abruptly intensified the pain in his temples. His vision seemed to come and go with the throbs, the images pulsing like a strobe light. He made out a white form through the windshield of the car and decided to concentrate on that, just to stop the vertigo.

The car started to move. The white form began to swim closer and Hatcher suddenly realized that the helmeted figure was a traffic policeman.

The car stopped again. The driver swore and slapped the wheel, and Hatcher suddenly had a plan. If the white figure of the cop would only stand there like that, long enough for Hatcher to concentrate, to remember that one small, everyday Italian word for "help."

Help. *Hilfe. Au secours.* What the hell was the Italian? He had heard it recently. Where? The Piazza Navona. Lena. Something about the fountain, Bernini's fountain.

Hatcher fought to collect himself for one effort. The car stopped again. The man in the white uniform began to loom up and became clearer, like a lighthouse emerging out of a fog.

Just as the car drew even with the policeman, Hatcher moved. He swung his arms as hard as he could at the side window, and he could hear the sound of breaking glass and his own rasping cry of *"Aiuto!"* before everything exploded and vanished.

20

Hatcher woke up in a room in the Salvator Mundi International Hospital on the Janiculum Hill. He felt awful. Then he saw Vittorio Pecci sitting in a corner of the room, and immediately felt worse.

When he noticed that Hatcher was conscious, Pecci smiled pleasantly and picked up a clipboard that was sitting on the table next to him.

"Well, Mr. Hatcher, I should tell you that you are quite lucky. I have to mention it, because you may not feel that way at present, but believe me. You are, for example, alive."

Pecci glanced at the clipboard.

"Let me see. A fairly minor concussion, multiple lacerations of both forearms, requiring a number of stitches, one rib cracked, and three others badly bruised. There seems to be no brain damage, although one might argue that the brain that led you into your present predicament was already suspect. You look terrible, but they tell me you looked worse when they brought you in."

Hatcher's throat was bone-dry. His voice was a painful croak.

"Painting. . . . Cara — Caravaggio . . ."

"The altarpiece is safe. Apparently when the *carabinieri* drove you here, you kept saying, 'Sant'Agostino, Sant' Agostino.' Everyone thought this was odd. If you had been calling out for the Madonna or Saint Christopher, they would have understood. But Saint *Augustine?* Then you began to mutter about Caraveggio, and some painting. One of the men came from the Campo Marzio and made the connection, so after they left you at the hospital they drove over to the church."

"What happened . . . to me?"

"Oh, you. Yes. Well, apparently you were being kidnapped, a colorful local custom in Rome these days. You made a scene on the Lungotevere up near the

Flaminio Bridge north of Rome, smashed out the window of the car, and caught the attention of a traffic policeman. This in itself would have done you very little good, since, as you know, the *vigili* have no weapons. Luckily there was a car full of *carabinieri* driving along the river. The *vigile* stopped them, and they began to chase your car. Your abductors decided to throw you out to divert the *carabinieri,* and the ploy worked. The kidnappers got away."

"Disappointed, Pecci?"

Pecci smiled, held out his hand and tilted it back and forth.

"Mezzo, mezzo. If the *carabinieri* had decided to leave you lying on the sidewalk by the Tiber you probably would have bled to death before anyone could have got you to a hospital. On the other hand, they might have caught the people in the car. I will be satisfied with the outcome, of course, if you can identify the kidnappers for me."

"Tough luck, Pecci. I can't."

"Oh? Then I guess the *carabinieri* made the wrong decision. Technically speaking, I mean."

Hatcher had bandages up to his wrists

on both arms, and a tight turban of bandages on his head. His chest was constricted by a sort of harness affair which made it hard to breathe. Both knees ached, and whatever medication they were giving him was strong enough to make him groggy but not strong enough to kill the pain. He had an intravenous tube in his arm, and a catheter in his penis. He also had Pecci, which was one thing too many.

"Pecci?"

"Yes?"

"*Ti ho in culo*, Pecci."

"What did you say?"

Hatcher glared at him for a moment. "I said, 'Have an *especially* nice day.' "

Later that afternoon Hatcher telephoned Landini from the hospital. Landini was at first shocked at Hatcher's account. Then he was relieved to find out that his friend was more or less in one piece. Hatcher was slightly abashed at not having informed him of his plan ahead of time, but Landini seemed to accept his passive role in the investigation. He had a wife, kids, and a job, and none of these factors provided any inducement for running around after armed criminals.

When he had hung up the telephone,

Hatcher was carted off for a number of tests. They all proved negative. The X-rays showed that his skull was not fractured (no matter how it felt to Hatcher), the EEG showed that Hatcher's brain was normal, at least from an electromechanical point of view, and chest X-rays reassured the doctors that none of his ribs was cracked severely enough to threaten the patient with a punctured lung. Hatcher's internal organs seemed to be roughly where they were supposed to be and doing roughly what they were intended to do, so the doctors were prevailed upon to remove the tubes and allow Hatcher a small amount of mobility. Hatcher had spent enough time in hospitals recently to savor the small triumphs, such as solid food and the privilege of going to the bathroom by himself.

That evening Hatcher was visited by Landini and his wife. She was a dumpy woman with a rather plain face which suddenly became radiantly pretty when she smiled. They had brought a huge wicker basket full of food, and after they had listened to Hatcher's story with what seemed to Hatcher almost parental solicitude, they all had a feast. The nurses, sisters of the Salvatorian order, did not exactly approve of the bacchanalia in Hatcher's room, but they did not do anything to stop it, either. Hatcher and Landini told stories of various high jinks they had been involved in years before during their student days, and Landini's wife, Anna, rewarded them with delightful peals of laughter. Then she told Hatcher about her meeting with Landini and their courtship in a number of anecdotes ranging in tone from bawdy slapstick to wry affection, most of them illustrating the proposition that boys will be boys, God help us all, and isn't it lucky they have us to clean up after them. At the end of the evening Hatcher felt more like a six-year-old who had fallen out of a swing than a man who had been beaten up and pushed out of a car.

Before they left, Hatcher made a request to Landini for some drawing supplies. He asked for two pads of paper, a number of lead pencils ranging from very soft to very hard, some charcoal pencils, erasers, and fixative.

Hatcher spent two more days in the hospital. His only visitors were Landini, who brought him the drawing equipment, and Pecci, who demanded a full account of all of Hatcher's activities between the time he had last spoken to him in his office and the moment he had been dropped out of the car. When Hatcher inquired about Pecci's activities, Pecci snorted and told him curtly that his own investigation was proceeding as anticipated. Somehow, Hatcher failed to find this information reassuring.

To Hatcher's surprise, none of his injuries proved serious. The headache eventually went away (except for the interval with Pecci), the cuts, bruises, and cracks turned out to be minor, and the doctors assured him that the only permanent scar might be the gash on his forehead caused by the pistol. Aside from Pecci, Landini, and the hospital staff, Hatcher was left to his own devices.

Most of the time he spent drawing. For some reason, the portrait of the man who had struck Hatcher turned out much better than the earlier sketch of the woman. He had a lean, angular face, with sharply defined planes. Hatcher found it easy to capture the large, heavy-lidded eyes with their thick, feminine lashes, the aquiline nose, and the tight, guarded mouth. What was missing was expression, life. Hatcher's drawing was as neutral and rigid as one of the Pharaonic portrait-sculptures from the Old Kingdom in Egypt. Yet he realized, examining the sheet of paper, that this was not a mistake in draftsmanship.

Hatcher could not recall having seen a single strong emotion on the little man's face: not fear, not anger, not even triumph. It was a face that expressed nothing and betrayed nothing, like the face in the drawing.

21

"Where've you been, Hatcher? Off tilting at windmills again? From that bandage on your forehead, I gather some of them have been tilting back."

"I cut myself shaving."

"On your forehead?"

"Silly me. Wasn't that clumsy?"

"All right, sit down, for God's sake. I'm not going to sit here squinting up at you for the next hour and a half."

Hatcher took a glass from the next table and put it down next to Crelly's bottle. Then he sat down with the drawing pad in his lap.

"You could have been my next article, Hatcher. Made me go and find a whole new topic instead."

"I'm sure you found one almost as

exciting."

" 'Italian virility,' Hatcher, that's the subject of this week's sermon. Want to hear a great metaphor?"

"I'm always in the market for a good metaphor, Crelly."

"Terrific. Well, Italian men love tight pants, right? Not just tight, but tight enough so you can see their cocks. Tell whether or not they're circumcised when they're fully clothed and half a block away. 'Male display,' the anthropologists call it, or just exhibitionism, take your pick. Anyway, there's a small side problem here, which is that if you wear pants that tight you cut off circulation to the balls, and if you do *that* long enough, you wind up sterilizing yourself. Eventually your testicles atrophy. So, in the effort to win the great virility sweepstakes, Italy is in danger of becoming a whole nation of *castrati.*"

"I sense an irony crashing down on my head."

"Isn't it perfect? What I haven't figured out, though — maybe you can help me here — is this just the key to Italian manhood, or does it answer the great enigma of Italian history, and Italian

350

culture as well? Is this the great Italian archetype?"

"Deep questions, Crelly. While I think about them, maybe I can ask *you* a question."

"Maybe."

Hatcher put the drawing pad on the table, flipped it open, and held it up for Crelly. Crelly looked at it, then looked quizzically at Hatcher.

Hatcher shrugged.

"Looks like a mean bastard. Intelligent, though. Where did the drawing come from?"

"I did it myself, when I was in the hospital recovering from the shaving accident."

"Ho, ho, ho! I'm beginning to get it. You were involved in the business with the Caravaggio altarpiece. The papers didn't mention you, Hatcher."

"Pecci told them not to."

"Well, well. So this is my boy, is it?"

"That's your hero. That's the man who's been organizing the art thefts."

"If you got close enough to him to do this drawing, I'm a little surprised that you're here now. So tell me, who's winning?"

"It's a standoff. So far."

"He has a gang behind him? The *Brigate Rosse,* right?"

"I don't know."

"You got *that close,* you didn't even interview him?"

"He was trying to *kidnap* me, Crelly."

"You got away? Christ, Hatcher, you should have stuck around, stayed on the case. What kind of a stringer are you?"

"If I had 'stayed on the case,' as you put it, they probably would have killed me. Then you'd have to find another source."

"Maybe not. Maybe the *carabinieri* could have sprung you. They sprung Dozier, after all. Still, I admit the odds would have been small. Dozier was unbelievably lucky."

Hatcher watched Crelly as he finished his wine and refilled his glass.

"Tell me, Crelly. There isn't much of anything that you take seriously, is there?'

Crelly smiled bleakly at Hatcher. "Not much. I used to be a very serious lad, all piss and vinegar. I started out in this game all set to win a Nobel Prize. I was hot stuff in Vietnam, for a while."

"I thought I remembered your name. I

must have read your dispatches."

"I was in 'Nam in the beginning, back in the Kennedy days. I knew the history, the people, the language. I could have drawn you a blueprint of the final act two years before it happened. I wasn't the only one, of course. Lots of people could have done that. Want to hear about how I came to stop taking things seriously?"

"Why not?"

"I was on assignment in a little village up near the Cambodian border. Not too near, but fairly near. Village had maybe three hundred people in it, men, women, and children. Very stable, almost no Viet Cong activity. We really figured we had the hearts and minds pretty well sewed up in that hamlet.

"Well, to make a long story short, I got my hands on some very hot stuff. A small raiding party of North Vietnamese regulars were preparing to attack the village. I had the whole plan: the time, the routes, the armaments — everything! Damn near got killed getting it, but that's another story. The point is, the info was absolutely first-class stuff. I took it to the commander. Know what he did? He confiscated my notes and had me locked up in solitary confinement.

"They waited until the North Vietnamese were just at the outskirts of the village. Then they flattened it. Gunships, mortars, machine guns — everything they had, for one solid hour. When they got through, there was nothing left of the village at all. About thirty North Vietnamese soldiers were killed, and about three hundred villagers. In the official dispatches, of course, these figures were reversed. It was proclaimed as a great victory. It was also one more village nobody had to worry about. Remember what Simon de Montfort said during the Albigensian Crusade? 'Kill them all; God will know his own.'

"Some people became junkies in Vietnam, some went mad. I became a millenarian. The only context in which anything made any sense was Armageddon, the end of the world. The only article of religious faith I accept is the Last Judgment, and the sooner the better. I saw the previews. Now I want the real thing. Other than that, I don't take anything very seriously."

"Why did you come to Italy?"

"You asked that before."

"You didn't answer it."

"I came to see the Colosseum. Don't you know that old saying? 'While stands the Colosseum, Rome shall stand. When falls the Colosseum, Rome shall fall. And when Rome falls — the world.' Keep your eyes on the Colosseum, Hatcher. It's got some new cracks. By the way — what are *your* articles of faith?"

"I was thinking about that earlier. I couldn't come up with much besides art."

"See? I told you you were an aesthete. 'Art' isn't much, Hatcher."

"Maybe not."

" 'Art' sounds like a pretty thin blanket when the winds grow cold."

"Everyone to his own foxhole, Crelly. At least the Colosseum is still there."

"Not for long."

"See you, Crelly."

"*Ciao,* Hatcher."

22

"I've been expecting you, Hatcher. You might as well come in."

Blake waved Hatcher into his apartment, which looked almost as disheveled as Blake himself. The air was stale and fetid, as if the windows had been kept closed too long. The room was dark except for the gooseneck lamp on the table where Blake had been working, and when the scholar turned on the overhead light, Hatcher noticed the source of the sour odor. Several dishes sat on the table, with food half-eaten and congealing. There were empty wine bottles, and one chair was occupied by a tangled gnarl of soiled clothes.

"How is the symposium going?"

"It will happen, I suppose. One way or

another. You didn't come here to talk about that."

"No."

Blake looked haggard. He had dark pouches under his eyes. His white hair was a tangled mat, and he had the appearance of a man for whom eating and sleeping were painfully effortful, or just irrelevant activities.

"I tried to get in touch with you after I read about that business in Sant'Agostino. You didn't leave any address. Bruni didn't know where you were, either, so I really didn't know where to go. I suppose it has to stop, doesn't it?"

The last remark was an admission rather than a question. Hatcher opened his drawing pad to the portrait, and handed it to Blake.

"Christ, he still doesn't look any older than that? Well. This face is a little harder and crueler than the one I remember, but I guess I should have expected that. Drink, Hatcher?"

"Fine. How about a Campari soda?"

"How about two double Scotches? This isn't a tea party. We're not going to sit around a table with watercress sandwiches . . ."

"Two double Scotches, then."

"That's better."

Blake brought in two glasses and put them on the table. He took the dirty plates back to the kitchen, and returned with a bowl of ice and a large bottle of Scotch. After pouring himself a hefty whiskey, he propped Hatcher's drawing against the wall, sat down in front of it, and stared at it.

"You said he murdered someone?"

Hatcher nodded.

"I suppose I should be shocked. Surprised, at least. Well, what do you know about him?"

"What I told you. Most of it is guess-work. In terms of facts, nothing."

"Not even his name?"

"Not even that."

"So it's got to be me, then? That's great, Hatcher. Well, do I get my thirty pieces of silver in advance, or should I bill you later?"

"You're talking to the wrong person, Blake. This man murdered a friend of mine in cold blood. Three days ago he tried to kidnap me, and if he'd succeeded I'd probably be dead by now. So don't expect me to get terribly sentimental about him. All I know is a killer."

For a brief moment Hatcher was afraid that Blake was going to change his mind. He started rubbing his forehead hard with his fist, his knuckles leaving long white tracks on his skin. Then he stopped, stared at Hatcher's portrait for a moment, and nodded his head.

"Will you be taking notes?"

"No. If it's important, I'll remember it."

"All right, then. But I probably won't want to repeat any of it."

"I'll listed closely."

"His name is Piero Capelli. He came to Rome about twelve or thirteen years ago, I suppose; I don't really know. He came here from Sicily. Maybe that's the most important thing about him, that he's a *siciliano*. He hated Sicily, and he plotted to get out before he was ten years old, but it stamped him. His pride, his crazy sense of honor, and his volcanic temper — the way he could jump from ice-cold to red-hot instantaneously, with no warning and no transition — all of that was Sicilian. Have you been to Sicily, Hatcher?"

"Very briefly. Just to Taormina and Syracuse."

"Those places are on the east coast, where the tourists go. Western Sicily is a different country, run by different rules. Capelli used to tell me that the distinction was that eastern Sicily was still a part of Italy; you could leave it. But western Sicily was a world that had nothing to do with any other world. It was like Corsica. If you were born there you could never get away from it any more than you could get away from yourself, no matter how hard you ran.

"Anyway, Capelli was born and grew up in a village on the northern coast, near Palermo. I don't know what his father did. He never mentioned him directly. I have the feeling that he hated him. Capelli grew up in poverty, like everyone else around him, and he said he could never rid himself of the memories of all that dust and hunger, and the sun hammering down relentlessly on the parched, useless soil.

"When he was six, his mother took him to church in Palermo. He couldn't remember which one. It doesn't make any difference; they're all similar; but one of those incredibly rich churches encrusted with sculpture from floor to ceiling. Capelli used to tell the story as a joke, because later he came to despise all that decorative profusion and ostentation, all those stucco saints and cupids. But as a six-year-old child, he stood there looking up at it in total amazement. He said it was the first time he'd ever experienced the feeling of joy in his life.

"His mother was equally jubilant with his reaction, of course. She thought it was a sign of his vocation, that it meant that he was destined for the priesthood. For the next two years little Piero kept demanding to go to Palermo to go to church, and while his mother had visions of her brilliant son rising up through the church hierarchy, Piero was busy developing his eye. Christianity meant nothing at all to him. He'd seen enough of the way the world worked, and formed enough of his own conclusions about it, to be an agnostic by the time he was eight years old. Nevertheless, he prayed and said the rosary and studied the Bible, because that was how you got taken to church. Piero Capelli was an art historian by the age of ten, even though he would have had no idea what that phrase meant. Am I boring you, Hatcher?"

"Not at all."

"Good. I've never talked much about Capelli before, except with my wife. Exwife, I should say. You're getting the whole thing, not just bits and pieces, whether you want it or not. I owe him that, anyway."

"I won't be bored, Blake. Go on."

"On one of his trips to Palermo, Piero was taken to the church of San Lorenzo, where he saw Caravaggio's *Nativity*. He told me that that was another revelation to him, that he couldn't understand how a painting could be so real, and yet so mysterious. Suddenly all the clamoring swarms of plaster angels seemed to be trivial and false beside those colossal, silent, brooding figures. At that moment, Caravaggio became his artist. It took me a while to understand it, Hatcher, but he meant that literally. He considered Caravaggio *his* artist in some moral sense, almost. I think it's very important to emphasize that."

Blake took a long sip of whiskey and lit a cigarette.

"By the time Capelli was fourteen he'd managed to see every Caravaggio in Sicily, the ones in Syracuse and Messina, as well as the Palermo *Nativity*. God knows how he got to those places, or where he stayed, or how he managed to eat. I never asked him. That's a pretty odd obsession for a kid twelve and thirteen, don't you think? Anyway, Piero Capelli had found his vocation. Not quite the one Mama Capelli picked out for him, though."

Blake paused for a moment. He got out of his chair, and began to pace back and forth in front of Hatcher with his drink in his hand, trying to get the story right.

"I'm not trying to justify or excuse anything, Hatcher. I just want to show you the kind of road Capelli carved out for himself."

"I don't want to interrupt you, but what about the Palermo *Nativity?* Wasn't that stolen around sixty-eight or sixty-nine?"

Blake laughed.

"You should have heard Piero go on about that. It's more than a little ironic, in retrospect, but he was extraordinarily shocked and offended when the altarpiece was stolen. He was certain it was a Mafia job. He said the Mafia were the only people strong and brazen enough to do a thing like that in Palermo."

"Go on."

"As I was saying, Capelli picked a hard

363

route. He didn't talk about it much, and I didn't press him, but getting to the University of Rome from that little village outside Palermo must have been like the son of a black sharecropper in Mississippi getting to Harvard. There wasn't any choice, though. He wanted to study seventeenth-century art, Caravaggio in particular, so where else could he go?"

Blake picked up the drawing pad and stared at Hatcher's portrait as if he meant to pose it a question.

"Let me ask you, when was he ever a child? When was he ever even young, for Christ's sake? When I met him for the first time seven years ago, he was just beginning his graduate studies, according to the records, but it was silly to call him a 'student.' "

Blake dropped the pad on the table and refilled his glass.

"By the time I got to him, he already spoke fluent French, German, and English. He used to do imitations of American actors — Stewart, Fonda, Bogart, Cagney, all of them. I found out that's how he taught himself languages. He'd go to foreign films and sit through them six or eight times until he'd memorized them. He never studied languages formally at all. The technical vocabulary, the art historical language, was easy; he picked that up when he was mastering the literature — and I mean 'mastering' literally.

"I had a one-year appointment teaching at the University of Rome. Piero Capelli was supposed to be my student. Tell me, Hatcher, have you ever taught? I mean, at the graduate level?"

Hatcher nodded.

"Good. Then you know how exciting it is to find a first-rate student. You look for certain things: intelligence, curiosity, quickness, a certain kind of intellectual flexibility. Part of the delight comes in watching students change, watching them grope toward their own methodology, helping them make discoveries, posing problems, and seeing them fumble toward solutions. It's all very satisfying, isn't it? Pretty manipulative and pretty narcissistic, too, but we try not to worry about that too much. Mostly we just bask in all that cozy ego-gratification, nurturing our young minds and helping them grow by fertilizing them with just the right admixture of rich, warm bullshit.

"It didn't work out quite like that with Capelli. He was as smart as I was, for one thing. Well, that happens occasionally, right? You can usually handle it fairly easily, though, because you know more than they do. Except in the case of Capelli, that wasn't true, either. What the hell, he was already supporting himself by that time making discoveries for the big dealers on the Via del Babuino. His eye was as sharp as his knowledge of the art historical literature, and I've never seen that before in anyone. It's always one thing or the other."

Blake closed his eyes for a few seconds. Hatcher assumed that he was drifting back into the past, and let him go. He wanted the whole story.

"After my first lecture, Piero came up and started asking a few questions, pointing out a few things, mentioning some examples of pictures that contradicted everything I'd been saying. At first I thought he was challenging me. He wasn't, at least not in the sense I thought. He was just telling me gently that he wasn't interested in playing student, and suggesting that we could talk, but only as equals. He wasn't really arrogant, and it

366

wasn't a matter of power of authority, as I quickly discovered. Capelli just didn't want to waste his time.

"He wanted someone he could talk to on his own level, you see. That eliminated all of his fellow students and most of the faculty. It didn't take long for me to realize the advantages of this arrangement, because I got someone I could talk to on *my* level, too. I'm not modest, Hatcher. There weren't many people around for me, either.

"Jesus, did we talk! Talk, argue, fight, scream at each other, get drunk together, wrestle with ideas until we reached the point of actual physical exhaustion. Baroque art wasn't just an arcane field to him, any more than art history was just a job to me. It wasn't a matter of genteel scholarly dialogue, either. It was a battle-field.

"I say we were equals. That isn't quite true. In certain ways I thought he was intellectually immature. Why not? He was only twenty-two. He viewed some things too personally, and when he became too involved his judgment got distorted. The business of Caravaggio as a populist, a 'people's artist,' the mouthpiece for some kind of proletarian 'truth' — I thought that was sentimental rot, and told him so. That was the closest we ever came to physical violence. Afterward, we steered away from that issue."

Blake took a drink of whiskey. Hatcher waited. He did not expect the next part of Blake's monologue to be easy.

"In the beginning, I thought of our relationship as some kind of curious brotherhood. Capelli had a tiny apartment over in Trastevere, and I found myself going over there late in the afternoons, bringing articles and books to discuss with him, or just some new idea or connection I'd come up with. By four-thirty, I always seemed to find something. Some pretext.

"I could see my life going slightly out of kilter. I could feel myself being pulled into a strange vortex. I began to find myself coming home late, and missing an occasional class. What did that matter, beside this extraordinary voyage of intellectual discovery? After a while I couldn't keep away from Capelli. There was an incredible intensity to him, an incandescence, almost."

Blake laughed sardonically and shook his head.

"They say the wife is always the last to know, don't they? Not in my case, Hatcher. In fact, *she* was the one who told me. 'You're in love with him, aren't you?' That's all she said. Oh, the tirade that question precipitated, the abuse! I must have ranted for a solid two hours. She didn't say a word, she just waited for it all to burn out before she asked the next innocent-looking, deadly little question: 'Why did that make you so angry?'

"I really *hadn't* known, you see. Not consciously, if that makes any difference. I was insulated by so many layers of fine old Yankee repression and self-delusion, and Janet cut through all of them with two short sentences. It never occurred to me that I was being seduced, that Capelli should have been named Svengali. I didn't really find out about Piero's dark side until we were lovers, and by that time Janet was safely back in the states. Smart lady!

"I'll spare you the details of our affair, Hatcher. It's a trite story, anyway. If you're curious, I can refer you to a couple of old Cole Porter songs. One of the rude shocks I suppose I should mention was the discovery that I wasn't the only one susceptible to Piero's incandescent appeal.

369

There were lots of other moths cheerfully flapping around that particular flame, and not just boy moths, either. Capelli turned out to be a regular Pied Piper.

"He didn't allow his friendships to overlap. We all had our compartments, all tightly sealed off from one another. For example, I found out quite by accident that Piero was a political leader at the university. We never discussed politics directly, partly because I wasn't particularly interested in it, I suppose, and partly because he knew I wouldn't be particularly sympathetic to his point of view, which was radical Marxist. Also, my compartment was art. Looking back, I realize how naive I was. Student politics in Italy in the seventies meant real revolution. What did I think Capelli was doing, anyway, running for president of the Young Republicans Club at Ohio State? More likely he was running guns."

For a moment Hatcher found himself wondering where this was all leading. The confessional tone was beginning to embarrass him. He didn't feel he could offer any comfort to Blake without sounding painfully condescending. What did he want? Understanding? Absolution? As if sensing

Hatcher's uneasiness, Blake picked up the pace of his narrative.

"At the end of that academic year I returned here, and Aldo Bruni returned to the Baroque slot in the art history faculty of the university. He became Piero's official adviser. I was angry and jealous, of course, but in a strange way I was also relieved. I was burned out by that time, my life was a shambles — I wanted time to regroup. I still wanted him, but I was tired of fighting for him, and tired of the humiliation. My relationship with Capelli had by that time degenerated into fights, jealous arguments, endless recriminations, followed by pleading, begging, forgiveness. Then the whole cycle all over again.

"Bruni went after Capelli like a shot. My God, he practically courted him with flowers. I assumed he wanted Piero in the same way that I wanted him. I think Piero did, too. We used to laugh about it. I always thought of Aldo Bruni as an ambitious mediocrity; a hard worker, but someone without any particular originality. Trustworthy, solid, but by no means brilliant.

"Capelli gave Bruni all his work for criticism. I asked him why, and Piero told me he was amused by Bruni's comments. By that time, Capelli was working on his dissertation. A large section of it concerned certain optical and anatomical distortions in Caravaggio's paintings, and what they meant —"

"My God! 'Realism and Reality in the Art of Caravaggio'!"

"Then you've read it? That's Capelli's work, word for word. I think that somewhere in the back Capelli is given a footnote, but otherwise Bruni never mentions him."

"He just *stole* it?"

Blake nodded.

"That happens, as you know. Ideas are stolen from time to time, passages plagiarized. It's probably more common in Europe than in the States, though, since the professor has a great deal more authority here. But to take a whole article, a concept that Capelli had been developing for over a year, was incredible."

"Capelli had no idea what Bruni was doing?"

"I assume none at all, until he saw his ideas in print."

"What did he do?"

"He went to find Bruni in his office. Luckily for both of them, Bruni wasn't there. Capelli waited, but Bruni never came. After a while, I don't know exactly how long, Piero apparently went berserk. People who saw the office the next day said that it looked as if a bomb had exploded in it, literally. Every piece of furniture in it was broken to pieces, books were torn apart, locked filing cabinets were wrenched open, and the contents shredded and strewn about like confetti.

"The police caught up with Capelli just before he got to Bruni's apartment. It took three of them to stop him, and one of them wound up in the hospital. Capelli spent some time in jail, and Bruni immediately took a leave of absence from the university and went abroad. In the end, it didn't make any difference about the article. Capelli's academic career was finished. He never went back."

"God, what an awful story. What did he do then?"

"I didn't see much of Capelli after that. I immediately went to the prison when I heard what had happened, but he didn't want to see me. I don't believe he really thought I had anything to do with Bruni's article, but still there was some vague sense of guilt by association. I lost track of him, then I heard he was working for a dealer again, on the Via del Babuino."

Hatcher poured his second drink. Blake was working on his third. Hatcher found it curious that everybody around him was so impervious to alcohol.

"I only know what happened after that from hearsay. Capelli was working for a man named Sagrestini. After a number of important discoveries that began to put Sagrestini's name on the map, Capelli apparently demanded a raise from the dealer. The dealer laughed in Capelli's face and said he should be grateful for what he was getting. After that, the stories diverge. In one version, Sagrestini was brought into the Policlinico Hospital shortly thereafter more dead than alive. In another version Capelli just spoke to him for a while, and didn't even raise his voice. At any rate, Sagrestini's gallery was up for rent a short time later. I recently heard that Sagrestini is in Genoa now, running a very small, very quiet operation out of a well-guarded apartment.

"After that, Capelli did some transla-tions for popular guidebooks. That didn't last long; I'll show you why. Incredibly, some of them actually got into circulation. I hear they're collector's items by now."

Blake pulled a book from the shelf over the desk. It was a cheap paperback guidebook full of glossy reproductions. Blake opened it, and pointed to a passage underlined in red ink.

"Of all Raphael's vacuous Madonnas," Hatcher read, "few are as totally insipid as this one."

"Then Capelli disappeared. I tried to track him, and failed. I suppose he went underground. I read about the thefts, of course, and I must have half-suspected that he was involved somehow. But I managed to repress it, even when the pictures from that show I organized with Bruni were stolen. I never wanted to face Piero Capelli's dark side; it seems I still don't. Anyway, I wasn't absolutely certain until you told me about that phrase painted on the wall of the Palazzo Caprese. I guess that joke was for me."

Hatcher got out of his chair and stretched. He suddenly felt exhausted. He was tired of looking at the face on the pad, and tired of looking at Blake.

"How do I find him?"

Blake looked at Hatcher for a while without speaking.

"Listen, Blake. It has to stop. You said so yourself."

"All right, then. For the symposium I'm delivering a paper called 'Patronage and the Myth of Caravaggio's "Populism." ' It was a deliberate attempt to provoke Capelli into attending by bringing up the old argument we had years ago. The papers are to be followed by a discussion from the floor. Maybe I'm crazier than he is, but I have the idea that Capelli would want to be there just to have the chance to refute me."

"I don't think that's a crazy idea. From what you've told me about him, it makes perfect sense. Will I need an invitation to the symposium?"

Blake shook his head. Hatcher swallowed the three fingers' worth of whiskey left in his glass, hoping it would do the trick.

"What will you do if he comes?"

"Stop him somehow. Turn him in."

"He won't be taken. He won't be caged, or dragged before prosecutors. You'll have to kill him."

"Maybe."

"I hope he doesn't come to the symposium. He's been betrayed enough."

Oh, Christ, Hatcher thought.

"Look. I had a friend named Jake Sloane. If you get too worried about 'betrayals,' I can give you a nice wallet-sized photo of old Jake slumped over his desk with the handle of Capelli's knife sticking out of the back of his neck."

Blake didn't react, and they were running out of whiskey.

"Okay, try this. I've been sitting here for hours listening to you talk about a man who is doomed. Does it really make any difference whose hand pulls the switch, whether it's mine or yours or his? Is there anything left of him anyway, besides rage?"

He could not tell if Blake was listening. Suddenly Hatcher felt empty and useless. He got out of his chair, closed the drawing pad, and tucked it under his arm. Before he left, he squeezed Blake's shoulder, and said the only thing he could think of to say.

"I'm sorry."

When Hatcher went out the door, Blake was still staring at the spot on the wall where Capelli's portrait had been.

23

Hatcher looked at the image on the screen and tried to focus his mind on the picture. The man at the podium was an eager young instructor from Harvard. The subject of his talk was "Caravaggio's Use of Classical Sculpture." Since Caravaggio's use of classical sculpture was limited almost to the point of nonexistence, the nominal subject of the lecture was exhausted in the first five minutes. This left fifteen minutes for irrelevant scholarly wool-gathering on the question of *why* Caravaggio didn't make more use of classical sculpture. Hatcher had heard too many similar lectures in his time to have much patience with this one; why not a lecture on "Caravaggio's Use of Trained Seals"?

Hatcher was in a seat in the back row at the extreme left of the small auditorium, next to the aisle. Behind him, only a few steps away, was one door. The other door was on the opposite side of the theater. Both entrances gave out onto small landings connected to flights of steps descending one story to two outer lobbies that faced a small courtyard. It was a nicely symmetrical arrangement which simplified Hatcher's job. Anyone entering the auditorium from outside had to come through one of the two doors at the back.

Landini was next to the door on the right. Hatcher was nervous about using him, but Landini had insisted, finally convincing Hatcher that he would play a passive role in any circumstances. Hatcher had the only gun. He had considered warning Pecci, then firmly rejected that idea. What was emphatically *not* indicated was an elaborate Felliniesque plot involving the swarms of policemen, *paparazzi*, camera crews, sharpshooters, politicians, and camp followers that Pecci would be tempted to deploy if he expected to make a major bust.

Hatcher's plan, such as it was, was simple. If Capelli came through the left door, Hatcher would see him. If he came through the other door, Landini would see him. Right next to Landini were the light switches for the auditorium. The overhead lights were governed by a rheostat. By playing with the knob, Landini could make the lights flicker slightly; this was his signal to Hatcher that he had spotted Capelli. After that it was simply a matter of getting his gun firmly placed in the middle of Capelli's back and taking him out onto a landing, where Landini could call the police. This plan seemed to have been simplified even further by Capelli's apparent decision not to attend the symposium.

"Thus we may conclude that Caravaggio's fascination with antiquity, no matter how subtly hidden and disguised, nevertheless formed a seminal element in the development of the artist's mature aesthetic. Thank you."

Balls, thought Hatcher. The young man sat down amidst an anemic smattering of applause. In his years as an art historian Hatcher had come to loathe certain words, and "seminal," with its obliquely naughty associations, was at the top of Hatcher's list. "Aesthetic" was not far behind it.

Hatcher wanted to take the "seminal aesthetic" out of art history and put it back in the bedroom where it belonged.

Blake was the next speaker. As he strode to the podium, he seemed assured, almost jaunty. Hatcher was amazed at his transformation. He began his talk with a witty anecdote, and launched into the body of his lecture with the panache of a seasoned pro. His arguments were well supported, his points were crisply made, and there was an elegance in his language totally lacking in the muddled cant of the previous speaker. Somewhat against his will, Hatcher's attention became increasingly diverted from the job at hand to the substance of Blake's talk.

"Were subtleties such as these intended for some hypothetical Everyman, the average poorly educated and probably illiterate Roman worker, or were they directed instead toward a small and highly cultivated group of *cognoscenti?*" Blake paused and took a sip of water.

Suddenly the overhead lights, which had been set very low to avoid interfering with the slide projection, went out altogether. This wasn't the signal. Why was Landini playing with the rheostat? Hatcher swung his head around, but couldn't see anything in the gloom. Then there were three shots and the sound of exploding metal and glass, and the screen at the front of the room went black. Hatcher heard gasps followed by screams as he swung out of his seat. The only light left in the room was the podium light, and all it illuminated was the white, stricken face of Richard Blake. Then there was another voice, a cry of rage cutting through the commotion.

"Your stupid speech is over, Blake. What do you know of Caravaggio? It was people like you who destroyed him!"

Hatcher stumbled along the aisle at the back of the auditorium in the direction of the voice. The pistol was in his hand; this was not going to be another Hamburg. Suddenly the door opened and Hatcher saw Capelli framed against a rectangle of light. He raised his gun to fire and then pitched forward, tripping over the shattered slide projector that had been shot off its platform. Hatcher got up again and started running toward the patch of light, now just a sliver left by the closing door.

When he finally reached the door and opened it, he found his friend on the landing. Landini was leaning against the wall, holding his forehead. He turned toward Hatcher, who saw a thin trickle of blood running down Landini's cheek.

"Amos, he —"

"Can't stop, Lou."

Hatcher ran past him, following the sound of Capelli's steps echoing in the stairwell. At the bottom of the first flight of stairs Hatcher heard the outer door slam. A few seconds later he reached the same spot. He waited for a split second, kicked it open, and dove out.

There was a shot. The bullet missed Hatcher, splattering against the marble wall behind him. Hatcher ducked behind a car, and listened. For a moment the night was quiet, then he heard Capelli's footsteps crunching on gravel, then smacking against stone as he veered out of the courtyard into the narrow street. Hatcher followed, running hard.

Normally Hatcher would have had the advantage. He was a natural runner, and had been a good track man in his day. But now he had bruised knees and cracked ribs, and each step cost him a sharp jab of pain. He kept up with the younger man, but he could not close the gap.

Hatcher followed Capelli the length of the narrow street, keeping a row of cars between them. Then Capelli cut down a short alley. Hatcher followed him, expecting Capelli to waste another shot, but he just kept going.

Capelli turned onto a wide thoroughfare. Suddenly there were bright street lights, activity, pedestrians; surely they must find it a little odd, Hatcher thought, two men chasing each other through the streets of Rome with pistols. He heard someone cry out. Hatcher kept running.

24

Capelli vaulted over the barrier and crossed the bridge leading into the large central hall of the ancient market built by the Emperor Trajan. Hatcher followed him, vaguely aware that he was not just crossing a bridge, but probably burning it behind him as well. He had only a few seconds before entering the great cavernous structure, to try to remember the building's layout.

Actually, it did not seem like a "market" so much as a vast antique department store or shopping mall. There was a concrete vault covering the central hall like a canopy, and on each side of the hall were rows of shops, each a square cubicle with a door facing onto the hall. This part Hatcher remembered clearly. He decided to take it step by step.

Step one was getting through the central portal into the market.

Hatcher crouched by the side of the door. He could hear Capelli's footsteps retreating into the back of the building. Hatcher broke through the entrance and raced for the first door on the left of the main hall. Just as he dove into the cubicle Capelli fired again. It was a wild shot, but the sound of the sudden explosion, magnified and refracted through the empty building, was deafening.

Hatcher sprawled on the concrete floor of the room and tried to catch his breath. The building was very dark but not pitch-black. At Capelli's end there was a large semicircular aperture open to the sky. The cold north wind had come from the Alps that afternoon, sweeping the Roman skies clean. There was a full moon which combined with the city lights to provide a faint, ghostly illumination at both ends of the building.

Hatcher felt his way along the walls, trying to remember whether or not the shops ranged along the central hall were entirely closed, or connected by a passageway. In the corner of the room his hands struck a molding. It was a marble jamb; the shops *were* connected. Moving as stealthily as possible, Hatcher groped his way from room to room. All he could see, as he moved down the length of the market, was the faint outline of the main hall framed in the doorways as he passed from stall to stall. Hatcher kept to the left. Capelli's shot had come from the right.

Hatcher reached the cubicle next to the last, crawled to the doorway, and looked out. He couldn't see anything but shadows. If his calculations were correct, Capelli was on the opposite side of the building, probably about forty or fifty feet from where Hatcher was crouching. If Capelli was still there.

Hatcher felt along the walls until he found a fragment of loose brick he could work free. As it happened, he did not need it. He heard a faint scuffling noise, another pistol shot, and the piercing scream of a cat. Hatcher wheeled and fired twice in the direction of the sound. They were stupid shots. Hatcher's nerves were frayed.

The crescendo of noise was immediately followed by an equally shocking silence, and then Hatcher could hear Capelli running again. Hatcher followed the sound of the footsteps. He raced across the hall and was about to plunge down the flight of stairs after his quarry when he reminded himself that Capelli was not trying to escape from him, but trying to kill him. At the bottom of the steps, there would be a doorway, and when Hatcher reached the doorway, Capelli would be waiting. Just like Hamburg.

Hatcher kicked off his shoes, peering around in the gloom until he saw another set of stairs. Very good, he thought; Capelli went down; then I'll go up.

Hatcher quickly mounted the stairs. When he got to the top, he found an open archway that led outside the building onto a small trapezoidal concrete platform like a ledge. Hatcher dropped to his stomach, crawled to the edge, and looked down.

Three stories below him was a concave hemicycle about fifty or sixty yards long. At the base of the ledge where Hatcher lay was an ancient road, paved with massive black stones. Across the road from the enclosed market were the ruins of more brick stalls, stubby little wall fragments that looked like dwarf hedges that had been unevenly clipped. Behind these was a concrete walkway with a short retaining wall that formed the border of the hemicycle. Behind the retaining wall there was a long drop to Trajan's Forum below.

Hatcher concentrated on the fragmentary brick walls. They were not much higher than three or four feet at any point, but they would be perfect cover for someone training a pistol on the opposite door.

Hatcher slid over on his ledge until he reached a point that he assumed to be more or less directly over the doorway below, then he felt around in the dark until he found a pebble. He pushed it to the edge of the platform, then nudged it over with the barrel of his gun.

The sound of the pebble made Capelli commit himself. He stood up behind his brick barricade and for a moment Hatcher had him silhouetted. Hatcher fired once. He saw Capelli spin around, the pistol flying out of his hand. He fired again, then raced for the stairs.

In a few seconds he was through the doorway. He sprinted across the road and vaulted over the stubby brick wall toward Capelli, who was trying to drag his body over to where his gun had landed. Hatcher got there first, and kicked it away. He hardly had the energy to pick it up. He staggered to a corner of the ancient chamber and dropped to the floor, spent. Except for the sound of the two men catching their breath, the night was still.

"*Noi, siamo solo.*"

"Please. You speak terrible Italian."

Capelli was curled up on the floor, and it was clear from his voice that even speaking was an effort. Hatcher wondered if the insult was worth the pain. Capelli was clutching his right shoulder with his left hand, which was wet.

"There's no Mario this time. And I have the guns."

"*Ebbene.* Shoot me."

Hatcher didn't answer. He was close enough to Capelli, and could see well enough, to note that the small man's face held the same impassive expression he had seen before. The blood, the beads of sweat on his brow, and the spasmodic quality of his breathing were the only evidence of his defeat.

"I have only three questions. I want to know where the art is, and I want to know who and where Mario and the others are."

The small man looked at Hatcher for a

moment, then turned his head and spat.

Hatcher forced his mind to focus on the memory of Jake Sloane. He waited until the image became so acute that he could almost feel Jake's presence, and then he moved.

He went over the Capelli and pulled his hand away from the wound. The small man cried out involuntarily, and Hatcher immediately saw why. The first bullet had caught Capelli just at the junction of arm and shoulder and had left a gaping hole. Hatcher guessed that there was a good deal of shattered bone and cartilage as well as torn muscle. It didn't make any difference that the second bullet had missed.

Hatcher ripped off Capelli's belt, rolled him over on his face, and tied his wrists together with the belt. Capelli shrieked when Hatcher pulled his arms back, but Hatcher was still thinking about Jake.

"The man you killed in New York was a good friend of mine."

"To hell with him."

Hatcher gripped Capelli's right wrist.

"The bullet went right through the process of your shoulder, so I would imagine that the slightest movement of your right arm would be exceedingly painful. Is that right, Capelli?"

Hatcher pulled the wrist a fraction of an inch to his left, and Capelli gasped.

"I would imagine that it feels something like trying to put your weight on a leg after you've been shot in the kneecap. Now, where is the art?"

"To hell with you."

"Not '*ti ho in culo,*' Capelli? Listen, then. As I pull your arm to the left, there will be a certain point there the pain becomes unendurable. Then you can scream, but that's all you can do. If I do it slowly, you won't pass out or go into shock, you'll just suffer and scream. Mario would be better at this, I suppose, but Mario isn't here. Again, where is the art?"

A while later Capelli did pass out, but not before answering Hatcher's questions. By the time he retraced his steps through the ancient market, Hatcher felt empty and humiliated. He was almost at the entrance when he noticed that he was not wearing any shoes.

Epilogue

"Are you okay, Amos?" Sheila's voice sounded a little foggy, partly because of the transatlantic connection and partly, no doubt, because he had waked her out of a sound sleep.

"I'm okay, Sheila. Really. No wounds, no scars, and I'm much fatter than when I left."

"That's not entirely what I meant."

Damn you, Hatcher thought. You have no right to know me that well. I cracked the case, I'm coming home; I have the right to feel pretty good.

"Semi-okay."

"I see. Anything that can't be fixed?"

Hatcher hesitated. Lena could be fixed, he knew that the moment he heard Sheila's voice, but he had been a damn fool, and it wasn't going to be as easy as he had kidded himself it was going to be. The business the night before with Capelli was a bigger problem. Capelli had held out much too long, long enough to force Hatcher into a kind of cold-blooded savagery that was more frightening to Hatcher himself, perhaps, than to Capelli. There were other things, too, that he couldn't quite articulate.

"I don't think so; I hope not. I want to see you."

"Good. Me, too. The show is set to close, so I can come to New York . . ."

"No. I've booked a flight to Boston. I should be arriving at Logan at the end of the afternoon. I'll come straight to the gallery."

"I can't wait. Shouldn't you report to Max Fleischmann, though?"

"Later. First I have to see you. See you, hold you, be inside you, be next to you. Then I need to be held by you, maybe for a long time. Then I need to take you to the little Italian restaurant on the Hill, and then I need to go down to the Charles with you and feed the ducks, and then . . ."

"So many needs. I like that. Amos?"

"Yes?"

"I don't think there's anything that can't be fixed."

After he hung up the phone, Hatcher rejoined Landini in the airport bar. There was nothing wrong with Landini other than a nasty cut on his forehead, which Anna Landini had wrapped in so many layers of bandages that her husband looked as if he was wearing a turban.

"Back to the story. The apartment was over in Trastevere only a few blocks away from your *trattoria*. What a bleak place. Naked bulbs, ancient furniture, the bed just a little platform with a mattress thrown over it. It really looked like the set from some road company version of a Tennessee Williams play. But in the corner he's knocked together a bin and thrown a shower curtain across it. You should have been there when we ripped off that curtain."

Hatcher smiled, leaned back in his chair, and languidly stirred his coffee. Landini, the master of the dramatic pause, was unamused.

"For God's sake, Amos . . ."

"Where was I? Oh, yes. Anyway, there must have been sixty or seventy paintings there, and the solution to about three-quarters of the art thefts in Rome in the last six or eight months. He had all the stuff from the Caprese Collection, the Procacci Museum, and the Caravaggio show. None of it had been fenced. Not just paintings, either. Sculpture, liturgical objects, manuscripts, everything. There were plenty of things that had never been reported stolen, stuff that must have come from dealers or private collectors."

"Pecci should have fun trying to locate the owners. Half the art in private hands in this country is only semilegal anyway, since it's really part of the underground economy. Lots of art collecting, so-called, is a euphemism for tax evasion. What about the other members of the gang?"

"They got Mario, the thug that was with Capelli at Sant'Agostino, and somebody named Alberto. The woman who calls herself 'Lena' had been sent off to Bologna."

"That makes sense. Bologna is a left-wing city, and also an important intellectual center. She shouldn't be hard to find."

"No."

"That's it, then."

"I suppose so."

This pause was real. Something was bothering Hatcher, and he wanted to locate it before climbing on the plane. He didn't want to take it back to Sheila. Landini looked at his friend with concern.

"Okay, Lou. Explain this to me. Explain to me about Capelli and Crelly. Did Crelly know Capelli, were they in contact? Because they seem like two ends of the same black thought."

"I don't think they were in contact, no. Do you want to go after Crelly, too?"

"No, if Crelly did know Capelli, I don't want to think about it. The two men scare me; Capelli scared me almost as much last night when he was on the ground, wounded, and I had the guns, as he did in the church. I had to force myself to concentrate on Jake Sloane to do what I did."

"Had to do. If you hadn't, Pecci would have, and it would have been worse."

"Thanks. Anyway, what frightens me about them is their blackness, their nihilism. I can identify with both of them, even sympathize to a point. I hate them, but I can't help thinking they're right about some things."

"You mean about Italy?"

"Partly."

Landini laughed.

"*Benvenuto a Roma,* as I said before. Let me explain something, Amos. Medieval theologians were very concerned about a sin they called *acedia.*"

"I thought *acedia* meant sloth."

"That's what it came to mean in the Renaissance, but originally it meant something like 'spiritual despair.' Perhaps that's what you sense in Crelly and Capelli, and perhaps, to an extent, in Italy, too.

"It's here. It's always been here. Northerners like you come to Italy expecting beautiful art and beautiful women, sunshine and Chianti, laughter and *dolce far niente.* The land of the lotus-eaters. If you hang around for a while, you can wander too close to the edge, and then find yourself looking down into a black pit and smelling the brimstone. The pit is there, all right. The trick is to remember where it is so you don't stumble into it. You should read Barzini's books. He has some marvelously witty things to say about all the simple, childish Northerners with their naive ideas about Italy."

"You think that's it?"

"Sure. The next time you come, bring Sheila. We'll all go off to some dazzling place like Capri or Positano and lie around in the sun singing songs and drinking wine. Why not? That part's just as real as the other. Crelly's wrong, you know, the Colosseum will still be here. People have been predicting it would come crashing down at least since the fifth century, and periodically people have tried pretty seriously to *knock it* down, but there is."

"What about the Red Brigades?"

Landini shrugged.

"They'll be around for a while, then they'll go away. An old story. In the history of this country, they hardly rate a footnote. Don't forget Amos. The Italians invented perspective."

"And *chiaroscuro.*"

"Exactly. Well, I'd better put you on the plane."

Hatcher paid for the coffees, and the two of them strolled off to find the boarding gate.

THORNDIKE PRESS HOPES you
have enjoyed this Large Print
book. All our Large Print titles
are designed for the easiest
reading, and all our books are
made to last. Other Thorndike
Press Large Print books are
available at your library,
through selected bookstores, or
directly from the publisher. For
more information about our
current and upcoming Large
Print titles, please send your
name and address to:

THORNDIKE PRESS
ONE MILE ROAD
P.O. Box 157
THORNDIKE, MAINE 04986

There is no obligation, of course.